THE TRESPASSER

ALSO BY EDRA ZIESK

Acceptable Losses

A Cold Spring

THE TRESPASSER

a novel

EDRA ZIESK

Southern Methodist University Press / Dallas

This novel is a work of fiction.
Names, characters, places, and incidents are either the product of the author's imagination or are used fictitiously.

First edition, 2008

Requests for permission to reproduce material from this work should be sent to:
Rights and Permissions
Southern Methodist University Press
PO Box 750415
Dallas, Texas 75275-0415

Cover photograph: "No Trespassing" by Todd Laffler, www.lafflerphotography.com
Jacket and text design by Kellye Sanford

Library of Congress Cataloging-in-Publication Data
Ziesk, Edra.
The trespasser : a novel / Edra Ziesk. — 1st ed.
p. cm.
ISBN 978-0-87074-551-5 (acid-free paper)
1. Mountain life—Fiction. 2. Strangers—Fiction. 3. Kentucky—Fiction. 4. Psychological fiction. I. Title.
PS3576.I298T74 2008
813'.54—dc22
2008013759

Printed in the United States of America on acid-free paper

10 9 8 7 6 5 4 3 2 1

For Ben and for Kika

1

SEBASTIAN BRYANT was driving the mountain road that wound endlessly upwards without breach or pause, like a long-held breath. The road was pallid, flattened to bleakness by the hot white afternoon sun and by the absence of apparent habitation: he hadn't passed another car nor seen another person. He suspected he'd been sent on a fool's errand by the man in the luncheonette in the town where he had stopped earlier today.

"Where you headed?" the man asked.

"No particular place," Bryant said. "I'm a photographer. Just driving around."

"Well, what kind of thing you after?" the man said.

Bryant shrugged. "Someplace pretty," he said.

"Oh, *pretty,*" the man said. "You best go up the hill and see the Day place then."

The man smiled, swiveling his counter stool away, then back.

"Where's that?" Bryant said.

"You want to drive through town to the hill road maybe a mile from here," the man said. "You take her to the county road, then—"

"How far is it to the county road?" Bryant said. "So I don't overlook it."

"Oh, you won't," the man said. "You'll see her, no doubt. She's gonna run right into you."

Bryant had been driving up the mountain a long time. He would have stopped and turned around and gone back, but there was no place to do it. The road was narrow, bracketed by the mountain and a low persistent ditch that his rental car wouldn't have been able to work its way out of. The sun lay hot across his lap, the car's air-conditioning puny in the face of its intensity.

He had never seen a mountain like the one he was driving. It was hollowed out, its solidity gone, held up by nothing but ribby stalactites, its meat picked out so it looked, now, like a carcass with its rib cage bones sucked clean. The hillside's collapse seemed imminent, and Bryant leaned hard against the driver's side door, due, only partly, to centrifugal pull.

The car slid around another curve on the frictionless mountain road—hill, the man had called it.

"Hill," Bryant said now. "This is a—"

And then he saw what must be the county road—a two-way blacktop. The mountain road ended and there it was, running perpendicular, and Bryant edged up to it and stopped, looking in one direction, then the other. No cars passed. The roadway stretched out, a chalky black, deeply pocked and rutted and empty. A melting tar smell thickened the air.

Bryant turned onto the road and headed slowly west. He was looking for a place to turn around and head back down the mountain, when he saw the cabins.

"Car," Cass Pomfret called out. He stood on the porch of the first in the line of three cabins separated from the county road by yard and a dirt road and a weedy field. He'd caught sight of the car coming slowly up the county road, its chrome a moving white streak in the sun, and he'd kept his eyes on it. Not too many cars came by here.

"Car," Cass said again. His wife Sylvie and their baby boy were inside the cabin behind him, but Cass's voice was low, and they didn't hear him. The car traveled a short distance on the county road, then it split off onto the dirt road and headed towards the cabins, a little dust storm kicking up around it from the parched dirt.

"Car," Cass said one more time and after a little while, Sylvie heard it too and came out to the porch, the baby's creased, meaty legs jouncing against her.

The cabins were small, and listing. They lacked crispness, like a white shirt all the sizing's been washed out of. Panes were missing from the front window of the righthandmost cabin, although pieces of cardboard had been razored to fit in the open places, a neat job done by Hesketh Day, who owned them. The cabins had been built, years ago, by Heke's father to take advantage of what looked like another coal boom that, then, never happened. Nobody lived in the righthandmost cabin, or in the middle one either, only the left one had people in it—Cassius Clay Pomfret, known as Cass, and his wife Sylvestrie, known as Sylvie, and the baby Christopher. Heke let the place to them at a low rent while Cass sought work.

Bryant got out of the car in the deep shade of the tulip poplars a little ways down from the cabins. There was a large house set well back off the road that he hadn't seen before. The house gave off the porous stillness of an empty place.

Nothing moved. There was no breeze strong enough to stir a leaf or a weed frond, but the ceaseless din of insects filled the air—crickets, cicadas, bees, bestirred and angry in the heat—and that noise felt like motion.

Bryant headed towards the cabins. The people standing on the porch looked more substantial to him than the cabins themselves, which were flyaway, fragile in the way of broken eggshells.

"Hey there," Bryant called to the couple, and waved an arm over his head.

Sylvie had come down the porch steps by then and set the baby on the plain bare dirt of the yard. She stood beside the boy not looking down and not touching him, but with her leg within touchable distance. Cass didn't move at all. He watched Bryant approach until he was within seven yards or so of Sylvie and Christopher, then he called, "Help you? You lost, or what?"

"Yeah," Bryant said. "Probably am, knowing my sense of direction." He grinned, but neither Cass nor Sylvie smiled back.

"I'm a photographer," Bryant said. "I'm putting together a book to commemorate next year's bicentennial. I was just driving around and I saw you. I wondered if you folks would care to be in the book?"

They stood and stared for a minute like they hadn't understood him. Then—"A book?" Sylvie said.

"A book?" Cass said. "What kind of a book?"

When Sylvie said it, "book" sounded impressive, large and encompassing, thrilling almost, but Cass made it sound not quite clean.

"Photographs," Bryant said. "Of America. How it looks today."

"Like a picture book?" Sylvie said.

Bryant nodded. "I'm traveling around the country taking photographs of whatever strikes my eye. Schoolteachers, farmers, Native Americans."

"You mean you want us to dress up?" Sylvie said. She bent and scooped up the baby and set him on her hip. She seemed smaller, holding him, than she had on her own.

"No," Bryant said. He dropped his head and stubbed his toe in the dirt.

" 'Cause I'm not dressing up. I'm not putting on any costume."

"I just want you, on your own. The three of you."

"What is it about here struck your eye, exactly?" Cass said. He had moved, come to stand at the top of the porch steps.

"I'm not sure," Bryant said. "The quiet maybe? And it's pretty."

"It's the bottom of the universe," Cass said.

"Well, it is quiet," Sylvie said. "You have to give him that."

Bryant looked at her, but she wasn't talking to him.

"I'll pay you," Bryant said.

Sylvie glanced at Cass. "Pay us," she said. "How much?"

"Fifty dollars. That's what I pay."

"Fifty dollars," Sylvie said. "What for?"

"For me to photograph you," Bryant said. His voice was patient. He'd had this conversation before.

"Photograph us. Photograph us doing what?" Sylvie said.

Bryant laughed, then he coughed. "Nothing," he said. "Standing there on your porch, same as a minute ago."

"Just to stand there," Sylvie said.

"Just to stand there."

"When?" Cass said.

Bryant was looking up at the sky. The light had begun sliding away from the cabins—there was already a triangle of dark blue shade across the rooftop of the righthandmost one.

"Now," he said. "Right away, before we lose the light. My cameras are in my car, I could just go back and get them." He took a few steps towards the road.

"Fifty dollars, you said?" Cass called after him. "Just so's we're clear. You said fifty, right?"

"Right," Bryant said. "Don't move. Stay there. I'll be right back."

The cabin door smacked as Sylvie came inside.

"What's taking so long?" Cass said. "He settin up out there or what's he doing?"

Sylvie shrugged. She couldn't see Cass who'd gone in before her, she was blinded by the glare outside and the beating colored dark within, but she turned towards the settee to the right of the door where Cass was most often to be found. The cabin was a square box divided down the middle—kitchen and sitting room in the front, bedroom behind.

"Here. Give him here," Cass said, and put out his arms for the baby. "He change his mind on us?"

"Don't know." Sylvie handed the baby to Cass, then swung her arms a few times back and forth over her head. The cotton of her dress pulled tight across her chest.

"Hey, old woman," Cass said. His voice was low and he tugged at the hem of her dress.

"Leave go, Cass," Sylvie said. "That man's right outside."

"So?" Cass said. "That mean I can't touch my own wife?"

Sylvie bent and plucked his hand off her skirt. "I got to get supper started," she said and headed for the opposite end of the room where the kitchen table and chairs were, the small icebox, the stove, the shelf above the sink, the paper towel holder where dishcloths were draped over the two plastic arms.

"You think he's still out there?" Cass said.

Sylvie shrugged. "I guess."

"Could use that fifty," Cass said.

There was a pause in their conversation. The sounds Sylvie made pulling things off shelves, opening and closing the icebox, sounded louder in the room.

"Thing I don't get," Cass said. "What he wants with up here in the first place."

"Said it was pretty," Sylvie said. "You heard him." She stopped moving around in the kitchen, a paper-wrapped package of chopped meat in her hand.

"You don't think he was askin us to do something weird, do you, Cass?" she said.

"No," Cass said. "No! He said just standing. No!"

Sylvie looked out the door they'd left open, the pale silky dirt of the yard framed by the porch posts.

"Pretty," she said. "Not to me, it isn't."

"Nor me," Cass said. "Wouldn't hinder me from takin his fifty though."

"No," Sylvie said. "Me neither."

Cass set the baby on the floor, then he went to look out through the screen door. He couldn't locate Bryant through the shadows beyond, though the rental car was still there, a white glow underneath the poplars. From the field beyond the road, a crow made its crow sound.

"There he is," Cass said softly, and pushed his finger against the nailed-on plastic mesh. "Hey Syl? Was there two of them?"

Sylvie looked up from setting the table—napkin, napkin, plate, plate. The baby was drumming his heels against the floor, she could feel it up through the soles of her feet.

"There wasn't," she said, coming to stand next to Cass. "I'm pretty sure he come alone. That other one out there, you mean? That's Heke."

2

HESKETH DAY was sitting on the front porch of his house, the house Bryant had taken to be empty. Most of the place—yard, the dirt road apart from the tulip poplars, the weedy field beyond the road, the county road beyond that—stood in full sun, but the porch, hooded by the roof overhang and by the valance of shade thrown by the trees, was dark. Heke was sitting where he always sat, his chair pushed back against the wall of the house. Bryant had looked directly at him, but hadn't seen anyone sitting there.

Heke had seen Bryant, though. Watched him drive up in his pale-colored car, get out of the car and head over to the Pomfrets. Heke stayed where he was, chair's front legs tipped up and his eyes nearly closed, only half watching the man move through the glassy heat. He seemed like he knew where he was going, headed for the Pomfrets, although they did not have many visitors.

But when the man didn't go inside the cabin, as if the Pomfrets had a reason not to ask him, Heke came awake, and after a while he stepped down off his porch and crossed the parched yard to have a look at the man's car, which had rental plates and ocher-colored mud splattered up the wheel guards that Heke knew wasn't local.

Bryant had crossed the yard again on his way to get his cameras from the car. The shade, when he reached the tulip poplars, was so deep, at first he couldn't see even the trunks of the trees, and he kept missing his footing because he was unable to measure the distance the ground was from him. He didn't notice Heke until he was almost upon him.

"Oh, hey," Bryant said, and took two little backwards hops, and put his hands in his pockets. "Can I help you?"

Heke nodded as if he meant yes, but he said, "That'd be the question I was about to say to you," and then he went ahead and asked it—"Can I help you?" adding, "Who are you?" and "What're you doin up here?" and "You don't even know the Pomfrets, am I right? Just up here nosing around?"—as if Bryant had deliberately tried to fool him, but couldn't.

"Whoa," Bryant said, and his hands shot up in the air, then he laughed at the picture he must have made with his hands up in a *High Noon* surrender.

"I say something funny?" the man said. His head was tipped sideways and he spoke slowly, which made him seem baffled, and as if he was waiting to have the joke explained. He was old, his frail white hair floating out of the shady gloom, but he was tall and broad-shouldered and he carried himself with the easy trust in his own strength of a younger man.

Bryant shook his head; then, because he didn't know if the gesture could be seen in the plum-colored shade of the poplars he said, "No. I mean I was just laughing at myself, what I must have looked like. Hands up?" He raised them again, but only shoulder height.

"Is that your house back there?" Bryant said.

Heke looked behind him as if to check that it wasn't some other house Bryant was talking about, though aside from the cabins, his was the only house here.

"It is," he said.

"Sebastian Bryant," Bryant said, and extended his hand. Heke didn't take it. He held his own hand low and inspected his fingernails. They were large, an opaque white, as if they had come into contact with bleach.

"What'd you say your name was again?" Heke asked. Only his eyes moved, slid up so he was looking at Bryant, though the rest of his head stayed lowered, and he looked baffled again, or shy.

"Bryant," Bryant said again. "Sebastian Bryant?"

"You sure about that now," Heke said. "Sounds like you might not be."

Bryant nodded. "I'm pretty sure about it," he said. He smiled, then felt obliged to laugh, again on account of the darkness, though the laugh was more than he was comfortable giving up.

"Brant," Heke said. "You kin to those Brants live over by the college?"

"Not Brant, Bry-ant," Bryant said.

Heke nodded. "Alvah Brant," he said. "And the girl, now what's her name again?" He looked at Bryant as if he was waiting for him to provide the answer.

"I know everybody livin up around here, and everybody not livin," Heke barked a laugh. "Lots of Brants," he said. "Once upon a time."

"I'm pretty sure I don't have any relatives here," Bryant said. "My family's from the east coast. New Jersey."

Heke looked at him for a slow minute. "Well, you never know," he said. "Names land all over, but they all start someplace. Now what did you say you wanted?"

Bryant shook his head. "Oh, no," he said. "I don't want anything. Take a few photographs, that's all."

"Well, see, that may be wanting nothing to you, but to me, that might not be nothing," Heke said.

"I mean, I'm not trying to sell you anything—magazines, life insurance, circus animals." Bryant paused, waiting for Heke to see he was being funny.

"You said 'take' though," Heke said. " 'Take' a few pictures."

"Photographs," Bryant said.

"If you're takin pictures on my place, and you're takin pictures of my place, the way I see it, that's wanting something that's mine."

"I'm sorry. It's really the Pomfrets I want," Bryant said. "And I'm paying them to let me shoot them." He laughed because he was back to *High Noon* again, but Heke didn't notice.

"What would you be wanting with them, old son?"

"Nothing," Bryant said. "I just want them to stand out on their porch. Be in a couple of photographs. For a book."

Bryant waited for Heke to react to the word, then he turned and looked behind him at the Pomfrets' cabin. The dirt where Christopher had sat patting his hands was already in shade, shade wrinkling back towards the cabins like a piece of silk pulled slowly along. He was about to lose the light.

"See, that'd be something of mine," Heke was saying. "Cabins belong to me, house belongs to me, that field, these trees you're standing under belong to me, and this road you're standing on. So the one you'd best be talking to about any pictures is me."

"Yes," Bryant said. "And I'm happy to. But if I could just have your permission to take the photographs and then come back and talk to you? I'm about to lose the light."

Heke went on in the same slow voice, as if Bryant hadn't spoken. "Tell me what it is you want those pictures for?" he said.

"Photographs," Bryant said. "For a book." Sylvie had made the word sound important and weighty, but it didn't sound that way now.

"I'm working on a book to coincide with the bicentennial," Bryant said. "Next year."

Heke said, "I do know about the bicentennial. Even way back to in here."

"No, I know, I didn't mean—" Bryant looked down. He took a deep breath, then he looked up again.

"I'm traveling around," he said. "I have been for some time. Photographing all different parts of the country. For my book," he said again.

"That right?" Heke said. "And which part of the country would this be? In your book. Wouldn't be the sorry part, would it?"

"No," Bryant said. "What? No. It's—"

"Don't like photographers up to in here. We had them other times—after a coal bump, other times, they all find their way up to here. The sorry part. Show everybody how sorry it is."

"The *peaceful* part," Bryant said. "That's what I was going to say. It's so quiet up here. And peaceful."

He took a step backwards towards the cabins behind him. Paint had blistered off their outsides and now there was no paint. The porches sagged like a canvas sling a fat man had sat on.

"How is it you found my place, all the peaceful way up to here?" Heke said.

"They told me in town," Bryant said. "Fellow at the luncheonette."

"They told you to come up here? To this place?" Heke said, his voice sharp.

Bryant shrugged as if he couldn't remember what had been said to him. There had been noises in the luncheonette. Dish sounds. The slow whump of the ceiling fan that repeatedly lifted the edges of the paper napkins.

"I asked for someplace pretty," he said.

Heke snorted. "And this is what you got? Somebody been fooling with you, old son. Somebody been pulling your leg."

Bryant looked out over the field, full of slack, leggy weeds and edged with scrub trees. He looked up to the county road, heat wavering above it. He could smell the melting blacktop, even this far.

"It is nice up here," he said. "The light especially."

"The light," Heke said. "It's just light. Comes and goes, same as elsewhere."

"It's very clear," Bryant said. "It's good for photographs."

Heke reached into his shirt pocket and took out a cigarette, one of several singles he always carried rolling loose. He lit it, cupping his hands around the match in a practiced way, although there was so little breeze, the gesture was unnecessary. When he exhaled, the smoke hung for a moment in the dark air.

"Well, the light," Heke said. "Here's the thing, I think you may just be out of luck there, old son."

Bryant looked behind him again. The daylight was all but gone, only a thin arc left behind the cabins as bright as a ribbon in a little girl's hair. A crow called from the field across the road. The overhead light came on in the Pomfrets' cabin, the interior leapt out, naked and colorless.

Heke exhaled one last time, then he dropped the cigarette butt on the road, flattened it under his heel, bent and picked it up, the paper a pale flick against his palm.

"Daylight's all but finished," Heke said. "It's getting on for night."

3

HEKE STOOD holding the door to Bryant's rental car open like a parking attendant, and Bryant had no choice but to get in and drive away. He headed back the way he had come, sinking into the remaining light, a deep gold that burnished to orange as he drove. He went slowly, as if the mountain were not just winding, but slippery, his brake lights lit up behind. He was on his way back to the Cherokee Motel, where he had stayed the previous night, putting it out of his mind this morning when he left like any other place to which he was sure he would never return.

The road twisted, unwinding from the mountain like a strip of the peel of an apple, and the roadbed was rough, parts of it didn't even seem paved, although Bryant knew it must be the right road, and that he was going in the right direction. Stones smattered underneath the wheels. Chipped scapulae of rock loomed high up, black and thin and craggy against the less black sky and more disconcerting than they'd been in daylight. It was stiller out than seemed necessary.

For a long time, Bryant didn't pass a single sign or a single light. Train tracks ran beside him for a distance, a rusted ferrous orange he couldn't see but smelled and tasted in the dark.

And then the town appeared—suddenly there when a second before it hadn't been—as if a door into a dark room had opened. Low brick buildings ran down either side of the street—storefronts, the luncheonette—all shut and dark now. The town was old, the bricks of its buildings a burnt black, but it was busy when Bryant had been here this afternoon, most of the storefronts occupied.

Bryant was through the town quickly; quickly its beginning gave way to the stores which gave way to the other end of the town and to the few large houses clustered there. After that, the houses got smaller, then there were no houses, then nothing but the dark road until he drove into the pink and blue neon of the motel's Indian war bonnet sign.

He parked in the empty lot and got out of the car. His shoes scuffed and echoed as he headed for the motel's office, the surface gritty as a parking lot near a beach. There was a momentary delay before the sound reached his ears, as if he was being followed. He turned to look behind him several times, and when he turned back again he was never exactly facing the direction he had been before, as if the parking lot was very slowly revolving. Martine, his wife, had once told him she did not like to swim in deep water—"its unfixity," she had said—and Bryant had laughed at the imprecision of her English, but now he knew what she'd meant.

The motel office was a glass box swaddled in heavy fiberglass drapes, slits of light escaping where the ends of the fabric didn't meet. There were things—a newspaper with its pages fanned, a flattened styrofoam clamshell from a takeout hamburger—in between the drapes and the glass. They had been here yesterday when Bryant checked in the first time.

Inside, behind the tiny counter, was a boy about seventeen—not the person Bryant had dealt with yesterday. He was lying on his side on a cot, head propped on his hand, watching a TV hung from the ceiling. He stood up when Bryant opened the door, though he didn't speak or turn to Bryant right away, his eyes on the TV. "Sorry," he said finally. "Critical moment"—and he tapped his hand over his heart.

"Could I get a room? With a working a.c., please," Bryant said.

The boy had stepped over to the rack where the room keys were hanging, all of them available. How did they make a living way out here? Bryant wondered. Who would choose to stay here?

"Well, they all have air-conditioning," the boy said, turning to Bryant.

"Yes," Bryant said. "But I stayed here last night and the one in my room was broken. It was very hot." He smiled, to show the boy he was not being a pain in the ass, but the smile was tight and unconvincing.

"It's not usually this hot," the boy said. "I mean it never is. Air-conditioning should work though. Works in here." The office was almost bone cold.

The tall and lanky boy came out from behind the counter bouncing a ring of keys on his palm. "I'll find you a good one," he said.

He and Bryant headed up the path that curved around the office towards the long row of rooms in the back. Lights the size and brightness of bicycle reflectors embedded in the path made the toes of the boy's sneakers look wet.

The boy turned on the lights then the air conditioner of the first room he opened. The unit cranked to life, pushing dust out in front of it.

"There," he said. "How's that?"

Bryant stood and looked at the room. It had the same grim interior, clean on the surface but not clean, as the room he'd had last night. "Don't you have something better?" he wanted to ask.

"There you go," the boy said. "She's working." He was facing Bryant, but his eyes were on the office, as if he could see the TV from out here.

"Is there someplace I can get something to eat?" Bryant said, setting his bag down at the foot of the bed. "I haven't had any dinner."

"There's the food court over to the mall," the boy said. His face brightened. "If you go, could you maybe bring me back something? I mean, I'll pay for it and everything, just I can't leave the desk."

"Where is it?" Bryant said.

"It's in Petty?" the boy said and then he was reciting directions that went on for some time.

"How far is this?" Bryant said.

The boy shrugged. "Not far. Maybe twenty miles?"

Bryant shook his head. "Too far, I'm afraid," he said. "I've had enough driving for one day. Nothing closer?"

The boy looked up at the ceiling again and Bryant looked at it too. There were dead flies in the overhead light fixture.

"Nope," the boy said. "Not this late. There's a Jack in the Box at the food court, though." He gave Bryant a plaintive and hopeful look.

"Sorry," Bryant said.

"We got a snack machine then," the boy said. "Best I can offer." He sounded tired now, the hopefulness gone from his voice.

Bryant bought a bag of Cheez Doodles and a pack of peanut butter crackers from the machine at the end of a narrow passage that smelled of sodden indoor/outdoor carpet. Two flies or mosquitoes were gliding into and out of the bathroom, they must have gotten in when the boy opened the door to the room before. They bumped into the mirror, but not each other.

Bryant sat down on the burnt-orange-colored bedspread. It gave off a complicated mustiness—dust, mildew, sex—and he got up and moved to the table and chair in front of the sealed picture window in the back wall. The phone was on the bedside table and he leaned over, moved it to his lap and called his wife.

The phone rang many times in their loft apartment in New York and he sat twitching the cord, counting the rings, letting it go on and on because it was a large loft and because he believed Martine to be home. Which she was.

"Yes?" she said, her voice terse and angry.

"Martine," Bryant said, rolling the "r" Frenchly, although usually when he said her name, he did not. "Cherie," he said.

"Yes," she said again, still sharp, as if the sound of his voice was not enough to please or mollify her.

"It's me," Bryant had to say.

"*Yes,*" Martine said. "What is it? I am in the shower. Give me the number and I will call you back."

Bryant hesitated. If she called him back, the call would have to go through the front desk. What if no one was there? What if the boy decided to drive to the food court himself?

"Sebastian. I am wet. I am in the shower," Martine cried—and Bryant started, having forgotten she was there. He gave her the number, then he sat on the stained orange chair and waited for her to call back.

For more than twenty minutes she did not. Bryant sat fingering, but not opening, the packages of junk food on the table because his wife could not stand the American habit of eating while talking on the phone. And when the phone did ring—after so long a time the call seemed reluctant—she said it again, sharply, "Yes?"—as if it was Bryant who had called her and, once more, interrupted.

"Can you talk?" he said.

"Can I talk? What do you mean?"

"I—. Nothing," he said. He laughed, a small sound, chirping and ridiculous in the face of her imperious Frenchness. "You just sound like I'm, I don't know, interrupting," Bryant said and laughed the small chirping laugh again.

"Yes," Martine said. "You are interrupting."

"What?" Bryant said. "What am I interrupting?"

"What?" Martine said. "Oh, hold the phone."

"Martine?" And when she came back—"Is somebody there?"

"Yes," she said. There was a long pause, as if she were reluctant to tell him what she had to say. "It's my dinner," she said.

Bryant laughed, an ordinary laugh, as he relaxed. "What are you having?" he said.

"Lean Cuisine," she said, and Bryant laughed again. Martine was disdainful of processed, prepared and packaged things—American *merde,* she called it.

"No, really," Bryant said.

"Sebastian," she said, making it four syllables. "Stop it. Do you really need to know what I'm having for dinner?"

"Yes," he said. "I think I really do." When he was traveling, they did not always speak every day. Martine couldn't comfortably talk on the phone at her office; when Bryant called in the evenings, she wasn't always home. The immediate intimacy of a phone call after days of not speaking was difficult. For a time, they were shy with each other, with the actual sound of the other one's voice, and in the face of the details they didn't know of each other's daily life—what they had dressed in that morning, what they had eaten for breakfast or dinner.

"Sebastian, please," Martine said. "I do not want to do this."

"Do what?" he said.

There was a pause. Bryant listened to her breathing

"Do you know what I thought of before?" he said softly, the receiver pressed close to the side of his face.

"No," she said, weary. "How could I know?"

"Remember the time we were at that lake? In Connecticut? There was a float, a raft, out a little ways, and you didn't want to swim out to it. You didn't want to swim with a lot of water underneath, where you couldn't touch the bottom. Remember?"

"You were swimming?" Martine said. There was shock in her voice as if, out of all the possible pictures of him she carried in her head, she would never have picked that—swimming. The heat that had been hugging the Cumberlands, topping off the valleys so that the air was fibrous and the tops of the rivers greasy, wouldn't reach New York City till the next day.

"No," he said. "I wasn't swimming. I was just remembering how you'd said that. I finally got what you meant."

He could hear her steady breathing again through the phone.

"Martine," he said. "Why don't you come down here. Meet me. We could have breakfast together."

"Where?" Martine said. "Where are you?"

"I'm in—" He looked over towards the front window, the air blushing then bluing as it was washed by the alternating neon of the war bonnet sign though, through the window behind him, it was impenetrably dark.

"Kentucky. Somewhere," he said. "Near a town called Petty."

The moment had passed; the moment when Martine might have said yes, she would come. The moment when she would resolve to call her office in the morning, pack quickly, take a taxi to the airport.

But: "No," she said. "Sebastian. I cannot. And what would I do there? You are working."

"I know," he said. "I just wish you would."

He listened to her breathing again, but it sounded different now, evener, quieter than before.

"Maybe the next time, I will come," Martine said.

"Yes," he said. "Someplace a little—" She wouldn't like it here.

"How is it going?" she said. "Your work. Anything good?"

"Maybe," Bryant said. "Today I found some people—this girl. Up in the mountains near here. Her face."

"Ah," Martine said. He was away, sometimes for months. What did he do in the evenings? "A pretty girl," she said.

Bryant yawned and stretched and when he spoke, his voice was at first distorted. "I don't even know if she's pretty," he said.

"No?"

"It's something besides that."

"You got good shots?" Martine said.

"I got no shots. This man who owns the place wouldn't let me shoot—long story. I'm going back tomorrow."

"If he doesn't want you to?" Martine said. "Sebastian?"

"It's fine," Bryant said. "I think I just surprised him. Lord, I'm tired."

"Yes," Martine said. "Me as well."

"Martine. Listen. Let's leave both our phones off the hook and go to sleep. Put the receivers on the pillows. Yes?"

"Sebastian," she said softly. "I cannot."

"Why cannot you?"

"Sebastian," she said again. "I have not even had my dinner. Thai," she said. "It's Thai food."

Bryant went on sitting in the prickly orange chair, the phone in his lap, the wire taut across his shins, after he and Martine had hung up. The packets of junk food, lurid and fake, sat on the table. The seat of the second chair was darkly stained. He got up and went to take a shower.

The soap was scummy, water having soaked through the wrapper during other guests' showers. When he got out of the shower and opened a towel, a dead fly fell out, crisp and compact as a baked raisin.

Bryant came wet and naked from the bathroom, pinched at the orange spread and pulled it down until it fell off the foot of the bed revealing a pilled and pitted blanket the color of split pea soup underneath and he pinched that down too, and lay on top of the fitted sheet. He closed his eyes but the sheet crawled under him and he opened them again.

And slapped at his neck. The fly or mosquito or whatever it was escaped through the spread of his fingers, then through the opened bathroom door.

"Jesus," he said and fingered the bite which, as the night went on, began to itch.

Which, in the morning, would be the size and color of a hickey.

He dozed, waking always after forty minutes or an hour, sweat in the trough of his spine, the creases of the backs of his knees. The room, in spite of the air conditioner, was stifling and smelled of paint. Or the busy back-and-forth of the flies woke him.

When the sky began to lighten, he gave up. He showered again and dressed and packed his things and went out to his car. There was a thread of coolness to the air, though the heat of the day was already crowding it.

Bryant wasn't thinking of the coolness, nor the incipient heat. He was thinking of what he might order for breakfast, and of what Martine would have had if she had called the office and packed and flown out here to meet him. Last night, she'd had Thai food.

4

THINGS SHIFTED.

Sometimes Heke was living in the nowaday, sometimes he was with Rudy and Royl, his mother and father, who had both passed years back, and with his sister Narcissa in the long ago. Sometimes it was quiet in his house, sometimes he had company. He didn't mind. He was pretty used to it. Either way.

"Hesketh? Get up," is what he heard now.

Rudy Day, his mother, stood in the doorway to his room, her voice tart, as if she couldn't see why he wasn't up and dressed even though it was still fully dark out.

"What time is it?" Heke said. He had gone to bed almost as soon as Bryant's headlights faded, but now here was his mother waking him. It took him a minute before he knew it was the long ago. Through the window on the side wall down past the foot of his bed there was not even a glimmer of daylight.

"Is it day out?" Heke said.

He could just see Rudy in the twitching light of the hearth fire behind her. The other side of the hearth wall, against which Heke's bed lay, was just beginning to feel warm.

Rudy jumped the paper bag she was holding at him.

"For Sal Bluitt," she said. "Greens, flour, bacon. I want you to carry it to her. Before your dad's up."

"Can't it wait till morning?" Heke said, but there was no answer, and he didn't need one. Royl hated Bluitts. He said everybody up here on this boundary would've been millionaires if Bluitts hadn't sold them out. Least you had to do with any Bluitt, better off you were,

Royl said. He wouldn't have liked it that Rudy was sending food off their table to Sal, but Rudy said the poor woman had nothing to live on and it was Christian and neighborly, both, to help out. She didn't say this to Royl, she said it to Heke. Heke had been running packages up to the Bluitts—food mostly, but sometimes his own outgrown clothes and shoes for the kids—since the coal bump at the mine on the top of the hill something more than a year ago. He'd woken then to darkness and what sounded like a blister of hail on the roof, but it hadn't been hail or weather of any kind, it was the mountain above them giving way inside itself. The coal heaved down and then rushed as though it were some other pent-up force: dammed water. Coal shot way up into the air pushed by its own charging weight, then it rained back down again, covering everything.

It had been Royl, Heke's dad, who'd pulled him out of bed that night and they'd trudged up to the mine together in the coal-thickened, impenetrable darkness. Rudy hadn't wanted Heke to go—"He's not but ten," she'd said—but Royl didn't heed her.

The coal ash made the air almost solid, Royl's lantern lighting nothing but a small cone inside the darkness, and Heke had begun to feel what it must be like to be trapped in the mine, to hear the hiss of the coal coming at you louder and louder, and what would be worse, to hear the sound and know you'd be dead a minute after, or to be cut off in some tiny hunchbacked space you'd picked out of the seam, waiting for your air to give out.

"Dad?" Heke said. "Which do you think would be worst?" but Royl didn't answer.

There were lights, a glowing pumpkin color, set up at the mine, which made the night seem both festive and ghastly. The raining coal made a ceaseless sound, and it never got light that morning.

Sal Bluitt lost her oldest son, Canaan, in the bump, the one who supported the family—her husband had run off long since—and Rudy had been sending Heke with packets of food and clothes and such whenever she could manage.

The Bluitt house was about half a mile uphill from the Days'. Heke had been there many times, playing with the kids, though Royl didn't know about that either. The house was built close to the road like a turnpike house, but Royl said it hadn't been sited, just put up out of laziness and hurry, both together. He said when Bluitts first got here, they tethered their mules to two trees, dropped their goods and started hammering. There was a sign nailed to the gate—"Trespassers Will Be Prosecuted"—but some long ago Bluitt had crossed out "Prosecuted" and written "Shot."

Heke came up through the woods that retained the smoky dampness of autumn, even though it was early spring. Something was different about the house as he approached it, and Heke stopped outside the gate, trying to figure out what it was.

The place was quiet. No kids running around, yelling in their tin can voices; no Sal Bluitt hollering out at them to quiet up. The yard was empty, not just of the tumble of the kids but of the usual, casual chaos of things scattered everywhere—toy parts and machine parts and little bits of leftover pipe and lumber and frazzled, darkened rope ends. They came off a primeval pile as old as the house, bits of it nosed out by the dogs from time to time, or the kids. "Pure, sinful bone-deep laziness," Royl said it was. "Typical Bluitt. If there was hidden deadly sins, they'd seek 'em out and violate 'em." The pile was still there, but the rest of the yard was so empty, it looked swept.

Heke leaned heavily on the gate as he opened it and shuffled his feet as he came up to the front of the house, making as much noise as possible. He kept expecting the kids to come rushing out at him from around back of the house, hooting and breathless with the joke they had thought up: to hide. He kept expecting noise—the sound of his name yelled once, yelled again, a choppy chorus with some high-pitched giggling and whoops—but no noise came and he thought, School? Church? and tried to remember what day it was, what time, what season. He stood in the yard and kicked at the dirt, the cardboard brown color mixed up with the black shininess of coal particles. The steady quiet began to be spooky.

Heke turned to go, though he put no weight on the gate this time, having been converted to quiet himself. The paper bag Rudy had given him was still in his hand, and he thought up reasons his mother would accept for why it hadn't been delivered—("I see. The house was gone, was it? Disappeared?")—but there were none; he had no choice but to return to the house.

The Bluitt porch was dark enough to be creepy; Heke tried not to think about it as he crossed the empty yard. He would go up the steps, he would call at the open door—"Miz Bluitt? It's Hesketh Day. My mama sent this here for you"—and if she didn't answer, he would leave the paper sack outside the door.

("You did what? You think I packed up good food for some raccoons to abscond with?")

Inside the door, then, and where it wouldn't be stepped on. No one could do anymore.

Silence pressed at him from behind as Heke went up the porch steps, the treads worn to gray and depressed in the middle like punched-down bread dough. He was all the way to the front door before he realized it was shut, a thing that matched the quiet of the yard for oddness. He was looking at the wood stripping that framed the wobbly glass of the top half of the door, the rusted nail heads and, in places, the mis-hammered tips showing through. He hadn't ever seen this door shut. Barring subzero temperatures, doors were hardly ever shut around here. Where was everybody? Something felt wrong.

Heke turned, heading for the steps again, when he heard a man's voice. He held still, pressing himself back into the porch shadows, the soft paper sack hugged loose in his arms. The bag had been used and used again and was as silent and supple as scored deerskin. Heke could smell the cold white bacon fat through the paper, and the pervasive smell of cold ash in the air.

"Well, that's one good thing about this place," the voice said, and then there was another voice, another man: "How good?"

"Well," the first one said. "The woman's had about a hundred kids so—" and both the men laughed. "But the price is right," he said and jingled the coins in his pocket. "I've had worse—and paid more."

"At least we don't have to see the muckety kids," the second man said. "Nothin puts a damp on romance like kids," and then there was a sound like water hitting against hard ground and Heke edged closer to the side of the porch where he could lean out a little and see what it was. One man was peeing—not inside the privacy, but against its outer wall, his head tipped skywards like a coyote. Heke did not know him, nor the other man either, but men—engineers, people from the coal company, photographers, newspaper reporters—came and went from time to time, less since they'd closed the mine after the accident. A lot of strangers had come around then, investigating things, interviewing the families of miners who'd been lost in the bump, their hard voices bullying the teary women.

"Lord," the second man said. "This about the sorriest place you ever seen?"

The blood left Heke's face; he went clammy, and cold. Sorry? What was so sorry about it? He looked out at the part of the yard he could see. It looked swept up to him. It looked clean. How could a place look good to one person and sorry to another?

"This is how dogs live where I come from," the first man said. He was finished peeing; Heke saw him shake himself and jump a little as he put himself away.

"Hey, watch out, I got a dog!" the other man said.

The first man laughed, a sound that seemed to take him by surprise and to please him because he laughed again.

"Okay," the second man said. "My turn."

Heke thought he meant to pee, and why couldn't they go inside the privacy?, but the man walked a few steps towards the back of the house. Heke couldn't see exactly where he went, but when the man spoke—"You comin or what?" he called to the other man—his voice came back diminished.

"What? You need company? I'll wait out here," the first man said. "Up front."

The sound of hard shoes chuffing through the dirt of the yard took up, heading for the front of the house, and Heke froze where he was, pressed to the wall near the door. If he bolted straight down the porch steps, the man would see him and chase him and probably catch him, and he began to have the trapped feeling again, like he got when he thought about the coal bump. Objects—the plain wood porch posts, the dirt yard, the trees beyond the road—looked crisp and, though it was overcast, edged sharply in color.

A shushing noise now became evident to Heke—the noise of the man approaching?—and he breathed fast, fast, like a dog, and his heart felt cold.

He was making the noise himself, though, his jacket was as he slid against the house wall. He hadn't even realized he was moving, heading for the far corner of the house where the porch jigged sideways and wrapped around the house. Royl said it had been braggadocious to build that porch; he said he would never have done it himself, sheer waste of wood and labor and nobody would ever use it, as the side of the house wasn't suited for sitting, it got neither sun nor breeze. He'd been right. The side porch wasn't used, except to store things on.

An old settee was pushed underneath the side window. Heke dropped down low in front of it, then hunched behind its far arm. A powerful smell of urine and mildew reached him from the cushions and he tipped his head back and up into the air, but he didn't otherwise move.

Slowly, the unnatural silence returned. The absence of the sound of the man approaching became apparent and another sound began to make its way past the rush of blood in Heke's ears. A clipped, steady hammering that Heke thought, at first, must be a consequence of his own racketing heart, but he put his hand to his chest, and though it took a while to pick out his own beatbeatbeat from the slower and slightly less regular alternate sound, he could discern the difference. The sound was coming from the house. He pushed to his knees and raised his head to the window.

The man lay on his stomach on the bed—Heke thought he was dead, maybe—but then he saw the man was moving and that he wasn't dressed, or was only partly, his pants tethered loose at his ankles, his bare-naked butt looming in and out of Heke's frame of vision. The bed was on the move, its feet battering the floor again and again—the hammering sound.

And then he saw Sal, underneath the laboring man, limbs flailed to the bed's four corners, head turned away. The taste of bacon stormed up in the back of Heke's throat and sweat cropped out on his neck and his forehead, chilling him further in the chilly air, and he boosted himself off the porch wall and bolted. He dropped hard, so his knees buckled and his bottom teeth clocked against his top ones, but he scrabbled up and started running, bypassing the yard and the front of the house and the road, heading sideways, instead, into the scrub woods, through cold sharp air that he relished for its smoky usualness, its lack of taint.

Heke ran hard and without letting up, in case the outside man had pursued him, even if he hadn't. He wanted to put as much distance as possible between him and the Bluitts and the sin he knew to be sin without exactly knowing how he knew it. He didn't slow down until he came to where the road hooked back around and descended the hill in the direction of his house, then he stopped and bent over to catch his breath, the zipper of his jacket flipping up and back as his chest heaved. He still had Rudy's brown paper sack in his hand.

Heke held the bag by its crimped and puckered neck and he jumped it up and down a few times, as Rudy had when she'd woken him early that morning. He pitched the bag over his head and into a clump of bushes, let the raccoons come and get it.

He never went back to the Bluitts' after that. Rudy asked him to a few times but when she did, the sick feeling rose in the back of Heke's throat again, and he said he couldn't, that he was ailing. When Rudy put her hand against his forehead he was clammy, and when she stepped back so she could see into his face, he looked peaked and wan.

Sal Bluitt remarried and moved away a little while after that. For years, the sorry house just stood there, home to squirrels and bats. Leaves heaped up in the yard. Heke never told anyone about Sal and what he'd seen, but it attached itself to Royl's everyday hatred of Bluitts and tagged along. From time to time Rudy would say it was a shame to let a good house fall to ruination, and that someone should go up and tend it, lest it fall down in splinters, but nobody ever did.

5

MATTIE WHEELER woke, alert to the stillness around her, or to the sound or sounds that might come to disorder the stillness. She had no need to be up at this hour, the school year was over, it was guardedness that woke her. In the quiet interval that preceded the dense chop and chitter of birds—one bird first then, suddenly, many—Mattie listened for the thing that, this summer, had invaded her garden.

But there was no sound, or none that could be heard over the birds, and Mattie got up and made her way through the charcoal-colored light to the bathroom of the little house in which she had spent her girlhood, and which was now hers alone. The bathroom leapt out when she turned on the light, vivid and rosy. Pink and white floor tiles covered the concrete sub-basement of the one-story house, and square pink tiles covered the walls above the pink tub and sink.

Mattie turned the taps on full in the bathtub, then went through to the kitchen and opened the back door and stood there, listening. Her vegetable garden took up most of the yard. She planted it every year, and always before it had been tidy, staked, weeded, under control, but this year she was afraid to step into it, afraid of whatever it was that had colonized the interior. Not rabbits, squirrels, chipmunks, snails with which she could peacefully coexist and whose work, nibbles and holes, was familiar to her, almost dear. This was something else. Everything had been bitten, mangled, then dropped. Tomatoes with one chomp taken out of them lay tossed and abandoned, crawling with ants. Vines were broken, plants torn out by the roots as if it was not forage, but mayhem and destruction this creature was after. Mattie was afraid to step into the garden, and had let it go. The neighborhood boys who came around offering to shovel snow in the winter had no interest in gardens.

The yard still held some nighttime coolness, although the heat of the coming day was already displacing the thinner, cooler air. When Mattie turned from the doorway and headed back to the bathroom and stepped into the tub, the water was so hot she keened sideways a little and put her hand out to the wall. Cool water would have felt better, but a hot bath left her asheen and pearly and with her skin adjusted better to her frame somehow, as if all the lacing had been tightened. A cool tub or a shower didn't have the same effect. Today was the day she went and did for Heke.

Mattie stood it as long as she could, then wrapped herself up in a big pink towel and cleaned off the mirror and stood looking at herself. She had her attributes, all round and creamy surfaces, which was not too bad for the steep and shady side of forty. Her hair curled against the back of her neck due to the steam from the bath, a nut brown color although, as she leaned closer, some wiry gray ones were visible around her temples. Time to have it colored again.

Bryant drove into town, heading for the tables and chairs, counter stools and teetering piles of coffee cups at the luncheonette, where he would get the cooked meal he had pined for throughout a long night. The light was now a smoky topaz color tinted by the mist, and his windshield dewed up so he had to use the wipers a few times to clear it. There was no one outside any of the houses he passed, reversing the journey of last night—the neon-tinted stretch of road lit by the motel's war bonnet; houses just beginning to be visible; whitewashed cabins that he didn't remember seeing the night before emerging now from the mist as if they had been slapped together in the dark. White laundry hung limp on some of the porches. He didn't see a living soul.

So he expected the luncheonette to be empty, possibly not even open yet. Instead, it was packed, every seat taken, torsos swiveled towards each other on the counter stools, the front window steamed from so many poured-out cups of coffee.

The luncheonette's hubbub, audible through the shut door, quit when Bryant walked in. One man stopped talking, the man next to him did, until no one was talking: they all sat and looked at Bryant, some frankly, some with their heads down, peering out from under their eyebrows. Except for the waitress, it was all men.

Then—"Hey," a voice called, louder than it had to be in the persistent quiet. "You the boy was in here yesterday?"

Bryant located the speaker by the turning of the bodies of the other men—burly, red-faced, like he'd been spiking his coffee.

"Well," Bryant said. "I was in here yesterday."

"You found the Day place up the hill okay? Where I told you?" The man grinned and threw an elbow at the man beside him, a small, bony-headed fellow with erratic teeth Bryant noticed because now, that man was also grinning.

Bryant nodded at them. "I did," he said.

"How'd you like it?" the first man said.

"I liked it fine," Bryant told him.

"Then I guess you didn't find it," the man said.

There was laughter. Parts of what the man had just said—"didn't," and "guess"—were taken up by other men and repeated. Bryant waited for it to stop, then he said, "I think I did. Mr. Day, right?"

"You found Heke Day's place?" somebody else said. "All the way up to in there?"

Bryant didn't answer.

"Heke Day let you come visiting him? No, because he's not usually what you might call friendly." There was more laughter and some jostling, nothing from Bryant, then all the men began to stand up. They shook down their pants legs and tumbled the coins in their pockets while they got into line behind the cash register. Their coffee cups and dishes lay strewn on the counter and the tabletops, the handles of the cups turned in all directions as if blown by the overhead fans. Outside, a steam whistle sounded.

Bryant was the only one who didn't move, so it seemed like it was on his account all the other men were leaving, as if there was something contagious or distasteful about him. But when they had gone, the waitress, gathering dishes and cups inside the curve of her arm and sliding them into a blue plastic dishpan as if they were not dishes but the light and unbreakable by-product of some other chore, say shelling peas—she told Bryant: coal shift.

Heke's front door was open. Mattie stepped inside and she called to him—"Heke?"—her voice tentative. The house was dark, not too many windows, like most houses built when heat was more important than light, and there was the shading front porch, though it was not darkness that disturbed her, nor oddness either. The house was old. It had started out two log rooms, then been added to by each new Day husband or boy grown to manhood, and each part of the house contained in it the tickings and soft exhalations of the generations who had lived here, cooked and washed clothes and clipped their hair and their fingernails. Once, she had thought she would be one of them, one of the generations, cooking, washing, raising children, keeping up the life of the house. But then she hadn't been.

"Heke?" she called again, then stood listening for him. He'd jumped out at her enough times when they were children.

Or young, they hadn't been children at the same time, Heke was older than Mattie. Their mothers had been cousins, Mattie had often come here with her mother to visit. Heke had almost always been around. Which raised certain expectations on everybody's part.

And then Mattie went off to a two-year teachers college and when she returned, that first summer, her mother told her Heke was to be married.

At first Mattie thought her mother meant he was to be married to her. That the offer had been brokered by their two mothers, Heke too shy to speak to her himself. And then she'd seen her mother's face and known this guess to be mistaken.

"We'll see," Mattie had said in her new, firm schoolteacher's voice, as if her mother's words could, in fact, be taken two ways. "I'm going up there."

"Mattie, don't do it," her mother said, her eyes pale and moist and bleary. But Mattie had ignored her and left the house. She was wearing a short-sleeved blouse with butterflies printed on it, a brown cotton skirt with orange stitching, her clothes vivid and fresh beside her mother's faded house things.

She'd hesitated on the porch, a hand on the iron railing.

"Mattie," her mother called again, and she came out, holding a sweater Mattie did not take, though that spring had been chilly.

"Heke?" Mattie called again, now. "Hesketh?"

And then there he was, standing in front of her, soundless as she had predicted, wearing a white shirt that was either one of many or the only one he had so that Mattie sometimes bought shirts for him, in her head. He was so silent.

They were a distance apart, maybe fifteen feet, Heke with his back to the kitchen, a dark shape surrounded by the early light from the kitchen window behind him. To his right was the parlor he never went into and Mattie never cleaned because the hulking boxes with the brand-new stove and refrigerator and washing machine in them were there. The things Heke had never used or unpacked or returned, all heaped together as if a giant broom had swept them into the middle of the room and left them. Things bought for the girl who had not come up the hill to marry him, after all.

Wouldn't, some people said. Balked. Didn't want to live all the way up here.

He wouldn't, other people said. And some said they didn't believe there ever had been a girl, to begin with.

Mattie had taken it, then, as a good thing: he had seen that he wanted a wife. Once a little time had passed and the sore-heartedness left him, there she'd be. For a long time, Mattie believed Heke to be a half step from speaking to her and, from time to time, less. There was something between them—an understanding, a sympathy—and sometimes there was more. From time to time a little flame leapt up between them, she could see it. And he had given her things—once a pair of bookends he'd made, once a pin in the shape of a starburst. She had waited for him to speak, for the little flame to gather and leap; she had turned down other men because she believed Heke to be on the verge of speaking but he hadn't. For a long time Mattie had been fixed on him; for another, longer time, she hadn't. But she'd developed the habit, in his presence, of waiting in this caught-breath way, as he transmitted the feeling, always, that he was on the verge of some kind of declaration.

"Mattie," Heke said now; he had to clear his throat and start again. "Mattie. I wasn't expecting to see you so early. It's barely come light."

Mattie had to blink before she could answer him, and remember where in her history she was: which Heke was standing before her, talking to which Mattie.

"I know," she said. "I couldn't sleep and, well, here I am."

Bryant pulled the car off the blacktop a little distance from the Pomfrets', trundling in beside a large Crown-of-Thorns bush. There was no shoulder here; there was blacktop, field, dirt road, yard, house, divided and distinct, like various gradations—the plains, mesas, steppes, tundra, ice caps—on old maps. He could see two of the three cabins. Heke's dark porch.

It was lighter out now, the shadows with less depth, though mist still whirled around everything like cigarette smoke shut inside a jar. Bryant sat and stared through the windshield. Both the elation that came from lack of sleep and the caffeine rush from all the coffee he'd just had and that felt like elation had worn off. He opened the door to get out of the car but he was parked on a tilt and it wouldn't stay open; the overhead light popped on and then off. Bryant leaned his head back against the seat and tried and failed and tried and failed to move.

Cass lay on his side in the bedroom of the cabin, staring at the window. Shapes were beginning to come out of the dark—trees, the edge of the road—sliding out of blackness as if only just arriving in these places. The baby was still asleep in the creaky portable crib at the foot of their bed. It was a small crib, though it jammed up the room; Christopher looked hulking and oversized in it. Cass kept his eyes on the crib but all he could see was the navy blue darkness.

Sylvie lay facing away from him, the right side of her face mashed hard into the pillow, as if in desperate pursuit of the deepest level of sleep. Cass said Sylvie went out before her head touched, dreaming in mid-air.

"I can't help it," Sylvie said. "I don't even know why you're not dead with it."

"I just don't need as much sleep as you do," Cass said, but he often napped when the baby did if he was not out looking for work or working the one-, two-, three-day stints he picked up now and then, hauling jobs, mostly. There wasn't any work around here. He'd been everywhere looking, and there wasn't.

Cass reached for Sylvie now, though she was still sleeping her desperate sleep, backfacing him. He slid his left hand slowly inside the armhole of the overlarge nightgown she had on, so his elbow lay on top of hers and his lower arm crossed her body. He stayed for a minute like that, breathing when she breathed, his exhales ruffling the tiny hairs at her neck. It was warm inside the nightgown.

And then Cass began to move his arm, slowly, like somebody bowing across an instrument. He thought about her, rosy and wet, and went on doing it, his hand flat, bowing. Still, Sylvie didn't stir.

He moved closer to her, tight up as he could, fishing the pebbled yellow nightgown out from between them, what felt like yards and yards, and under which she was naked. He was not stealthy now. He hitched her up a little, and still she didn't speak, though Cass knew she was awake from the little twitchy breaths, the long sigh as he slid into her and began moving.

Christopher stirred, pedaling so the sheet slipped off the foot of the plastic-covered mattress and his feet made a sandpaper sound. Sylvie opened her eyes and watched the crib.

Cass kept on, and now he put his hand on her breast that was small, not bigger than a halved orange, and he squeezed and Sylvie bit her lip, but she didn't cry out, so he squeezed harder, as if it was a question he needed some answer to, and then she couldn't help it.

"Cass!" she said out, and he said, "Girl."

The baby, on the lookout, heard Sylvie. He sat up and cooed and when she didn't answer, pressed his face to the crib slats and when she still didn't come to him began to whimper and Sylvie's eyes were open but she didn't call to him, knowing her voice a second time would make it worse. She clamped her teeth hard so she wouldn't call out again and she reached for Cass behind her; she reached back, slid her small hand between his legs hunting the slippery underside of his sex, riding her thumb there over and over.

"Oh," Cass breathed against the back of her neck, his eyes rolled back, eyelids aflutter, and Thank You Lord for the tricks this little girl knew.

It was getting lighter, the sky and air simultaneously brightening like a single piece of cloth lit from behind. Bryant opened his eyes—he had been asleep in the front seat for ten minutes maybe, or fifteen.

"Jesus," he said and hauled himself out of the car.

It was already warmer, the heat jellied on the surface of his skin. Bryant brushed at the back of his neck, touching the bite that had been dormant for hours but that now began to itch with a pestilential fury. He scratched it as he went around to the trunk, where his cameras were and the tripod he'd decided to use, to take a slow timed exposure of the three cabins emerging from the mist, an image he now wanted almost as much as the one of Sylvie and Cass and the baby on the porch.

Cass heard clanking sounds, or thought he did, and buttoning his jeans he went through the house to the front door.

"Don't you at least intend on washing?" Sylvie called around the rubber band in her mouth. She was scraping her hair into a hasty ponytail, and her own hand smelled of plain soap. Christopher lay on the bed happily burbling, though tears still sat like droplets of glycerine in the outside corners of his eyes.

"Hey you boy," Sylvie said, and she smiled down at him.

And then Cass called back to her—"Syl. You know what I bet it is?"

Sylvie knelt by the edge of the bed. She lifted the baby's T-shirt and blew against his belly.

"Syl?" Cass called again. "It's that photographer fella. I bet you a fifty I'm right."

Because she had started on Heke's house so early, Mattie finished early too. There wasn't all that much to do anyway. Heke was used to doing for himself, and if he did not sweep in all the corners or polish the drip trays on the stove and the bathroom faucets or wax the kitchen floor—well, a lot of other people didn't do all those things either.

Mattie sighed and went outside to sweep the porch floor clear of the frill of pollen that lay thick enough to skate through. She had barely seen Heke this morning. To keep out of her way, he'd taken his breakfast into his bedroom, first right off the front door, part of the original house. He wouldn't let Mattie in there to clean, where he had piled-up newspapers he was intending to get to, the stacks high enough to be useful as end tables, and where his dish and his coffee cup now rested.

"Heke," Mattie called when she was finished sweeping. "Heke? I'm done, I'm going."

She stood with the broom in her hand and waited for him to come out and talk to her or, at least, say good-bye, but he didn't. Tears came up in Mattie's eyes, even though every time she came here was more or less like this. Heke made conversation or he didn't; said good-bye, or he did not. Her ministrations didn't make much difference to him that she could see, though her toilette on the days she came up here was nearly bridal.

"I'm not doing this anymore," Mattie said now to the broom, to the sparse, chipped paint of its handle. "A person can stand only so much total neglect. Hesketh?" she called, meaning to tell him—Not that you care; not that it's here nor there to you. "Hesketh?"

Still there was no answer, the silence, in fact, so deep and complete, Mattie began to think something might be wrong, perhaps something had happened to him—he was not young, though he seemed not to have noticed this about himself—and she turned and headed back towards the house.

Heke stepped out on the porch then. He looked bleary, as if he did not know where he was, and though he looked across the yard at Mattie, it took him a long time to speak. He'd been somewhere else, caught up in the long ago.

"Mattie," he said finally. "That *was* you. You going already? We didn't even get a chance to chitchat. I wanted to tell you—"

They looked at each other across the distance of the yard. Mattie even leaned towards the house a little so she would not miss whatever he might say next.

Heke raised his hand. "My thanks to you, Mattie," he said. "As always. Bye."

The smell of bacon stayed in the cabin all day. It faded as the day passed, as air stirred through the windows and the open door, until it was met by the next morning's breakfast, and the bacon smell thickened back.

"He's takin a long time just getting up here," Cass said.

Sylvie looked up, plate in her hand to fork the cooked bacon onto. "Maybe it's not him," she said.

"You think I should go out there and see?"

"Cass," Sylvie said. "Just sit down and eat your breakfast."

Bryant smelled the bacon. His head came up and he sniffed at the air and his mouth watered, even though he'd just eaten enough at the luncheonette for two people. He had come from his car to just short of the dirt road, stopping for a minute to rest and to scratch the bite on his neck that was now the circumference of a quarter. His equipment was arrayed on the ground, the grass underneath his things tamped down. The metal gear box, the tripod, a black canvas shoulder bag inside which were several stiff black leather cases that held lenses of increasing size and magnification. Everything was heavy or sharp-edged or awkward to carry. Bryant was wearing jeans and a short-sleeved canvas jacket with many pockets, soft from years of washing.

Driving away from Heke's house, Mattie saw the man standing as if at attention. The grass at his feet stirred in the car's hot breeze. His hair lifted from his forehead. A salesman, he must be, hardly anybody made their way all the way up here, and know it or not, he, too, would be wasting his time. Heke was not big on company, except for the kind in his head.

Mattie looked again for the man she had seen in her rearview mirror, but he had bent down by then, and was gone.

Mattie drove into town and parked, then she sat with the car door open, swiveled around so both feet were on the pavement. She looked down at her feet in the old moccasins she wore to clean in.

"I think I'll buy a nice new pair of shoes. Sandals," she said and held her head up as if in defiance of anyone who might be going to tell her how impractical sandals were here, where it was hardly ever this hot.

The shoe store was at the end of the street, past the drugstore and the appliance store, the fans in its window with little tags of cloth waving from them to show they worked. There was a storefront office—accounting, notary public—and a bed store, then the five-and-ten. The dusky interior tempted Mattie as she passed it, and she stepped into the opened doorway.

"Miz Wheeler? That you?"

Mattie turned. A boy, Bruce, one of her old students, he must be about twelve now.

"Bruce," she said. "How are you, you enjoying your summer so far?"

"You see? I told you it was her," Bruce hissed over his shoulder.

Mattie stepped out into the sun again. She squinted in the direction Bruce had called and saw a little girl peeping out from the top of the alley in between the luncheonette and the sharp-sided brick wall of another store.

"Is that your sister, Bruce?" Mattie said.

Bruce said, "That's Bliss. You'll be teachering her in September, so she's shy."

The little girl's face slid away, and then Mattie saw her running across the lot behind the stores to a wooden staircase that led to an upstairs apartment.

"Teaching, Bruce," Mattie said. "Not teachering."

Bruce looked up at Mattie like he had not understood her, then he said, "You goin in here Miz Wheeler?"

"You know what, I'm not," Mattie said, looking as far back as she could see into the dim interior. "I have to run a few errands. You enjoy your summer now, Bruce. And Bliss," Mattie said, and she resumed walking. She had not gone far when she was stopped again, by a timid woman with two small clinging children. She told Mattie her name straight off, starting with, "You probably don't remember me."

"Well of course I do," Mattie said, though there were so many former students from the twenty-three years of teaching she'd done so far, and it was hard to remember them all.

A little farther on again a man called—"Hey Miz Wheeler"—and Mattie stopped once more.

"Who's that?" she said, shading her eyes.

"Guess," the man said, and grinned and waited. It was always the men who said guess, the women never did. As if the effort of trying to remember some old former student without even a hint of who he was could bring Mattie nothing but delight.

It took her a long time to get to the shoe store, the walk a progression of tribute and acknowledgment that slowly warmed her. She had to stop and talk to this one and that one. She was invited to the luncheonette for coffee. By the time she bought shoes, had lunch and drove home again, hours had passed. Inside her house, the telephone was ringing.

Bryant, making his way up the dirt road to the cabins, thought it was Heke who drove by in the car, and he stopped walking and held himself as still as possible. The car that had passed him—white and wide and well kept—didn't strike Bryant as the type Cass and Sylvie would own. He didn't know who Mattie was, or that she had been here.

When the white car was gone, Bryant began to load himself up again—the tripod under one arm, the shoulder bag and the sharp-sided, weighty gear box in the other—and he headed again towards the Pomfrets' cabin, moving with the spiky, gawk-legged gait of a stork or a crane or some other improbable species of bird.

"Here he comes," Cass said. He folded the last piece of bacon into his mouth and wiped his thumb down the leg of his jeans and got up, swinging his leg over the kitchen chair that had once been green and before that red and brown and on which there were now generations of color, visible over and under each other.

Cass went to stand behind the screen door. Sylvie looked at him; he was still bare-chested, his back smooth and T-shaped, the muscles at rest but clear, as if ready to catch and couple under his skin.

Christopher started to cough. Sylvie patted him idly, but he went on coughing and she pulled her eyes from her husband and looked at the baby who was red-faced now, and still coughing. She swooped her finger inside his mouth and hooked the piece of bacon, wet and flabby, from the back of his throat.

"You're okay, Pa," she told the baby, putting the piece of wet bacon on the table. "You okay?"

"Here he comes," Cass said. "I can see him."

"Get the fifty first," Sylvie said. She went on rubbing Christopher's back until he stopped fussing, then she put him down on the floor and got up to clear the dishes. Christopher trailed her, sliding in between Sylvie's feet, scooting along on his left side, his own version of locomotion. Sylvie had to watch where she walked to keep from stepping on him, and she didn't look up at all until the screen door slammed.

"There goes your daddy," Sylvie said.

Sylvie could hear the low underburble of the two men's voices outside until she turned the water on and lost them. She never waited on a chore; if she waited the thing would not ever get done. Things would pile up like laundry, stacked, but never put away.

This was the third place they had lived in the last two years, this place that felt like an attic, the same grubby bareness and hot still air. The walls were bare wood, and though there was cold running water in the sink, there was no indoor bathroom. Sylvie hadn't hung a picture on the walls, not even a calendar, as if she didn't want to know how many days and weeks and months were passing. Even Christopher's gaudy plastic toys looked cheerless. One more downward slip would bring them to sleeping on relatives' couches or floors. They were already in arrears on this place.

Sylvie shut off the water and dried her hands on the dish towel. She could hear Cass again; the overly loud and perky sound of his voice—the fifty dollars would bring them almost up to date on rent. Then the screen door opened and Cass stuck his head in.

"Come on, Syl," he said to her. "He's out here waiting." His voice was low, but he was beckoning furiously where Bryant couldn't see him.

Sylvie looked at him, but she didn't move.

"Sylvie, something wrong with you? Come on. He's ready. He's got to catch the light."

"You some kind of expert all of the sudden?" Sylvie said. "And what light is that exactly? It's just all mist and whatnot, is what I see."

"Here," Cass said. "See if this makes it any lighter for you."

He laid a fifty dollar bill down on the table, smoothed it end to end with his thumbs.

Sylvie looked down at it. "It does," she said.

"Come on out then," Cass said, and when she was still not quick enough, he scooped the baby up off the floor himself and put his hand underneath Sylvie's elbow.

Tears pricked hard at Sylvie's eyes at the kindness of the gesture, and she dragged in a breath.

"What is the matter with you?" Cass said. "That time of the month, or what is it?"

Sylvie shook her head. "Let me just go change real quick," she said, spotting her eyes with the bone of her wrist. The dress she had on was a baggy, shapeless thing. It was too hot to feel the press of cloth of any kind, and things had begun to feel tight on her. Again.

"Mr. Pomfret?" Bryant called from outside.

"My hair," Sylvie said, poking at the bristly ponytail as Cass drew her to the door. "It's not even brushed yet. Cass. *Cass!* Aren't you even gonna put a shirt on?"

"Said not to," Cass told her. "Said he wanted me like this. My natural self." He tried not to smile; failed at it.

"Why?" Sylvie said. "Why, Cass?" She worked her elbow from his hand and frowned up at him.

"Don't you think there's something, I don't know, not right about that?" she said. "Not decent?" She could see Bryant standing just beyond the porch steps and kept her voice low.

"I don't think he craves me, if that's what you mean," Cass said.

"It's not. It's—well, why us? What's so special about us? Really."

"Speak for yourself, darlin," Cass said.

Bryant was ready for them. He'd set up the tripod with the 500 mm lens on it for the time exposure of the cabins; he'd take the rest handheld.

"Let's do it now," he said, as the Pomfrets came outside, Sylvie shrinking a little against Cass. Her face, in this morning's particular light, had the pale luminescence of certain kinds of stone.

Sylvie looked out across the yard. It was gloomy. Scarves of mist traveled across the ground so dense, ten yards ahead you couldn't see a thing.

"Where you want us?" Cass said, standing in front of Sylvie. She could smell his warm bare skin, a scent somewhere between boring and erotic, and she leaned in briefly and touched his back with her forehead.

"Get where you feel comfortable," Bryant called to them.

Cass perched on the railing, Sylvie stayed where she was, half a step away. She held the baby on her left hip, the fabric of her dress hiked up to just below her underwear elastic.

"Yes," Bryant said, already snapping. "That's good, hold it just like that."

"No, uh uh, you hold it," a voice said. Bryant turned. Sylvie and Cass held their poses on the porch, but their gaze shifted. It was Heke.

He came walking out of the mist. Mist tongued at his hair and coiled at his ankles.

"Oh no," Bryant said under his breath. "I thought you'd gone out, old man."

"Good morning, Mr. Day," Bryant said, loudly and brightly. "How are you this morning?"

"You are trespassing here, old son," Heke said. "I already told you."

"This is perfectly legal, Mr. Day. I asked the Pomfrets' permission, and they gave it to me."

Cass was ready to confirm this, but he wasn't asked. Heke didn't even look his way.

"Ain't Pomfrets owns this place. Days own it, which is me. Around here, trespassing on another man's land isn't no way legal. I got a friend here backs me up," and he held up the shotgun he was carrying.

Bryant almost laughed. The gun was old, an antique, it looked like Daniel Boone's gun, a blunderbuss, like it had to be loaded with pellets and plugs of pig fat.

"I respect your privacy, Mr. Day. Truly. But what is wrong with me taking a few photographs? It's for a book, remember I told you yesterday? For the nation's bicentennial."

"You deaf or just stupid?" Heke said, his face a dangerous red. "This is my land. Private property. Nobody's taking pictures to show 'the nation' how sorry it is here."

"I don't know what you mean by sorry, Mr. Day. To me, it looks pretty wild up here. What appeals to me is, it looks probably not so different from what it looked like when your ancestors first—"

"You have any idea what the hell you are even talking about?" Heke said. "What it used to look like? It used to be timbered up to here, they came in and took out all the trees. Used to be coal. Always somebody wanting something from up in here. What I got, I'm keeping."

"You could tell me what it was like," Bryant said. "I'd really like to know."

"I'm not telling you nothing," Heke said. "Except one thing—you get yourself the hell offa here. I already told you last night." He made a sweeping gesture with the hand that did not have the gun in it.

"Stop," Cass said under his breath, his eyes fixed on Bryant.

"You know, Mr. Day, I believe there are two sides to this."

"There's not. All the sides here are mine, little man. This is my land you are stepping your shoes on."

"One second," Bryant said, and took a step towards Heke.

And Heke shot.

"Oh shit," Cass said. "Holy—" and his arm went out as if he were driving, Sylvie next to him, and they'd stopped short, all of a sudden.

Bryant went to his knees. He looked down at the khaki jacket, soft with so many washings.

"Oh," he said. "You didn't have to—" and he fingered the jacket, darkening with wet.

And then he was down on his hip, knees bent, arms pushed up, like a child who has wakened in the night and looked around and is about to go back to sleep. Who is seeing someplace other than where he is now.

6

NOBODY MOVED except Heke, who had turned and was walking away, slowly, as if his visit had been only neighborly.

Sylvie held still, Cass went on holding his arm across her front like the restraining bar on a roller coaster, they all held still, even the baby. For a minute, it was just another hot morning, one in a string of hot days. Heke went on walking, silent, though disconnected from the overall silence, as a plane is, flying way up.

A car went by on the road. A crow cawed, then it cawed again. Christopher's face crumpled at the bitter raw sound though it was another minute before he cried.

Then Sylvie yelled. Breath returned and "Noooo," came out of her, raucous, high-pitched, late, though it set her in motion. She put the baby down on the top step and, still bent, she ran down the steps to Bryant. He didn't move, but there was something soft in the way he lay, curled around, and Sylvie thought she saw him blink.

"Heeey!" Cass yelled, his voice angry and assertive. Sylvie turned, frowning at him—what did he think, did he think she was flirting?—but Cass wasn't looking at her.

"Heey!" he yelled again, flapping his arm over his head so that Sylvie looked then at the ground beyond Bryant to see if there was something predatory out there. The crow maybe. But Cass was flapping at Heke.

Heke paid no attention, partly deaf as he was from the report. He went on walking, the gun still in his hand, though he carried it with his arm down and equal to the other, empty, one. Cass let his arm drop.

Bryant's eyes closed.

Run! Sylvie told herself then, and her breath came out in ragged hiccups. She took off, hectic and wheeling.

"I'll be right back," she said as she passed Bryant. "I'm going to get help. I'll be right back."

"Syl," Cass called after her, but he didn't call again. By then, the baby was crying.

Heke kept walking—old man taking his old, slow time, black pants standing out wide from his waist as if they were made of some inflexible material, of tin, and held up by suspenders. Sylvie passed Heke as she ran hard towards his house, stirring up the dry dirt as her feet moved through it. The limp little ponytail at the back of her head danced.

She was at Heke's porch, then up it and inside where she stopped in the smoke-smelling dark and stood, trying to get her mind to slow down and think where the telephone was. She took a step or two straight ahead towards the kitchen, then something turned her, carried her into Heke's room, though she'd never been in it before.

The phone was on a tower of newspapers fully two feet high beside the bed pillows, as if Heke called somebody late at night, whispering into the phone in the starry dark, and Sylvie was, for a tiny moment, reluctant to touch it, to scar that pretty story with this new, harsh one.

Then she heard Heke. He had not run, but now he was here, feet stub-stubbing up the porch steps. The hairs at the back of Sylvie's neck rose and pulled against the rubber band she'd used for the ponytail, and she didn't hesitate anymore. She reached for the phone, her fingers awkward with haste and nervousness, sure Heke would get to her before she made the call.

She dialed 9, and there was a long, slow wait while the dial fanned out, then crept back, then 1 and 1. Her breath came and went, blurring the rusty-colored black of the mouthpiece—It was taking so much time!—and where was Heke now? Sylvie stepped over to the window overlooking the porch though the brown, crisp, ancient shade was pulled down and she was afraid to touch it. She put her hand up and flipped the ponytail. The back of her neck was wet, slippery, as if she had been swimming.

And then somebody answered the phone and she was blabbering into it fast and loud till she remembered Heke was right outside and quieted her voice a little, though she couldn't slow it down nor think of a way to say what she had to say that would sound like she wasn't blaming anybody, in case he was listening.

"Somebody's been shot here! Somebody's been shot!"

"You got to send out a—something," she said.

"Ambulance!" she said.

"Ohhh, I don't know." (Her voice broke.)

"I saw him blink a coupla few times. Where he is. Just lyin. Outside."

(Outside, the chair Heke was sitting in creaked loudly, as if he might be standing up.)

"Please," Sylvie moaned into the phone.

"I already told you. I don't know! I don't know! I don't know!"

7

HEKE LEANED the gun against the right-angled jut of the front door, next to the broom, then he sat down in his customary chair.

A girl edged out the door behind his right shoulder, trying to make her way past him inconspicuously, and he laughed, it was so useless, and she was so comical at it.

His sister Narciss was who he saw—Narciss young, in the long ago, not as she'd look now, if she'd been around to be seen—and he called to her—"Narciss! You think I don't see you?" and he laughed again.

"No," the girl said. "It's me, Sylvie Pomfret." A little whimpering sound came out of her.

"I just come up here to use the phone," she said. "I hope that's all right. An emergency for the baby. Christopher? He might be sick."

"Well I don't have a problem with you using the phone Narcissa," Heke said. "It's your house too."

Sylvie didn't know what he meant nor who he was talking to. She didn't know he was in the long ago. She leapt the porch and took off.

"Narciss," Heke called after her. "Don't you be late for dinner, now. You know dad."

Heke sat on, his hands spread like doilies on his knees, quiet, so his mother would not find him and assign him some chore to do.

"Hesketh. Hesketh?"

Heke sighed. "Out here, Mama."

"What're you up to?"

"Sweepin," Heke said, though he knew she'd hear him not sweeping, the absence of the shushing of the broom.

But Rudy only said, "Dinner's soon."

Inside, the air was thick with the heat from the oven. His mother had been cooking all morning. On the table was a turkey, roasted and prettily carved, the slices feathered out across the platter. Beans were in one bowl, peas with bacon in another, and greens, all out of the kitchen garden, and there was corn bread and white bread and dressing and gravy for the turkey and stewed lady apples in a garnet-colored syrup and a sweet potato pudding.

"Thanksgiving back again already?" Heke said.

Rudy didn't answer. Her wide face was pink from the heat; her sparse hair, combed back in a tight little bun, was stringy with sweat.

"Who's company?" Heke said, counting the five place settings.

"Just never mind and don't take up with what don't concern you," his mother said. "Come on anyway. I hear him."

She meant Royl, who was out on the back porch, and then Narcissa came in from the front and she had this boy tagging with her, JoJo Jones.

"That's the company?" Heke said.

Royl came in from the back. He looked surprised to see JoJo and, when he walked in, JoJo looked surprised to see him.

"Mr. Day!" JoJo said, bouncing on his heels. After they shook hands, Royl and JoJo both turned to face Rudy, like two dogs waiting for rewards after a trick.

"Doesn't it smell good in here," Narciss said, in her pretty voice. The two dogs nodded.

Narciss had put an apron around her waist when she came in, and Heke noticed for the first time how nicely dressed she was, like she was going to a dance or something, and now she went over to Rudy and put an arm around her waist and kissed her.

"Thank you, Mama," she mouthed.

Heke watched the two of them, then he looked again at JoJo and Royl.

"What's going on?" Heke said, and everybody turned to him.

"Sit," Rudy said. Her voice was pleasant, but she was frowning at Heke like he'd said or done something spoiling or stupid.

"What?" Heke said.

Royl began filling his plate in a diligent way, as if he intended to enjoy his food even if it was too hot for eating. Rudy pinched Heke's leg under the table.

"Ow! What?" Heke said again.

When it looked like nobody was going to do any more eating, Narciss got up. Rudy pushed her chair back too—"You sit, Mama, I'll do it," Narciss said, which made Heke look up at her, and made Royl laugh. Narciss never voluntarily cleared the table, claiming she might get something on her clothes and those were just her regular things; today she was so dressed up. The dress she was wearing was a pinkish tan, and she had on jewelry, a pin in a starburst pattern she had borrowed from Rudy. The rays were all tipped with faceted glass.

"Here," Narciss said. "Mama?" And she put five small dessert plates down on the table in front of Rudy and the five forks she held bunched in her hand. Royl was already rolling a cigarette for himself.

"No dessert for me," he said.

"Royl," Rudy said. "This dessert's special."

Narciss came back to the table holding a cake bigger by a long way than any cake Heke had ever seen before.

"Wow," Heke said, thinking of the size of the piece he was likely to get.

Narciss stood there with it, everybody watching, though nobody said anything, which made the cake, in every way exceptional, seem a little out of reach.

Rudy gestured with her chin towards Royl, and Narciss headed for him. The cake moved before the rest of her did, floating towards her father, as if it was a birthday cake she was delivering. Her hands shook a little with the cake's weight, JoJo half stood to help her, but Rudy put a hand on his arm and he stayed put.

"What's this?" Royl said. "This for me?" He tried to keep his voice indifferent, but pleasure seeped out anyway, and he dragged on his cigarette to keep his smile hidden. "It wasn't you made this, Narciss, I hope," Royl said and they all laughed as they were meant to, at Narciss's reputation for cookery. JoJo joined in, last, least and slowest.

Narciss slid the cake over to her father, and Royl's face one hundred percent changed then; it caved in on itself as if his teeth were missing all of a sudden. Later, years after this day, Rudy would still be saying her mistake had been to put those initials on the cake—JJJ and NJ. She'd cut them out carefully from two sheets of paper and laid the papers on the cooled top layer of the cake and snowed powdered sugar over them so the initials had come out clean-edged and smart.

"I shouldn't have done those letters," she said. "That's what changed everything."

"What is this?" Royl said, he couldn't seem to stop saying it. "What is this?" over and over. His face had gone a dark red.

Rudy looked at Royl and said, "They are, Royl. Married. Already done."

"No," Royl said. "Uh uh. She's not but sixteen, and he ain't but half-witted."

"Mama," Narciss said, and Rudy said, "Royl."

"You got a job, old son? You able to afford yourself a wife? And where is it you planning to live?"

"I've got a job, Daddy," Narciss said. "I'm working. And we thought we'd live here. For a little while."

"Well, think again," Royl said. "He ain't what I got in mind for a son-in-law."

He stubbed his cigarette out on his empty cake plate and pushed away from the table.

Heke didn't know all the details of what happened after that, he'd been sent out of the kitchen. But when it was done his mother was crying, his father had stormed out the front way and Narciss and JoJo were gone. Nobody knew they'd never see the two of them again. Royl never yielded.

Heke sat on for a long while. Hours passed. He looked out at the daylight from his seat on the porch. It seemed fuller now, brighter. A man was walking towards him from the dirt road, heading for the house. Heke craned his neck forward and he squinted, then he stood up. He didn't go all the way to the edge of the porch, but he peered out from it at the man, watching him come.

Then: "Well what do you know. Mama?" he called. "See who's on his way up here now. JoJo Jones!"

8

THE AMBULANCE appeared finally up on the road, or Sylvie thought it was the ambulance—a bee-yellow stripe across the center, the rest white—though from a distance its pace seemed more dirge-like than swift.

"Come on, come on," Sylvie said, and pounded her fist against her thigh, to make it go faster. She did not look at Bryant.

Cass was up on the dirt road. As soon as Sylvie had come running back from Heke's waving both arms and yelling to him—"Ambulance is coming!"—Cass had headed up to the road to direct it, because where they were was tricky to get to. Heke was sitting quiet up on his porch by then, but menace and volatility hovered around him like heat above the surface of the highway. What if he came back and there was Sylvie alone with the baby, Cass up on the road, too far away to do them any good? He could picture it—his calling, Sylvie never answering, the house bursting with the noise of the baby's inconsolable wailing—and he turned and jogged back to where he could see them.

"Go inside," he yelled to Sylvie as he came back through the poplars, but Sylvie didn't.

The day felt unfamiliar.

Bryant hadn't moved, and nobody had moved him. All this activity happening to him or around him or because of him, but it did not seem to include him; he was outside the circle of scatter and rush. He lay in the same place, cheek to the ground, eyes closed, like he was listening to something through the earth.

The ambulance bumped off the blacktop onto the dirt road, passing into and out of the tiny ravine where Bryant had left his car. It finally stopped, no movement at all came from it for a minute, then the door opened and the EMTs tore out, running before they'd straightened up, heads down, equipment bumping against their legs. They dropped to their knees on the powdery dirt of the yard where Bryant lay, their movements quick, precise, economical. It seemed backwards to Sylvie, their speed, when the ambulance had approached so slowly.

The EMTs rolled Bryant over and started CPR, their movements forceful enough to make it look as if Bryant was resisting. Sylvie shut her eyes and turned her head to a different place before opening them again. She saw Cass, who'd come closer and was standing now between the cabin porch and where Bryant lay. Cass winced and his head pulled sideways in a movement of retraction and when Sylvie looked back at Bryant again, what the EMTs were doing to him seemed an unnecessary pummeling, a kind of abuse.

Cass came up the porch steps passing behind Sylvie where, a few minutes ago, Bryant had told them to stand, and went into the house. Sylvie remained, turned staunchly front, a kind of necessary hostessing the situation seemed to call for. She couldn't leave any more than if this had been another sort of company.

The EMTs never looked at her though. Sylvie knew it was because all their effort was focused on Bryant, she knew that; still, the absence of acknowledgment of any kind felt judgmental, as if they were saying this whole thing was her fault. Tears pricked at her eyes; Sylvie mashed them away with her thumbs. All the men were gone soon.

Christopher had fallen asleep on the porch, cheek to the old wood. He'd continually forced his eyes open at first, to confirm that Sylvie's ankles and legs were still there, but sleep had compelled him. He woke at the sound of the siren's small mewl. He didn't cry, though. The siren made only the one sound.

Sylvie heard the baby move and looked behind her. She wondered what the time was. He'd be wanting lunch soon, probably. It seemed a long time since breakfast.

9

"YES?" MATTIE said into the phone.

She was breathless, she had heard the phone ringing as she got out of the car and had rushed up the driveway and the three stone steps to her porch.

She was sure it was Heke. Pictured him standing, formal, in his bedroom while he made the call to apologize to her (although also, simultaneously, she could not picture this: Heke calling at all. She wondered often why he even had a phone).

"Yes?" she said into the phone.

"Mattie? That you?"

A man's voice, not Heke.

"Yes," Mattie said. "This is she."

"Well, Mattie," he said. "It's Junior Major. I don't know do you remember me?" There was a heartiness in his voice, a delight in the offered surprise of himself that was familiar to Mattie though not here, in her own house.

"I—" Mattie said.

"I was in your very first class that you ever taught over at the school. Didn't you let us hear about that enough times? You weren't but a few years older than me. I was a big lunk of a thing—seventeen? Eighteen?" He laughed, as punctuation.

"Well," he said when Mattie didn't speak. "You might know I'm the sheriff," he said. "And I'm sorry to have to be calling you up like this, Mattie, on so-called 'official business,' but we've got Heke—Mr. Day—down here. And Mattie, yours was the number he gave us."

"Oh," Mattie said. "The sheriff. Is that true?" She was lost, unmoored in the conversation—of course she knew he was the sheriff—caught by the fact that Heke knew her telephone number. Memorized, or did he have it on a paper he carried with him?

"Yes, well, see, that's not why I'm calling, Mattie," Junior said. "I'm calling about Heke. Mr. Day. I've got him down here with me."

"Oh," Mattie said again. "Heke. You do? Why? Is he lost or something?" She laughed, this didn't seem impossible to her—Heke hardly ever went into town. He did his shopping in bulk, canned things, mostly.

"No," Junior said. "He wasn't lost." He wet his lips and began to tell Mattie the progression of events, feeling a little bit tested, either because she'd been his teacher or because he hadn't been at this job very long.

"Ambulance went up to the Day place," he said. "EMTs commenced working on the victim."

"Victim?" Mattie said.

"Photographer," Junior said. "Didn't I say that?"

"What photographer?"

"Name of—" Mattie heard Junior flipping the pages of his notebook.

"Go on," she said.

"I arrived after the ambulance had already left," Junior said. "Heke was setting on the porch and he stood up when he saw me coming. Called me JoJo though," he told Mattie.

"Oh," Mattie said. "He did? JoJo. Hasn't it been a long while since I heard that name."

"Thank you for telling me, sheriff," she said. "Um, did you want me to come in and get him?"

"Not him, his things, I thought you might want to bring him a coupla few things," Junior said. He had lowered his voice as if to keep from rattling her further and the conversation took on an intimate cast that he hadn't intended but did not know how to reverse.

"Pajamas," he said in this voice. "Socks. He's going to be with us awhile."

Mattie was in her car again, heading back up the mountain, back to Heke's the same way she'd come before. The only difference was—well, there were a lot of differences. But it was light out now; before, it hadn't been.

She drove through the flat, shadowless sun, up past the precipitate slides of earth and scrub trees that had skated down almost to the edge of the road in a recent hard rain then stopped, their heel ends only inches from the blacktop. She passed the sharp cragged escarpment of mountain—leveled, lowered, hollowed as a mouth with every other tooth gone—but she didn't lament the sorry, ruined landscape as she often did; she didn't even notice.

Junior's phone call had left her feeling odd, displaced inside the day, or less connected to it than to another phone call, a different day.

Heke had called once, years ago. Rudy had been stricken, he said. He and Royl were down to the hospital with her. Could Mattie run up to the house and bring her down a few things?

"Yes," Mattie said, emphatic. "What happened? Is she all right?"

"A few things," Heke said. "Nightgown. Robe. Such as that."

She had met them at the hospital. Royl and Heke both looked up when she stepped into the room, and their eyes stayed on her as if they were attaching themselves to her fresh and galvanizing brightness.

Royl sat in the chair beside the window, Heke stood at the foot of the bed where Rudy lay, neat, her arms outside the blankets, pinning the rest of her body within. Her hair was down, though, and Mattie knew Rudy would not have wanted people to see it that way, scant and untidy. Mattie turned her eyes so that she was looking at the wall above the bed, the clean white space hung with a crucifix.

She stayed with them at the hospital, carried them coffee in a thermos from home, or soup. Rudy had lingered three days, and afterwards, Mattie went up to the Day place every evening and cleaned and cooked supper for Heke and Royl, and sat at the table with them while they ate.

It had been summer, though cool, fall in the air. Mattie thought about how it would be to make the drive up here every evening after school, the wool of her coat broadcasting its chill into the kitchen as she came in carrying groceries.

One evening, a few weeks into this time, Mattie came outside after washing the dishes and drying them and putting them away. It was not dark yet, but the light had begun to gather in, as if a piece of loosely knit weaving had tightened. Mattie came down the porch steps and leaned against the railing. There were a few lightning bugs out, just one or two, but your eye went to them.

Heke was sitting on the porch steps as he did most nights after he'd eaten and smoked two cigarettes, one after the other. He was tall and his long legs reached from the top step to the bottom.

"Goodnight, Heke," Mattie said. "I'll be back again tomorrow."

Heke took a drag off his cigarette then held it out to see if it was worth another one. Royl rolled his own cigarettes but Heke smoked store-bought. In his large hands, Mattie thought, they looked elegant.

"Mattie," Heke said. "Would you sit down with me for a minute?"

"It's getting dark, Heke. I best be getting down the hill. I'll be back again tomorrow."

"That's what I wanted to talk to you about," Heke said.

He asked her to sit again, but Mattie didn't. She knew, all of a sudden, what he was about to say; she had waited a long time for him to speak to her and she wanted to see his face while he did it.

"I want to thank you," Heke said. "All you've done for us. There's something I'd like for you to have."

He fished in his shirt pocket where his cigarettes usually rolled loose and drew out something that gave off a dim shine in the unfinished daylight, like the lightning bugs.

"Rudy's," he said. "I know she'd be glad of my giving it to you. I know she'd of wanted you to be the one to have it." He turned around and looked at the front door, as if Rudy was watching from behind it.

Heke held it a minute, then handed it to Mattie—a gold pin in the shape of a starburst, tipped with diamondy pieces of glass. It was not exactly the present she'd thought it might be, but it was a present nonetheless.

"Isn't that pretty," Mattie said.

"Mattie," he said. "I want to thank you again for all you've done. We just wanted you to know how much we do appreciate it. But we won't need to be bothering you to come all the way up to here anymore."

"No?" Mattie said, and she still thought he was about to speak to her in the capital S sense of the word.

"Why's that?" she said, and expected Heke to say, because I'd like it if you'd stay. No need for you to go running back and forth—something in that family of words—but no. What he said was, "We'll manage. You have our thanks for your fine help. We'll be good on our own from here on out."

Mattie looked out across the lawn, hunting the lightning bugs but, just at that moment, there weren't any. Why did he do this? Come to the verge, but not go over?

"Heke," she said. "You know I—"

Heke stood. He came down two steps and touched Mattie on the shoulder. "You've been such a help," he said. "Such a comfort. I want you to know that." He looked at her a long moment, then he looked away.

Mattie nodded. She looked down at the pin. She told herself it was grief, he was grieving Rudy, the brooch meant something, the promise of a promise. The metal was warm from the heat of his hand.

But almost as soon as he said it, Mattie began to move away from the idea of a future with him. It was the closest Heke had ever come to speaking, and it was the day Mattie realized he wasn't ever going to speak. She'd been a comfort to him. A help. What woman wants to be that?

Mattie parked now, under the tulip poplar farthest from the house, in the shade that was hot and sticky. She walked through a curtain of midges, fanning the air with her hand, then across the dirt road and the sparse grass of the yard, careful where she stepped as she always was here, where a hundred different kitchen gardens had been put in and abandoned over the years, and where vines sometimes sprung out from the ground. She'd never stopped coming up here to do for Heke, that had become a habit. And though she'd stopped thinking he was about to speak to her, she hadn't stopped wondering if he would speak, or what she'd say to him if he did. That had become a habit too.

Something moved in the dark lip of shadow on the porch, something seemed to. Heke? Mattie thought, hovering in the shady back part of the porch the way he always did. Heke, it must be.

"How'd you get back here so quick?" she called, her voice light with relief. She was ready to sound annoyed, to tease him about how he'd dragged her all the way up here for no reason; she was ready to relish that oh so ordinary annoyance. Maybe the sheriff had been wrong. Maybe she'd dreamed the whole thing.

"What you just put me through!" Mattie said. "I have made this whole drive up here again for nothing."

"'Scuse me?" a girl's voice said.

Mattie stopped. "Narciss?" she said. "Oh my gosh! Do you know somebody just spoke JoJo's name this very afternoon."

"I wish people would stop calling that to me," the girl said—a girl: how old must Narciss be?

"I mean, it's me. Sylvestrie Pomfret."

"What are you doing up there?" Mattie said after a pause. "Who told you you could be up on that porch?" Her voice was tight and high up.

"I'm not doing anything," Sylvie said. She had come to the foot of the porch and now held her hands up, as if to show Mattie they were empty.

"I just come up to use the phone. See how that photographer fella was doing."

"And did you find out?" Mattie said. She stopped, waiting to hear Sylvie's answer.

"Dead," Sylvie said. "He died."

"Oh," Mattie said. "He did not. I don't believe it."

"That's exactly what I said when I found out," Sylvie told her. "I never knew a shot-dead person before."

Mattie looked up and she blinked. "What are you doing up there?" she said, as if she had not said it before. "You come down off of there right now. You shoo out of here right this very minute." She advanced as she spoke—head down, arms pumping—a staunch pony of a woman.

Sylvie backed against the house wall, but she laughed at the sight Mattie was. "Wait," she said, laughing. "Hold up a minute."

"What are you doing here, you little—" Mattie yelled, her voice rising.

"Wait a minute," Sylvie said. "I'm not doing nothing. I came up to use the phone is all, like I just told you."

"Off!" Mattie yelled. "Get off of here!"

She'd come up the porch steps now and there was the broom, back in its crook behind the door where it always was, where she had returned it early today, just as she did every time she came up here and swept—neat and tidy, she was, neat and tidy. Always such a help. A comfort.

Mattie grabbed the broom and swung it out by the tip of its handle so it made the lowest, widest possible arc, causing Sylvie to have to jump over it to keep from being swatted, then jump as it came back again. Sylvie wasn't laughing anymore, though a sound did come out of her each time Mattie swung the broom around. She had to fold over small to make the jump. The position squeezed the air out of her chest forcing her to make the sound over and over, of the highest, faintest note on a concertina.

10

THEY'D PUT Heke in the single cell behind the sheriff's office. Junior had led him in and backed him to the edge of the cot and sat him down, and Heke had gone on sitting with the patience of an old man waiting for a slow, late bus. The sheriff's building was new, one story, built with a barracks-like rigor out of cement and corrugated steel, temporary-looking, though not temporary, and only recently inhabited. The old building stood in its old place beside the courthouse, everything as it had been the day of the move—desks with the chairs pushed back, toilet paper on the racks in the putrid, fly-swarmed bathrooms—as if the building had been quarantined and everyone had fled.

The new building reeked of its spareness and newness—the combined smells of fresh concrete and new wool blankets, and the big bar of yellow laundry soap on the edge of the sink. The cell was almost mockingly austere, like a room assigned to political detainees in other countries. There was a drain in the center of the slightly canted floor, so the place could be hosed down.

Junior went back there as little as possible. He'd gone pretty often at first—Heke was the first inhabitant—but Heke never spoke, never answered any of the polite questions Junior put to him—"How you feelin this morning? How was your sleep?"—and now Junior just stayed up front in the office that was as bare and stark as a winter tree. Heke didn't have any visitors, except Mattie.

"And here she is now," Junior said, as Mattie came through the front door, her face pink and moist from the heat, though she had only walked across the parking lot. She had a brown paper shopping bag looped over her wrist.

The sheriff paid her a kind of attention. Mattie liked it, though it also made her self-conscious, as if his notice pointed to her age, came with an "in spite of." She wasn't sure there wasn't something of mockery in it.

"I've brought him some more things," she said, and peered into the bag that she had taken from the stack of bags her mother had kept and used again and again. The paper was worn to the silent pliancy of cloth.

"Oh yeah?" Junior said. "Like what?" He leaned all the way back, so that his chair groaned.

"There's soup," Mattie said. "Biscuits. And a few personal items."

Junior frowned. "Personal items?" he said. "Such as?"

"Oh just some socks and a sweater. And underwear," Mattie said, after a pause, looking away.

"Now I'm not sure that's regulation," Junior said. "Gotta check the book on that. Underwear."

Mattie flushed.

Junior laughed and reached across his desk as if he was going to swat her, though he stopped before he did it.

"I'm just playing with you Mattie," he said. "Mmm. Something smells tempting. What is it you said was in there?"

Junior got up and came around the desk and peered inside Mattie's bag. "Soup, you said?"

"And biscuits. Can I offer you some?" Mattie said.

"You wouldn't be trying to bribe an officer of the law, would you Mattie?" Junior said.

Mattie said, "Is that what I was doing? Wouldn't you have to know whether or not the soup was any good, before it was considered a bribe? Maybe it's bad," she said. "Maybe it's not safe to eat it."

"I'm playing. I'm playing with you," Junior said. "Joking."

"I'm joking too," Mattie said softly. Junior laughed, although his face looked hard, because he didn't get it.

"I tell you what," Junior said. "Whyn't you go on ahead and bring him that food. What Heke doesn't eat, I'll have. Split the difference. Save you the trouble of carrying it home again."

"Yes," Mattie said. "That would be such a savings."

Heke looked up when Junior swung the door open, or he seemed to, though when Junior spoke—"Hey there, Heke. Here comes Mattie in to see you with a whole big bag full of food, lucky dog"—Heke didn't answer, and he didn't look at either one of them.

"Heke," Junior called, to jar him, but he didn't move then either.

"It's okay," Mattie said. "I can take it from here."

"I hope so," Junior said. "I hope you can get him to eat something too. Look at this."

Junior picked up Heke's untouched breakfast tray and tutted at it. "You on a hunger strike, Heke? You don't know what you're missing."

"He doesn't eat," he said to Mattie and held out the tray so she could see how the silverware was still rolled up tight inside the paper napkin, the food smeared down under a tight covering of plastic.

"Well, where's his eating place?" Mattie said. "Is he supposed to just eat off the bed?"

Junior looked around the small room before he answered, as if the question hadn't occurred to him before.

"Yeah," he said. "I guess so."

"That doesn't seem right," Mattie said. "The man should be entitled to eat his meals in a little human comfort, don't you think? He's not a dog!"

"Yeah, well, we're not really in the comfort business," Junior said. "We're not the Howard Johnson's here."

Mattie looked up at the slight change in light as Junior headed towards the door. She was pulling Heke's sweater from the shopping bag, a gray wool cardigan, once robust, now frail, the wool fretted with holes, the elbows worn down to ossification. It gave off the same cool, smoky odor as the inside of Heke's house.

"You don't think he's gonna need that, do you?" Junior said, and his voice rolled back at him from the cement walls and floor and ceiling.

"It might cool off," Mattie said. "It's not like this heat's normal."

"Not gonna be here long, is what I mean," Junior said. "And the place they're most likely to send him—this *is* the Howard Johnson's compared to that."

"Well, or they might just send him home again," Mattie said, refolding the sweater against herself. "You know what the Constitution says: Innocent until proven guilty," though she was suddenly not sure this was correct. Something said it: the Constitution? It dismayed her, the sudden elusiveness of this fact.

"Oh, he's guilty all right," Junior said. "That's a provable fact."

"Not by you it isn't," Mattie said.

"Mattie."

"Were you there?"

"There's eyewitnesses," Junior said. "He walked right up to the man and he—"

"Maybe he had reasons," Mattie said. "Anybody consider that? Maybe there's more to it than meets the eye."

"Like what?"

"Defense of self or property—the Constitution does speak about that."

"Self-defense," Junior said. "He never said word one in his own self-defense."

"He's right here!" Mattie said. "He's right in the room! And why are you calling me 'Mattie'? Who gave you permission to do that?"

"Mattie. Sorry. Miss Wheeler. I wouldn't worry too much about saying things in front of him. Heke's gone; he's present here in name only."

"You can go now, sheriff, if you wouldn't mind. If it's not bribery or something to ask you. I'd like a few private minutes."

"Whatever you say," Junior said. "Call if he gets rowdy," and he pulled the barred door shut behind him.

Mattie went back to unloading the paper bag, forcing herself to breathe slowly through her nose to calm down. She pulled out a pair of socks and held them to her cheek. They were egg-colored and egg-round and warm from sitting on top of the foil-wrapped biscuits, which also made them seem like eggs.

"Look what I brought you to eat," Mattie said, and fished out the tinfoil package of biscuits. "These are the biscuits you love," she said.

Heke didn't take the biscuit she was offering him though, didn't answer, didn't even turn his head, and Mattie set it on a napkin and put it on the cot, then she sat down beside him. They sat side by side looking straight out, as if they were sitting on a davenport, watching TV.

"Oh, I almost forgot. There's soup." Mattie jumped up and reached for the bag again, for the red-and-black-plaid thermos with a red plastic cup, the same one she had carried to Royl and Heke in the hospital when Rudy was there.

"You remember this?" she said, but Heke didn't answer.

"Here you go. Heke?" Mattie said and touched him gently on the shoulder with the cup.

Heke turned to her then; he looked right at her, his gaze as direct and clear as a boy's. Mattie set both cup and thermos on the floor beside the cot and sat back down beside him. They were both turned now, towards each other.

"What?" she said gently. "Heke?"

Heke shuffled his feet out as if he meant to get up, then pulled them back in again.

"Heke?" Mattie said. "Do you have something to say?" She had that feeling, large and anticipatory, that was not unfamiliar to her in Heke's presence. She felt him to be always on the verge of declaration; sure, every minute, that he would speak the next. The way he looked at her, even now.

But then he did not speak. Of course. Heke looked at Mattie, but said nothing. He blinked—his breath touched her right above the eyebrow—then resumed his original position, huge hands resting almost dainty on his knees. It was true what the sheriff had said: Heke was not really here; he was elsewhere.

Something slid across Mattie's foot, bare in her brand-new sandals. Something crawled. She held still, she didn't look down, concentrating only on the sensation waiting to discover she was mistaken in it, nothing was crawling, of course not.

It didn't stop though, and she finally did look. The soup. Heke had kicked over the thermos when he'd slid his feet out.

"My shoes!" Mattie said. "My new shoes! Sheriff," she called. "Junior."

Junior came at a run at the sound of her voice. "What's wrong?" he said, as he slammed the door open. He looked in at Heke, still immobile on the edge of the cot.

"What's he done?" Junior said.

"My shoes," Mattie said. "They're new—" and she was crying, crying and crying, she couldn't seem to stop.

Junior took a step forward and patted her shoulder, then he stepped back again. "It's okay," he said.

"I'm sorry," Mattie said finally, when she was able to speak. "I just overreacted. Some soup spilled, that's all. It's a bit of a mess. It's just—these shoes are new." She looked at Junior. He smiled at her. "Women," he said. "Women and shoes." Which made them both feel better.

"Don't worry, okay?" Junior said. "There's a hose, I'll take care of it. You all right now?"

Mattie nodded. She crossed the floor, the soup slimy and animate between her bare toes, then stopped.

"Those biscuits," she said. "In that tinfoil packet. Please have them. I couldn't get him to touch anything, either."

11

MATTIE EXPECTED to be called at the inquest. She expected to be asked to come to the front of the courtroom and testify to Heke's character, and she had planned what she was going to say—he had taken long, good care of his parents, Royl in particular; there had never been any trouble of any sort before—not just the words, but their emphases, soft stresses, so that she would not appear to be protesting too much.

It had taken her some time to dress. Her words, when she spoke about Heke, had to sound weighty and grave, her clothes grave to match. She hadn't lain in bed that morning listening through the opened back door for the noise of whatever was outside in her garden, nor for the daily aggregation of the sound of the birds. She'd spent that time dressing—a navy blue skirt and a white shell. It was hot and so she didn't wear, but carried, a matching blue jacket that she planned to put on when they called her, covering her shoulders as she would in church.

But she was never called. Even Cass wasn't. Only the EMTs. And Sylvie.

Sylvie had on a pink blouse that day. She stood when they called her, in the midst of the stirred-up talk that followed the EMTs from the room, one sound made up of more than one, like the wakening birds. Sylvie and Cass had been pushed down to the far end of the row and she had to squeeze her way past all the men in front of her, who sucked in their stomachs, but didn't move their legs. The talk in the room went away voice by voice, the way it had started, until the only sound was the creaking of the chairs as the men in Sylvie's row leaned back.

Sylvie was pink- and damp-faced by the time she got to the front of the room. Her palms were sweaty and she wove her fingers persistently and turned her hands up and over to the air.

"Start already," she muttered, silently, speaking down to her hands, but Cass saw her lips move.

"What if they ask me a question I don't know the answer to?" she had said to Cass before, at home, when she was dressing.

"Hey," he said. "What're you wearing that fancy thing for?" and he plucked at the edge of the thin pink blouse she was putting on.

"What?" she said. "It's the lightest thing I have," but she did always get compliments when she wore it.

"Commere," Cass said to her. "We got time."

"We don't," Sylvie said and slapped at his hand. "I can't be late to this thing. Nor you either"—and she turned and buttoned the buttons that were shaped like small, round, pink pearls.

"That thing getting tight on you, Syl? You getting bigger on me?" Cass said. His hands had moved off her but his eyes hadn't.

"Bigger off what?" she said. "All those meaty steaks you've been carrying home?" She hadn't yet told him she was pregnant. She curved her shoulders and pushed them against the fabric of the blouse to get it to give a little.

The courtroom was hot, airless, though the big windows were open at the tops and the overhead fans blatted slowly. There was a sound of shuffling papers from the front table, but Sylvie didn't look up. Mattie was right in her sight path, stern and forbidding in her navy blue.

"Okay then," said a voice, a man, the room was mostly filled with men, other than Sylvie and Mattie.

"You ready to begin?" It was Turner Ward, the state's attorney.

"I'm here," Sylvie said and looked at him, her chin tipped up a little. He was tall and big, thick-limbed. He had the dimensions and trustiness of a grown tree.

Turner laughed, then he stopped. He peered at her a minute, knees bent so he could see into her face because didn't he know her?

A chair scraped; somebody cleared his throat.

"Okay then," Turner Ward said. "I'm just going to play this tape back to you Mrs. —" and he looked down at the paper on the table beside him. Her name had just been called out—Pomfret, Mrs. Cass—but it hadn't meant anything to him.

"Mrs. Pomfret," he said. "Can you confirm for me please that this is you, on the tape of this telephone call?"

Sylvie nodded and she folded her hands and cocked her head to indicate sharp listening. Turner pushed a button on the tape player and her voice leapt into the room.

"Somebody's been shot, somebody's been shot!"

The audience of men mumbled and looked at each other.

Sylvie covered her mouth with her fingertips. The screeching urgency of the voice on the machine was embarrassing. There was no emergency here now. There was dust pouring in the slats of sun through the windows, and the calm pale pink of her blouse, shy against the other, staider colors—the browns of the tables and chairs, the green of the windowshades, the men.

Turner Ward stopped the tape. The room was perfectly quiet. A glassy hum came from one of the overhead fluorescents.

"Mrs. Pomfret?" Turner Ward said.

"Yes," she said. "That's me," and she held up her hand. "I swear it. From when I called the 911."

"Who were you referring to?" Turner said. "In the phone call."

He waited for Sylvie to answer; when she did not, the expression on her face both worried and expectant, Turner asked, "Who'd been shot, Mrs. Pomfret? You said 'somebody.' Who?"

"Oh," Sylvie said. "You know. Photographer fellow."

"And where'd the shots come from?"

"From a gun," Sylvie said. "Heke Day's. Well, I don't know was the gun his, but he's the one fired it. He didn't do it skulking or anything. Came right up and did it."

The men began talking again—a muddled sound reached Sylvie—and she looked out towards the back of the room, but her eyes snagged on Mattie as they had before, and she looked back at Turner. She remembered Turner; her sister Lusa had dated him in high school for a time, before he went off to college and law school and all his big things, it had to be ten years ago, more. He'd come back, though. It was Lusa didn't live around here anymore.

"And then what happened?" Turner said.

Sylvie blinked and held up a hand as if she'd been coughing and was going on coughing but would be finished soon.

"Pardon?" she said.

"After you made the telephone call. What happened then?"

"Well, I mean, he died," Sylvie said.

There was a rumble of sound in the room, an underburble of chat and some laughter and Mattie's cold, hard and persistent glare.

"Well, he did," Sylvie said, and pulled at the front placket of the blouse.

Turner waited for the noise to subside without asking it to. Then: "How do you know that?" he said. "That he died."

Sylvie shrugged. "Called the hospital," she said. "After."

Sylvie Neery, Turner realized. Sylvestrie, Lusa's little sister, she couldn't have been more than eight or so the last time he'd seen her. He smiled; it made his next question—"What happened after the shot, I meant?"—sound kind.

"Two," Sylvie said, holding up two fingers. "There were two shots."

"Two shots," Turner Ward said. "After the two shots. What did you do?"

"Well, I ran out. I tried to. He stood in front of the door and put his arm out, blockening me." She flung her arms out now, demonstrating.

"He?" Turner said.

"Cass. Cassius Clay Pomfret. My husband. There." She pointed at Cass, then quickly looked away, not sure if she had just accused him of something. She had sworn to tell the truth, but what if she wasn't? What if the way she'd seen things wasn't the true and actual way they'd really happened? A ribbon of nausea came up in the back of Sylvie's throat. She pinched her lips together with her fingertips and shut her eyes for a second against the rising taste of bacon.

"You all right?" Turner Ward said.

Sylvie opened her eyes and nodded and he handed her a glass of water from a tray on his table.

"Here," he said. "Here you go. It is *hot* in here." He fanned at his face while Sylvie moved the glass to her lips, hesitated, then handed it back to him.

"My mouth's willing but my stomach's not," she said. Her voice was low, not much above a whisper, it was Turner she was talking to, but there was a microphone in front of her and everybody heard. There was laughter again. Not from Cass, though, and not from Mattie.

"Mr. Pomfret put his arm out," Turner said.

Sylvie nodded.

"Like so," she said, and flung her arm out as she had before.

"To stop you?" Turner said.

"Yes. No! I mean yes, to stop me, but not for bad. He was scared for me and our baby boy. That's Christopher Pomfret. He's not here right this minute. He's with my sister right now. Not Lusa," she told Turner Ward. "My other sister. I don't know do you remember her? Naneen."

A sound came from Mattie, something between a moan and a howl. This unbearable girl and her tight, tight blouse. Turner Ward looked in the direction of the sound, then he looked back.

"Your husband was afraid of Mr. Day?" Turner said.

Sylvie nodded. "No. I mean, Cass wasn't afraid of him, more he was afraid for me, you see? Didn't want me running down there in case Heke was, you know. Dangerous all around."

Heke looked up then, the one and only time, as if he'd just now caught onto the fact that he was being talked of. He looked right at Sylvie and she said, "Not that you would. I mean, I'm just trying to be wholly truthful."

She stopped. She used to think truth-telling was simple, a clean, straight road. She hadn't ever noticed before how it branched.

"He's a good husband," Sylvie said. "Cass Pomfret, I'm talking about, not Heke. I mean, tell me I'm wrong, but I don't think Heke's ever been married. I mean, it's Cass I'm talking about. He's a good man, but 'cept he just doesn't have a job. But that's not his fault."

"It's not," Sylvie said: more underburble in the room.

"It's not like he hasn't looked. He's looked everywhere. Just, times are terrible. Ask anybody."

Cass had turned away before Sylvie finished speaking, his mouth a line of bitterness. Sylvie leaned in his direction. The fabric of the blouse pulled across her back, the cheap little stitches taxed almost to bursting.

"What did you do then, Sylvie?" Turner said, his voice mellow and coaxing, and Sylvie turned back to him: she had to. "Your husband tried to hold you back, and you . . . ?"

"I ran over to Heke's house anyway," Sylvie said. "I mean it didn't take more than two seconds, Cass stopping me. Not even. And then I called the 911." She pointed at the tape recorder.

"After that," Sylvie said, "the ambulance come."

"Come," Mattie said, shaking her head. "Come." She ground her back teeth to keep from speaking aloud. She hated this girl.

Sylvie flushed. "You know, what is your problem?" she called out to Mattie. "I am not making this all up, it's what happened. I'm sorry if you don't like it, but I don't much like it myself either. And I'm the one who seen it, not you."

"All right now," Turner said. "You can meet her outside later in the parking lot and duke it out."

The men all laughed.

"Okay then," Turner said. "Now, why didn't you make that telephone call from your own house?"

Sylvie hunched her small shoulders and tilted her head and looked at Turner, abject, begging for something.

Somebody cleared his throat.

"I can't make any calls from my house," Sylvie said. "We're not on the phone."

"We got the electric, though," she said. "Lights and a fridge and everything."

The laughter in the room got louder—a satisfied laughter, as if the morning was turning out to be entertaining. Cass thought it was him they were laughing at, but Mattie knew it wasn't—it was Heke, or Heke's father, Royl. How they'd been cheap in the building of those cabins, how cheapness was a Day family characteristic—and she drew herself up, about to stand and walk out, back straight, neck rigid, no mistake about what was sending her from the room, but Cass beat her to it. He stood up so fast his chair knocked akimbo from the others in the row, and he made his way through to the aisle, slamming against all the other men's knees, and then he stalked to the exit, shaking off the guard who tried to catch him and calm him and tell him maybe he should take a few deep breaths and sit back down.

Sylvie slid to the edge of her chair and leaned towards Cass, the tight pink blouse straining against her, but Cass didn't come back, he didn't even turn around. Later on he would say to her, I didn't know it was me on trial in there. I didn't know it was me who did anything wrong.

12

CASS LEFT the courtroom as if he were being pursued, though no one did pursue him. His heart was beating fast, the skin of his face was mottled and as he opened the outside door, he put his fingertips to it.

There was a great blare of light as he stepped outside, light bursting from the bare hard surfaces—storefronts, sidewalk, the ragged empty lot beyond—and what seemed like a solid wall of heat. Cass held up at the top of the steps in the refuge of a narrow gully of shade. His heart was still laboring; he waited for it to calm, until long past when it had, and he saw himself not as an enraged and righteous man paused at the top of the steps to catch his breath, but a man with nothing to do and no place to be. After that, he crossed the street.

Once, Sylvie had played a game of ping-pong; more than once, but this one particular time, back when she was in high school. It was on a homemade table and it was at a friend's house and she'd been playing the brother of the friend, a boy she'd liked second or maybe third. And then the boy she liked first came by.

They were in a kind of outside room the friend's father had put up. It had a packed dirt floor and a sheet metal roof held up by paired two-by-fours but no walls, a kind of shed nothing could be stored in because it wasn't enclosed. The ping-pong table was out there and a cooler, empty that day, though it was sometimes filled.

"Hey," the boy said. He said it to the boy Sylvie was playing, then his eyes moved to Sylvie, slowly, as if he was just casually searching the room. Sylvie stood smacking the fleshy part of her palm with the paddle, shifting her weight from foot to foot. Her palm stung, then the stinging went away.

After that, the ping-pong game took up again, but every ball that came to her Sylvie hit into her side of the net or else way past the opposite end of the table. She wanted to be free to go talk to the boy. The game was over in a minute.

Now, in the courtroom, it was like that. Sylvie watched Cass stalk out, balanced on just the edge of her seat, and she stayed that way. She answered the other few questions put to her, but her answers were quick or one-worded, her eyes fixed on the door. Turner Ward tried to get her to slow down, but Sylvie wouldn't. The thin and winding path of truth no longer concerned her. She wanted out.

When she was told she could step down, she caught up her purse on its long white strap and went fast up the aisle. The too-long strap slid off her shoulder to the middle of her arm and she raised it with the opposite hand, then left that hand where it was, arm slung across her chest. The blouse seemed tighter now than it had been, tight enough so that she noticed it with a kind of dawning horror as she went and thought, Could she be bigger since the morning?

Sylvie stood at the top of the steps when she got outside, as Cass had before. The air hung like a hot wet rag and she put her hand up to her throat.

"Where is Cass, now?" she said, and she frowned and came down the steps, the purse slipping from her shoulder again. She went across the street to the parking lot. Cass was in the truck. Sylvie opened the passenger door and got in.

"Lord," she said. "This has been a morning."

Cass looked at her while he started the truck, but he didn't speak.

"I swear to God, Cass, does this truck have to be the hottest place on earth?" She flounced in the seat and pulled on her window crank though the window never went any farther down than midway.

Cass pulled out of the parking lot. They rode in silence for a while, then Sylvie said, "Don't forget, we got to get Christopher at Naneen's," and she pointed ahead to where they'd have to get off the highway and onto the county road, then drive a little ways on that to her sister's.

"Slow down, Cass. We got to get off."

"Cass! You're going right past—"

"Hold up," Cass said. "Don't be so bossy, Syl. I got things to talk about. Your sister's gonna keep him a little bit longer."

"How come?" Sylvie said. "What 'things'?"

Cass shrugged. He kept his eyes on the road and held the wheel with two fingers.

"How do you know Naneen'll keep him?" Sylvie said.

"Because," Cass said. "I called her up and asked her."

Heke's house seemed different when they drove past, a kind of pressing quiet shut inside it.

Cass was driving slow, eyes on the road, the way he always did here—it was a walking road, not a driving one, he said—but Sylvie turned her head and watched the house, the front, then the side going past.

"You think he's coming back ever?" Sylvie said. She turned front again. In the moment before Cass gave his answer, she could hear how quiet it was. The quiet felt tighter than it should have, compressed alongside the heat like two bad things ganged up together.

"No," Cass said. "I don't think he ever is."

"What brings a man to think about killing somebody?" she said.

"I don't think he did think about it," Cass said. "You saw him. Photographer fella was trespassing, how Heke saw it. The killing part just stampeded out."

Then they were home.

Cass went heavily up the wood steps of the cabin, his feet turned sideways because the treads were narrow. He went in, the thin wood framing of the screen door smacking against the outside of the house. The inner door stood open, the way they always left it.

"Maybe you might want to think about closing this door when nobody's home," Cass said, and swung it back and forth between his palms a few times.

"Why?" Sylvie said. "We never do. Besides, you just said he wasn't coming back here."

"No," Cass said. "Not because of Heke. Well, just never mind."

It was dim inside the cabin. Sylvie slipped by Cass and reached for the light cord that hung above the table, swatting at the air until she found it.

"Aw, Syl, don't," Cass said and he shaded his eyes.

"What?" Sylvie said, but she snapped the light off again and stood where she was. The string swung.

"You want something cold to drink?" she said, then remembering what she had said before about how they had electricity, she looked away. Maybe Cass was thinking the same thing; he didn't answer. If there had been a fly anywhere inside the cabin right then, they would have heard it. Or a clock.

"Come on over and sit down by me," Cass said, and sat himself on the too-small settee underneath the window.

Sylvie sat down and looked at him.

Cass lolled back against the settee, legs tangled out in front of him. "God, I hate this place," he said. He didn't move when he spoke, except to close his eyes.

"Cass," Sylvie said. "Forget about that. Slide on over here to me." She was the one who moved, though, leaned up against Cass and ran a finger down the back of his neck, but he shook her off.

"What?" Sylvie said. "You're saying no? *You* are?"

"I gotta get out of here," Cass said.

"We will, baby," Sylvie crooned at him. "You just say where you want to go."

"No," Cass said, and he stood up. "I mean me. I have got to leave here."

"What do you mean?" Sylvie said, and then she was crying. It started slowly, tears just leaking from her, but soon she gave herself over to it, crying hard, like a child, face tipped to the ceiling, hands in her lap.

"You finished?" Cass said after a while.

Sylvie nodded. She jammed her thumbs into her eyes, then she reached for Cass and pulled him to sit back down beside her. She placed his hand on the buttons of the pink blouse.

Cass rubbed his thumb over one.

"I'm glad now Christopher's still at my sister's," Sylvie said. She spoke in a soft voice, and she smiled at him, as if her tears had wiped out the things Cass had said before, and now they could start over.

Cass played with the button for a moment, then he let go.

"Syl," he said softly. "I'm still going."

"You can't go, what do you mean? What about me?" Sylvie said. "What about the baby?"

"You'll be okay, I promise. You'll be altogether fine."

"Where to? Where are you going? What for? Are you scarpering on me, Cass, or what is it?"

"Ohio," Cass said. "I'm going on up to Ohio, to my sister's. Find work, find us a decent house to live in. Then I'll be back and get you."

"No you are not," Sylvie said, but Cass didn't answer.

"How long's all that supposed to take?"

"Don't know," Cass said. "Not too long. Don't know."

"We'll come now," Sylvie said. "It's not like there's aught to keep us."

Cass shook his head; he was looking at the door as if it was the door he was talking to. "Peggy's place is too small," he said. "You know that."

Sylvie didn't answer because she did know. They'd been for a visit once, she and Cass. Peggy's husband Steve got drunk and then he came after Sylvie like she was interested and he was available. She couldn't be left alone in the house or the car or the whole state with him. Peggy was never too keen on Sylvie after that.

"Well how long?" Sylvie said. "And how'm I supposed to manage? Pay for rent and groceries and everything?"

"I don't think rent's about to be a problem," Cass said. "Anyway, I'm'n'a get work, something, right away. I'll send you money. And there's that fifty he give us."

Sylvie shuddered. "I'm not touchin that."

"Why not?" Cass said.

"Because," Sylvie said. "He was payin us to take our pictures and he never did."

"He took some," Cass said. "He took a few."

"You can tell yourself that if you want to," Sylvie said. "That's not the way I'm looking at it. And I am not touching that money."

"Well, fine, suit yourself," Cass said. "I'll be sending you money anyhow, soon as I can."

"Why're you so sure there's even jobs in Oldhio?" Sylvie said.

Cass shrugged. "Big place. And I'll do anything."

He stood and went to the open door.

"But I'll be up here alone," Sylvie said from behind him. "All by myself up here on this hill."

"Go stay with your sister, then," Cass said.

"My, you've about thought of everything."

Cass didn't answer.

"Cass," Sylvie said. "Are you doing this to punish me?"

"I'm doing this *for* you. This is what I'm supposed to do, take care of my family."

"If I hadn't of said that, in the court? If they hadn't of asked me those things, would you still be going?"

Cass shrugged. He turned to the open doorway again. "Maybe not today," he said. "Or maybe I never would of at all. But that'd be worse.

Things'd just get worse and worse. We'd end up—You'd hate me, Syl."

"I never would."

"After a while. You would. It's what needs to be," Cass said. "There's no jobs here. I have looked and looked and looked."

"I know that. Don't you think I know that?" Sylvie's voice was loud. "I'm sorry," she said. "It's all my fault and I am so sorry."

"It's never your fault," Cass said. "Today just gave me a little boot, that's all. It's for good." He smiled, but Sylvie was crying again, or her face was wet when Cass came over to her and touched it.

He pulled her up against him. Her head only reached to his third shirt button from the top.

"A lot of men do this," Cass said.

"I know that," Sylvie said. "I just never pictured it'd be us."

"Yeah," Cass said. "Well, I never pictured this either. Living in a dump like this."

He was looking around over her head, Sylvie could feel the torque and flexion of his ligaments like distant ropes and pulleys against the side of her face. They stood that way a long minute, until Sylvie saw herself waiting for the minute to end.

"Well," she said. "If you're going, I suppose you should get on with it"—and almost immediately something in him released or dropped down as if it was ropes and pulleys; as if he'd been rigged by invisible tension. There had been no boys she'd liked third or second or first once she'd met him; there had been only Cass.

"Come on," Cass said now, looking down at her. "I'll carry you to your sister's. You can stand it for one night."

Sylvie rolled her eyes. Cass laughed. "You can try," he said. "Or we can find someplace else for you to go, if you're nervous on your own up here."

"I'm not," Sylvie said. "I'm fine. What's gonna happen to me here?"

She waited while Cass threw clothes and his razor into a paper sack, then they both went outside and got into the truck. Cass backed up and turned in the dirt in front of the first cabin, then headed back on the dirt road, slow as they'd come in. Heke's house sailed past again, weighty where it stood.

Cass paused to check the traffic before he pulled onto the highway, though there never was any. The only cars that made it all the way up here were cars that were looking for them.

13

THE TRUCK veered wide as Cass cut the wheel and pulled over on the highway, and Sylvie, nausea creeping just behind her rib cage, braced herself against the dashboard.

"Cass," she said. "What's wrong?"

Cass had stopped at the place where the off-road to Naneen's slid away from the highway, and when he didn't answer her, Sylvie figured maybe he didn't want to deal with her sister, no surprise. He got out of the truck and started around the front, heat radiating fiercely through his open door. Sylvie was about to get out too—had her own door pushed open—when the heat met her, and she couldn't move. She just sat there, one leg draped over the edge of the seat, her skirt hiked up, and with her head against the seatback and her eyes shut.

"I'm'n'a get out here," Cass said, leaning in at her door, and when Sylvie opened her eyes, he was gone, he just wasn't there anymore.

"Cass," Sylvie called, and flung herself out of the truck, but the nausea sloshed behind her breastbone and she had to stop and reach for the truck door and bend over.

Cass hadn't gone anywhere though, or only back to the truck bed, where he was collecting the clothes and shaving things that had rolled out of the paper sack.

"Cass," Sylvie called again. She came towards him, the distracted air of dyspepsia still on her face.

"Hey, Syl, watch yourself," Cass yelled. "This is the highway." And Sylvie said, "I know," and looked in the direction she was facing, but there weren't any cars. The highway was dry and chalky, as empty as a desert. It had been fought for by local politicians and finally won but nobody used it if they didn't have to. The road washed out in big rains, there was no drainage ditch or bunker of any kind, mud oozed down from the stripped hills and with nothing to stop it, slid out over the roadbed. Cold buckled it and left it pocked and fissured. It was never fixed.

"You could be a slow ant and still get across here," Sylvie said, and then something—the way the heat made the air waver up ahead, or the road's stretched-out emptiness—made her stop talking and walk back to the flag of shade thrown by the truck's open door.

"I'm'n'a leave you here," Cass said again, and he looked away down the highway in the same direction Sylvie just had.

"What do you mean, 'leave me here'?" Sylvie said. "I'm all by myself"—and pregnant, she almost said, then didn't: how fair would that be? She put her hand on her stomach though, let Cass ask what for if he wanted.

"Hitch," Cass said, and Sylvie's eyes bugged out and she yelled it back at him—"Hitch! Are you crazy? You want me to stand out here by myself in this heat?"

He was coming towards her by then, frowning against the glare and with his hands out like he meant to push her back, off the road, clear of the nonexistent traffic.

"Not you, me," he said when he reached her. His hands went one to each arm and he pulled her tight up against him. "I'm hitching. You take the truck," he said, his voice soft now.

Sylvie pulled away from him. "Take the truck your own self," she said. "Big daddy."

"Syl," Cass said.

"God, Cass," she said. "What kind of ride you even think you're going to get? How long've we been standing out here and how many cars have you counted?" She leaned against the truck with her arms tight across her chest and her head tipped skywards and her eyes shut. The pink blouse felt like it was about to split right down the back.

"How am I going to bear it?" she said. "You just tell me that?"

Cass stepped in, and he kissed her. For a moment, Sylvie wouldn't kiss him back, then she reached one arm around him, and she did.

Naneen's house was small—like the cottage of the wicked witch in Hansel and Gretel, Cass said about it—and severely neat. Sylvie had never seen the house out of order—or no, she had, small temporary ditches of mess—what she'd never seen was Naneen defeated by it. Her sister attacked disorder, a frown stitched between her eyes—Your face'll stay that way, Sylvie was sometimes on the point of saying, as their mother used to, but the things Naneen would have taken from other people she wouldn't take from Sylvie.

Naneen lived in the tiny house with her husband, Tucker, and their unidentical twin little boys—one yellow-haired, one dark. Tucker wasn't ever home, he was a mill foreman fifty-five miles away. ("Coincidence?" Cass said. "I don't think so.") Their wedding portrait—Naneen seated, light bouncing off her rounded, smiling cheek, Tucker standing behind with his big paw on her shoulder—sat in an easel frame on top of the TV.

"So the boys won't forget what he looks like," Cass said. "Since that's mostly where they're always looking."

Sylvie laughed, but when she was not with her sister, or when she had recovered from the last time they were together, her opinion about Naneen softened and was replaced by the warmth of nostalgia.

"She's not the way you always think she is," Cass tried to remind her. "She's not so nice," but Cass wasn't here now, Cass was getting smaller and smaller in the rearview mirror as Sylvie came off the highway, and a longing for her sister rose up in Sylvie, the word "sister" like a bowl filled up. She pictured the two of them, sitting across the table from each other in Naneen's clean bright kitchen, picking at a bowl of popcorn, talking all night, the little boys asleep upstairs, a fan clattering the hot air.

As it turned out, though, Sylvie didn't stay.

"What have you got on, Sylvestrie? That blouse is too tight on you, don't you have a mirror? It's like a doll clothes blouse or something," Naneen said before Sylvie was even inside the house. She stopped halfway, the door held open behind her with her foot.

"Come in," Naneen said, gesturing furiously. "Shut the door for God's sakes. Cass said you weren't picking Christopher up or I would have worn my company clothes too," she said. She was wearing baggy light blue shorts and a flowered blouse.

"Well, I don't think he could've said that, Nan," Sylvie said. "And you look fine. I was in court, is why I'm dressed up." Her voice was light and she sounded eager to say the right thing.

"Well, he did say it," Naneen said. "That's what he told me on the phone: you weren't picking Christopher up." She put her hands on her hips and Sylvie turned and looked at the bright hopping colors of the TV. Naneen's boys lolled on the sofa that was gold damask underneath its thick plastic cover, staring at the TV with their mouths open, the blond head beside the dark one. Christopher, propped up with bed pillows, sat beside them.

"Hey Sweet Pea," Sylvie whispered at him. A craving for him rose in her, she wanted to scoop him up and hold him, but it was better not to walk away from Nan while she was speaking.

"I know what he said," Naneen was saying, still in the same contentious tone. Sylvie couldn't tell her story now, about how she was pregnant, and Cass was gone. She could hear Naneen's answer—"Gone, I knew he'd be gone sometime. What a good-for-naught."

Sylvie sighed.

"What?" Naneen said. "What is the problem now?" And Sylvie said, "God, Nan, I'm just breathing."

She picked Christopher up from the sofa then, and stuck him on her hip. Underneath where he'd been sitting, the plastic cover was beaded with damp and she hoped it wasn't pee. He smelled good though, sweet and powdery—Naneen's doing—and the fondness she felt for her sister in her sister's absence rushed back.

"Nan," Sylvie said. "Thanks for taking such good care of him. Did he sleep?" She was looking at the baby, waiting for Naneen to speak—one word of softening or encouragement and she'd stay—but Naneen was already banging on the bed pillows she'd brought out for Christopher to sit on, a job she was doing with noise and vigor.

"Okay, well. I'm'n'a get a move on now I guess," Sylvie said.

Bang, bang, bang.

"Well okay. Bye then," Sylvie said, and blinked back the tears that had ambushed her. She stopped at the door, turned and waved at her two nephews, but the boys didn't say anything to her either, craning around Naneen to keep the TV in view.

Christopher fell asleep almost immediately. He looked like a dangling sack—egg-shaped body restrained, head dipping almost to his knees—when Sylvie strapped him into the front seat beside her.

"Poor little thing," Sylvie said. She rubbed her thumb over the silky, frictionless skin of his thigh.

She could have gone to sleep herself, she felt almost drunk in the hot, heavy air, and drove with her eyes skinned open, blinking against the grit floating in through the window. She hooked her thumb into the underarm seam of the pink blouse where it was cutting into her flesh and pulled.

And then they were home—she had passed Heke's empty house without noticing, and the dirt road, and the spot where that photographer had once stood.

"God," Sylvie said, getting out of the truck. "I hope it's planning to rain soon."

She unbuckled the baby and plucked him, still heavily asleep and sweaty, from the seat and carried him up the wood steps and through the cabin where she laid him down on her bed. Then she undressed, fighting the pink blouse that cleaved to her. It had become smaller and smaller as the day went on till it was as tight as the skin on a plum. She dropped the blouse and shook her skirt down, stepping over the puddle of it on the floor, then she lay down beside the baby, dressed only in her underwear and slip.

"I'm not going to go to sleep," she said to the sleeping boy. "I'm just going to rest here one quick minute."

14

THE AIR did not cool in the darkness, or at least it was no cooler inside the cabin. The heat persisted, heavy and unbreathable.

Sylvie woke at three A.M., stiff and logy. Christopher slept on beside her, his legs in the L's of frog legs, his chubby fists clenched. Sylvie leaned close so she could see him in the dark, waiting until the regular rise and fall of his breath became visible to her. She wasn't going to sleep anymore tonight. Too many things crowded into her mind and besides, she was no longer tired.

Sylvie got up, pulling the slip over her head and stepping over it where it fell, and she put on an old T-shirt of Cass's, the material dry and smooth and covering. Her breasts were now, almost suddenly, tender.

The cabin was utterly silent. It was so quiet Sylvie could hear the faint tink of the filament in the lightbulb once she'd located the string and turned it on. Its glum brightness brought no comfort to her, though. She stood out, alone inside a bubble of brightness while the dark cohered around her, and she grabbed at the string and shut it off again. After that, the dark seemed softer.

The smell of bacon hung, faint but discernible, around her, and the dark flickered and jumped. Things seemed to move, silent and furtive, through the air and along the edges of the floor. She turned once, sure Cass was on the settee behind her, long legs looming out from the surrounding dark.

The quiet was unbelievable.

Sylvie got up and opened the cabin door—there was some sound now, as the fullness of the outside air reached her. Or not sound, for it was quiet out too, but the capacity for sound, like a held breath that would soon be exhaled. It was better with the door open, she felt less separate from the outer world. The white T-shirt she was wearing gave off a soft glow.

Where was Cass now? Had he made it to his sister's by this time? Sylvie knew, if Cass had arrived late he would not ring Peggy's doorbell. He would sit in a park or out on the curb in front of the apartment house where Peggy lived, knees drawn up almost to his chin, waiting for the hour to be decent.

"Like a vagrant," Sylvie said. "Like a bum of some kind. I mean God, Cass, she's your sister for God's sakes," but her voice caught then, and she pressed her thumbs into her eyes because he was neither a bum nor a vagrant: he was some version of its opposite. Courtly. Thoughtful. Kind.

Sylvie turned back into the room that seemed smaller to her now, either because she had stood facing the expansive dark or because she had just been picturing Cass, out in Ohio. She went and rummaged in the drawer beside the sink—the white T-shirt made one soft white blur, the porcelain sink another—looking for the oblong paper calendar book they'd given away at the card store one year that had pages in the back for phone numbers. "Cass's sister Peggy" she had written there.

In the bedroom, Sylvie knelt near the top of the bed as if she meant to put the book beneath her pillow, but instead she leaned over until Christopher's face and tidy compactness became visible to her and she checked, once again, that he was breathing. Then she went outside. She stood for a moment on the porch as she had that day Heke had come walking through the mist like Moses through the parted sea, but she was not thinking of that day: she had stood just so many times.

She came down the porch steps and began to move slowly across the dirt patch in front of the cabins, her legs bright flashes. Heke's house shone as she proceeded towards it. She held the little telephone book in her hand.

The porch was blacker than the darkness—Sylvie would not even have known where the door was if a gleam of light from someplace hadn't licked the glass—and her bare toes bruised against the backs of each step because she could not see them. There was a quick sound as she opened the door and stepped inside, a skittering she knew to be only mice, though it still made her shiver and she thought of Heke and what he'd done.

Sylvie wandered through the dark house with its old and indelible smells—stale cooking and cold ash and the sweet ancientness of the logs the house had been built of. The room to her left was full of cardboard boxes—huge, taller and wider than she was. They were heavy, full of something, and their tops were covered with a talc-thick coating of dust she trailed her fingers through.

In the kitchen, Sylvie wondered what Heke cooked and ate but aside from the persistent smell of coffee she could not pull a strand from the overall muddle of smells and it was too dark to see into the pantry or cupboards. Turning on a light seemed more like trespass than actually being here.

The house was so cool.

Sylvie left Heke's house and returned to the cabin. She didn't know how long she had been gone—she stopped on her way back, chin raised, alert to any sound—but there was no sound.

Christopher was still asleep, still on his back though he had scooted somehow closer to the edge of the bed. His arms were flung up, one on either side of his head, which someone had once told Sylvie meant a baby was contented. She knelt down beside him and blew the hair off his forehead. She wanted to watch him open his eyes and see delight crowd up in his face at the first sight of her, that chippy smile that made him look like an old man with his teeth out. Pa, she sometimes called him.

But her breath didn't wake him nor her touch, as she stroked the baby hair back, so she pushed up from her knees and went to the kitchen to wash.

The kitchen was the only place in the cabin with running water. When they'd first come here, when Heke had taken them up to the row of three cabins and pointed out which one they would occupy, Sylvie had walked through to see where everything was. She'd gone from the kitchen back into the bedroom and out again.

"Where's the bathroom at?" she said to Cass, whispering even though Heke had gone away by then. "Where's the toilet?"

Cass nodded. "It's out back," he said, and lifted his chin in that direction.

Sylvie shook her head. "No, it isn't. I been back into the bedroom."

"Out back," Cass said. "Outside. There in the yard." His voice was sharp and he wouldn't look at her.

"Well," Sylvie said. "We can't stay here then. We can't, Cass. That's settled."

She was used to it now, or at least she did not complain every time she had to go outside to pee, though when she got to where she could smell it, the chalky lime smell never quite masking the other, her head whipped sideways and for a second, she couldn't get herself to go in it, despite the however many times she already had. But it was the washing she really didn't like. No shower, no tub except the tin one leaning against the back outside wall because it embarrassed her to have it on the front porch where people could see it. Where she would feel, every time, like she had to explain—"This is only for temporary, us here. Until Cass gets a job."

They hardly ever used the tub anyway, it was too much trouble, hauling it inside, filling it, dumping it out again. And there was no place to bathe, other than the kitchen. Sylvie washed at the sink with a washcloth and soapy water and she did it when Cass was asleep or not here.

He was not here now. Even so, she was furtive, aware of herself in here and the dark beyond. She kept the T-shirt on and washed underneath it, as though it was a tent.

There was a sound; used as she was now to the almost pure quiet, Sylvie did not at first know—she did not at first remember—what it was. A deep inward rushing, a clicking and she held still, the washcloth in her raised hand, the T-shirt mostly soaked, silver and transparent.

It was Christopher, gathering breath so that he could begin to wail, which he did right then.

"Okay, okay," Sylvie called as she went in to him, pushing her arms through the wet shirt. "Here I am," she cooed. "Here's your mama," and gathered the boy into her arms, but he would not stop crying even then; for a long time he wouldn't. It sounded to Sylvie more like outrage than anything, as if he had woken expecting to find it morning and it was not.

After she settled him, Sylvie cleaned him with the same washcloth she'd used on herself and put him in dry things. She put on a thin cotton dress so faded it looked like she had it on inside out. Then she cooked bacon and fried bread as she did every morning, the dark frying pan hard to see in the room even though, now, it was less dark. She was sweating by the time the meat was cooked, the table set, the bacon fat drained off into the jar she kept for the purpose on the back of the stove, the room blazing hot though it was barely past 4:30. Christopher sat in his high chair slapping the tray with his palms. The broken up pieces of bacon Sylvie had put there jumped.

"Hey don't do that, Pa. Eat it," Sylvie said and put a piece into his mouth.

"And don't choke on it this time either," Sylvie said, holding his chin in her cupped hand to make sure he chewed.

It got truly light soon after they'd eaten. "See?" Sylvie said to the baby, carrying him to the opened door.

"I told you it was going to." Although she was relieved herself, as the night had seemed to take such a long time to pass.

By noon, it was too hot to stay in the cabin, which grew smaller as the heat increased. Sylvie hauled out the tin tub, a mustache of dirt clinging to the part that had rested on the ground, and dragged it around to the front one-handed, holding Christopher stuck to her hip with the other. She set him down on the fine, sieved dirt in the yard while she went in and out, filling the tub with potfuls of water. She stopped at about three inches, but it still took a lot of coming and going.

"We'll go call your daddy about suppertime," Sylvie said, sitting on the porch steps while the naked little boy splashed in the water. "Don't let me forget."

She meant six or so, the time Cass was likely to be back from his job hunt and eating, but by that hour, Sylvie and the baby were asleep again. Christopher dropped off in the high chair, head on the plastic tray, his boneless body held by the chair's webbed straps as, the day before, he had been held by the seat belt in the truck. Sylvie brushed a piece of flattened bread from his cheek, his cheek imprinted with the bread's large pores. She lay him on the bed, then lay down beside him. When she woke this time, it was two A.M.

She went out to Heke's again, bringing the little paper phone book with her. This time, she brought Christopher as well. He didn't wake when she gathered him up from the bed, pressing the round and rolling marble of his head to her shoulder. Nor when she went back to the cabin to get diapers and a washcloth, things she would need. She returned to Heke's house and stepped into the same smoke-suffused smell, the same appreciable coolness that had been there last night. As she lay Christopher down on Heke's bed, he drew a long, deep breath, then exhaled, but still he didn't wake.

15

ANOTHER HOT day, the heat didn't seem to want to quit. Every evening, Chuck Go, the local TV weatherman, said the same hot air mass was stuck on top of the Cumberlands. "Like a blanket," he said, his hands pressing down.

Mattie had braced herself for change after the inquest—for Heke to be sent elsewhere. But days passed, then weeks, and nothing did change. Heke was still in the new jail here, she was still visiting him, cooking him foods he did not eat, bringing him magazines and newspapers he did not open.

Early on the morning of the twenty-fifth day, Mattie was sitting at her kitchen table near the opened back door, drinking coffee. The whatever-it-was in the garden had quit for the day. The rustlings she heard from time to time were of rabbits or chipmunks, creatures that seemed familiar, domestic, almost like pets. The doorbell rang.

"Bruce," Mattie said when she opened the front door. She looked at the twelve-year-old boy with his slightly buck front teeth and his gold burr of summer-cut hair. His body was turned toward her but his face wasn't so that he looked shifty and it came to Mattie, suddenly, what he might turn out to be: a quiet and sly man, someone who snuck into empty houses, who snitched wallets out of women's purses when they were left untended on the tables at church suppers.

"What are you doing here, Bruce?" Mattie said.

Bruce was looking in the direction of town, and he did not answer.

"*Bruce!*" Mattie shouted.

He jumped before he turned and looked at her.

"Why are you here, please?" Mattie said, pleasant-sounding now, a teacher's trick: it let the student know she'd only raised her voice because she had been forced to.

Bruce blinked at her. "Thought I'd just come on here and tell you. About Heke," he said.

"*What?*" Mattie said. "Heke?" Was the whole town talking about him, saying "Heke" this, and "Heke" that like he was a goat or a half-tame neighborhood dog?

"What did you say?" Mattie's voice was sharp again, and Bruce shut his mouth and looked furtive.

"Well," he said. "What I said was, Heke—"

And then he must have seen what she meant.

"Or," he said. "I mean, Mr. Day."

"What in the world are you talking about, Bruce? Speak up!"

"They moved him, is what," Bruce said. "Came out and got him in a van. I thought you'd want to know about it, if you didn't already. I mean, if the sheriff didn't call you." He sounded unruffled and forthright, not like a future pickpocket.

"Oh," Mattie said. She stood for a second not speaking, caught between the picture of sneaky Bruce and this other one.

"And how is it you know he's being taken someplace? What gave you that idea? Maybe the sheriff just took him out for a walk, Bruce. Did you ever think of that?" Mattie had herself under control now, and spoke in the voice of patient, if distant, encouragement she used in school when a child stumbled, excruciatingly, through some sort of recitation.

Bruce had his eyes on the lit-up doorbell beside the door. One screw had popped loose and the light sometimes flickered on and off without being touched. "Does this bell work?" he said.

"Bruce," Mattie said. "You were telling me how you knew Mr.—"

"Saw," Bruce said. "A van come, I live right back of the new jail, I can see the parking lot. When they bring him the food and whatnot, I can see it."

"Food," Mattie said. "There. I'll bet that's what it was."

Bruce shook his head. "This wasn't the food," he said.

"Well," Mattie said slowly. "But maybe it was. Maybe they switched to a different purveyor and you didn't recognize the van. You know what 'purveyor' means, Bruce?" She smiled at him.

"No," Bruce said. "I mean, it wasn't that."

The blood dropped straight down from Mattie's head then, and she shut her eyes and leaned against the door frame.

"Bruce," she said when she opened them again as if, in the interval, she had forgotten he was there. "Time for you to go now."

Which was clearly not what he'd been expecting.

"But—"

"Go on. I can't spend any more time now. This is a very busy day."

The living room, as Mattie turned into it, was a vacuum of light where nothing was visible to her but her coffee cup on the table amid the brightness of the kitchen beyond.

She tried not to believe him—it was Bruce after all; odd Bruce—and she reminded herself of the thieverous man. But she did believe him. The thieverous man had disappeared. The sheriff had told her Heke would be moved. Somehow, she had lost sight of that. The jail was new and empty, as if it had been built for Heke, so he wouldn't have to live too far from town. And every day Heke was still there added itself to the days he had been there already. Mattie had let herself see them with the collective authority of fact.

Well, she'd go talk to the sheriff and straighten this out. She wouldn't drive though. Parking was always tight in town.

The sheriff raised his chin as the door opened. He had been clipping his nails into a wastebasket held between his knees. His face colored.

"Heke?" Mattie said. "That is, I came to—"

"Not here," Junior said, setting the basket on the floor. "Heke's out, matter of fact. He's unavailable," and he grinned.

"There wasn't any van," Mattie said. "I didn't see the van."

"Van's gone," Junior said. "It was here till a few little whiles ago. Gone now. You know, I sure am going to miss your fine food, Miss Mattie." He leaned way back in the chair and pointed at her with the nail clipper. "I didn't know you wanted to be here for the send-off."

Mattie had gone pale, her skin waxy and with an undertone of green.

"Miss Mattie?" Junior said at the sight of her. "You all right?" He sounded stricken suddenly, as if the lazy cruelty he'd displayed had just become visible to him, and he jumped up and came around the desk and fetched a paper cup of water from the brand-new bubbler in the corner.

"You're sure you don't want to sit down?" he said, watching her drink.

Mattie shook her head at him over the top of the paper cup. "May I have a look?" she said when she'd finished. "I mean, just to see if he left anything."

The door was open, the cell had been hosed down, the wetness already beginning to contract away from the edges of the floor leaving an area rug of darkness. It smelled of the dampened concrete.

The cot had been stripped, the bedding folded at the head as if an overnight guest had just left here, somebody inconspicuous, and tidy. Heke was gone altogether.

"His things're here," Junior said. "I bagged them all up."

When she left, Mattie was carrying the brown paper bag of every single thing she'd brought since Heke had been here, books, magazines, things she had carried over from his house or her own. Junior hovered around her, holding the door open when she got to it—"Here, let me. This door can be heavy"—then stood out on the top step beside her. She'd been here every day, but she wouldn't be coming back.

"Miss Mattie?" Junior said, when they'd been standing that way a few minutes. "Why don't I drive you home? You can come back for your own car later on. Tell you what, I'll even feed the meter for you, so you don't get a ticket, how's that?" and he grinned, though Mattie didn't notice.

"Miss Mattie?" he said again. He put out a finger and touched the bag.

"Hmm?"

"I said did you want me to drive you home."

"No thank you. I walked, I didn't bring my car. I thought I'd have a hard time parking."

"All the more reason," Junior said. "You don't want to be dragging around in this heat carrying that heavy sack."

"I'm fine," Mattie said. "It's fine. Really. The bag doesn't feel heavy to me. It hardly weighs anything at all."

"It hardly weighs anything to you now," Junior said. "Will do in a minute. Wait here. I'm'n'a drive the cruiser around."

"It's really not necessary," Mattie said.

"I say it is. Executive decision. You want to sit down while you wait, Miss Mattie?"

"Junior," Mattie said. "You don't have to call me Miss."

16

CASS WAS in Ohio, but it wasn't any different than it had been at home—a day's work here and there, two back-to-back if he was lucky. It had taken him a long time to flag a ride, until well into the night. He'd crossed the Ohio River around dawn, the air in the cab of the truck that had picked him up lightened by cigarette smoke. Cass had smelled it when the driver first opened the door and did not speak but looked over, waiting for Cass to say where he wanted to go. When they got there, the light was the same color as the air in the cab had been, foggy and white.

Cass had been in the mid-sized town one giant-sized step into Ohio, for six weeks, sleeping on Peggy and Steve's fold-out sofa, looking for work. Whatever he earned he sent home to Sylvie, minus what he gave Peggy for his keep. His brother-in-law thought he was stinting, Cass could tell by the way Steve looked at Peggy and by the way Peggy didn't look back. He's my brother and welcome here, her look said. And, He's doing what he can.

Cass was doing what he could. He kept almost nothing for himself, enough for a couple of packs of cigarettes, that was all, and when there wasn't any work, he didn't buy cigarettes either. He sifted through the ashtrays before Peggy emptied and washed them every morning and collected the butts left there. Peggy had taken to stubbing out her cigarettes half finished, like she was leaving them for him, but Steve smoked his right down to the filter. Cass was grateful to his sister, even though she smoked menthols.

Steve was a small, mean bull of a man with a sunburnt snub neck and short arms on a fist of a body. It seemed like he watched every forkful of food Cass put in his mouth, every sip of beer he swallowed; that he counted every cigarette Cass offered him when he had enough to buy a pack.

"Yeah," Steve said at these times. "Big man."

Steve was worst at night, his meanness sharpened when he was tired and cranky and had had a few beers. Cass was always vowing to himself he'd stay out till late, walk around the chipped gray sidewalks, go sit in the little broken-bottle-infested park that only looked green from a distance. But then he knew Peggy would hold dinner for him thinking either something good had happened to him, or something bad; that she'd be waiting for him to come in, her face anxious. He didn't want to worry his sister nor show her disrespect when she went to the trouble of cooking every night, so he undermined the vow each time he made it, and was back by six o'clock.

"Here he comes now," Steve said. "What do you think, he's gonna miss a meal?"

"Not one of Peggy's fine feasts, I wouldn't," Cass said, laboring to keep his voice cheerful.

There was no work. Early on, Steve had taken Cass over to the plant that manufactured household cleaners where he worked himself. Put in a good word for you, Steve said, but though he sounded officious and boastful, proclaiming "My brother-in-law" in a dime-shiny voice to the hiring people, it seemed they didn't know Steve at all, that his recommendation counted for nothing. And there were no jobs.

Cass looked for work elsewhere, but he didn't have a car. He had to take buses, watching out the scratched and smeary plastic windows for some kind of landmark because he had no idea where he was. He got on the buses and went after jobs he saw listed in the paper, but no matter how early he arrived at a mustering site, there were always dozens of other men there before him and he was never picked. After a couple of weeks, he stopped making the trips and saved the bus fare.

At night, low fierce whispering seeped out from the bedroom.

Cass lay on his back in the dark and he smoked, expelling the smoke upwards so that the dark turned diffuse and cloudy, like the cab of the truck that had brought him here. If he lay particularly still and flat and didn't turn his head, it was like Sylvie was there beside him, her basketed rib cage visible, the gleam of her pale, pale skin.

"I truly do hate the son of a bitch," Cass told her. "And being here."

"You know, maybe I should go home," Cass said one morning, Steve already gone, Peggy busy wrapping up her own lunch and the one she made and left for Cass before she went to work herself. Cass sat at the table smoking one of the whole cigarettes Peggy offered when Steve wasn't around.

Peggy worked as a maid for a cleaning service and was wearing the brown twill pants and milk-in-coffee twill shirt and the short green stock-boy smock that was her uniform. The clothes looked like they'd been cut out of unyielding cardboard. Seen in them from the back, Peggy looked squared off and mannish.

"Why do they make you wear that stuff?" Cass said. "It's so, I don't know, stiff-like."

"They don't want the customers thinking of us as—"

"As what?" Cass said. "People?"

"I was going to say sexual objects," Peggy said, and Cass colored, then laughed.

He was turned towards the window. The door to the bedroom was behind him, the bathroom beside that. The apartment seemed not so different from the cabin where he and Sylvie and Christopher lived. Get rid of the paint, the bathroom, the furniture—new but cheap, its lacquered veneers the color of dried glue—and there wasn't a whole lot of difference.

"I should just quit out and go home," Cass said again. He was conscious of the noise of the passing traffic, though he couldn't see the cars.

"If you want to know what I think," Peggy said, heading for the door, for the elevator, for the street where she would wait for another girl to pick her up and drive a car full of the cardboard-suited maids to work.

"I think you ought to stay put and see what happens here. It hasn't been that long. You never know."

Cass stayed. A week went by, another week. He went in and out with the extra key Peggy kept at the bottom of a canister that had dog biscuits in it although they did not have a dog, nor had Cass heard of them ever having one. When Peggy left, Cass took the stairs down to the basement. He didn't trust the small, low elevator and they were only on the third floor, tree-house level. Piles of magazines, bundled to be thrown out, sat on the basement floor, and newspapers from the day before, one of which Cass took back upstairs with him to hunt for a job. It didn't matter that the papers were day-old. Most of the ads for laborers and the like were generic, they ran every day, permanent in the way of franked government envelopes.

Someone else in the building was job hunting. Sometimes, the paper Cass picked up had ads circled in red—receptionist, typist, word processor—girl jobs. He wondered if the red circles had been made with lipstick.

When he was done, Cass returned the papers to the pile near the laundry room. He had asked Peg once if he couldn't take care of the laundry.

"Oh no," she said, and looked distressed. "Steve wouldn't like that."

"It's just clothes, Peg," Cass had said, but his sister, thinking maybe of her bras and pants or of Steve's odiferous work clothes, pressed her lips together and shook her head. She never let Cass do a thing in the apartment—there was never a thing left to do. The surfaces of the glossy furniture were always glossy, the bed tightly made, the drips wiped off the shower door and faucets. Cass wondered how many places Peg cleaned every day, working as fast as she did.

After replacing the newspaper that made him feel he was spying on the job-hunting girl, Cass went out. He looked in the windows of the nearby, single-story shops for Help Wanted signs, but there weren't any signs—there weren't any customers, hardly, in the little stores. There was a dump where he got a day's work now and then, sorting through junk for usable electrical parts, and sometimes he got delivery work at a little market. When there was nothing he went back to Peg's. He drank water and he smoked the butts he'd collected from the ashtrays the night before. He did not turn on the radio or the TV or lights, so as not to waste the electric he wasn't paying for. He sat at the table, his long spine curved.

And then one afternoon Steve came home and stood, as he always did, on a page of the previous Sunday's newspaper comics which he kept stacked on the floor inside the door to leave his shoes on. He was grubby, like he always was from work, a patina of oil and sweat and dirt in rings around his neck, and he strode by Cass on his way to shower, hostile and silent as always.

But this day, Steve slapped the table in front of Cass as he went by, and when he took his hand away, there was a paper on the table.

"Work at home!" the paper said. "Earn good money in your spare time!"

So Cass called the telephone number and was hired after only a very few words had been exchanged, and the next day Steve stopped on his way home from work to pick up the thousands of envelopes Cass had verbally contracted to stuff with thousands of sheets of paper. Steve set the boxes alongside his empty shoes on top of the square of hilariously colored newspaper near the door.

Cass had been doing this job for almost three weeks. When Steve and then Peggy left in the morning, he pulled out the boxes of empty envelopes and the announcements that went in them and the filled envelopes from underneath the sofa and he took them to the kitchen table and he folded and stuffed and sealed, folded and stuffed and sealed.

He earned one cent for every envelope that he did, which had sounded good to him when he spoke to the man on the phone, but which meant he had to stuff 10,000 envelopes to make $100. At his fastest he could do five in a minute. In eight hours, that was 2,400. It took him five full days to earn $100. And it wasn't $100. They withheld money as security against the paper they gave you, to make sure you were doing it neatly and correctly—$25 per lot of 10,000. Cass still owed the first $25 to Steve.

He would never catch up.

He'd stopped thinking about home, about anything. He counted the envelopes as he stuffed them, or he counted the minutes that passed or his breaths: 100 more and he could have a drink of water. He could pee or stand up and stretch or smoke one of the cigarettes that now he could afford, though he could afford little else. Day after day after day after day. Until one night the telephone rang, and it was for him.

17

HEKE SAT in the van on the ride out to the prison, a ride so bumpy his backside left the seat more than one time, and his hands flew apart in his lap.

Now he sat sideways on the cot, same as he'd done in the new jail at home. This jail wasn't new. A huge gray wad of stone loomed up as the van approached, barren and isolated. It grew larger the closer they got until there was no other landscape. Inside, it was a dark and shrouded green, as if vegetation grew up over the one small, high window in Heke's cell. All the windows were slits, invisible from the outside so that the structure appeared smooth from a distance.

The murky light enhanced the high humidity of the place, or vice versa. Everything was green—the sprung spring cots and stools placed on the floor of the oddly large cell, the jungle-like light. Moss, slimy as slug trails, grew on the inner walls.

There was a toilet and a tiny sink with a rusty container of paper towels hung above it. The sink had dirt permanently scored into the cracked enamel, the way grease works its way into the invisible lines on a hand. It smelled of urine and a strong, piney disinfectant.

They'd put Heke in with another old man, older than Heke, though they shared a generation. The man—his name was McGee Brown—was pleased as anything when he found out Heke was coming, almost wifely in his preparations, washing everything with the rough brown paper towels. The guards laughed at him and called him Mother Brown.

McGee jumped up when Heke was brought in. Eagerness and excitement made his limbs tremble as he rabbitted around, asking Heke this and telling him that.

"You'll be okay, Mr. Day," McGee said from time to time over the first few days. "Just need to settle down a bit. Get used to it."

McGee had decided to address Heke as Mr. Day until invited to do otherwise, but weeks passed and Heke never invited him, never said a word, as if he was someplace else. After a period of fury at Heke—"What? You think you're too good to speak to me?"—followed by a period of despair at having what looked like this last mean trick played on him by the guards, McGee decided he didn't mind it. It was *him* Heke wasn't talking to, after all, and wasn't there something personal and intimate in that?

Heke went where they made him go, shuffling from one destination to another, then back to the cell again. McGee's talking didn't even penetrate: it took a louder noise than that. The cell door swung on its heavy weight-bearing hinges, like the gate in front of the Bluitts' house that was never latched and that sang when you pushed it.

Heke never went by the Bluitts' since the day he'd seen Sal and the man in bed; he turned his head downwind if he so much as passed the place. But then one day, there he was, right in front of it.

"Now, how'd I get to here?" Heke said, his voice wondering, and McGee jumped up, fast as an attentive waiter.

"What's that, Mr. Day?" he said. "Do something for you?"

But Heke had retreated again into the long ago, and had, anyway, not been talking to McGee. He sat on, unmoving, except for the blinking of his eyes.

He'd been making a long loop around the Bluitt place on his way back from hunting nuts. He was somewhere early in his twenties. A sound had gotten his attention and he'd followed it and all of a sudden he saw where he was, and then a face loomed out at him and he thought of Caan Bluitt, maybe haunting this empty place nobody had taken any care of.

"Hey," the face said.

"Oh Lord," Heke said. "I thought you was a ghost or someaught."

It was a girl. She laughed. "No," she said. "I'm real. Here, pinch"—and she slid up the sleeve of her red jacket and danced a pale arm out at him.

"No, I do not want to pinch you," Heke said. "You trespassing, or what are you doin up here?"

"Do I have to be doing something?" the girl said. "I'm wandering is all. Not trespassing. Come for a walk."

Heke said nothing. Looked off into the trees behind the house where the leaves had gone auburn and the speckled yellow of bananas and a brown that was like oiled supple leather.

"You know the people live here?" the girl finally said.

"Nobody lives here," Heke told her and turned slightly so he could see the girl who was standing up the hill at a little distance from him, but put the house outside his range of sight. That slight nauseated tilt in his stomach that always came upon him when he thought of Sal Bluitt was there, working on him again after all these years and years.

"Used to," the girl said. "Folks called—"

"Bluitt, I know. Moved," Heke said. There was a pause, then he eyed the girl. "You wouldn't be named Bluitt, would you?"

"Francie McCready," the girl said. "What's wrong with being named Bluitt?"

"Who said anything was wrong with it?"

Francie shrugged. "Your voice went all smoked," she said.

"Just some ancient history. What is it you said you wanted up here?"

"Nothing. Some nuts maybe," Francie said, eyeing the burlap sack in Heke's hand.

"No nuts grow where you are?" Heke said, and Francie looked right at him. She had a wide frank face that was loaded with freckles, the skin underneath or between them showing pink as if she'd spent time trying to scrub the freckles off.

"Not really," she said.

"Well, I'll show you a good spot then," Heke said. "So you don't go home empty-handed. Just don't take all of 'em, nor bring squads of folks back to do it either."

"I won't," Francie said.

They were walking higher up the hill towards the stand of hickories Heke had already visited that day.

"I'm going to show you some hickories here today that're the last of their kind."

"How come?" Francie said.

"How come what? Hickories?"

"How come they're the last?"

"Lumber companies. They come in years ago and took out most of the timber in here—chestnut, oaks, beeches, the sugar trees, poplars. Big trees, some more than two hundred feet, took it all down."

"You saw them big trees?"

"Well, no, I did not see them. This is more'n a hundred years back. If I had of seen them, they wouldn't of got nothing off my land."

Francie grew shy when she saw the trees, a sturdy circle of them tall and straight, as if the trees were important people whose company she wasn't sure she ought to be in.

"How'd these get spared?" she asked, looking way up to see their tops.

"Don't know," Heke said. "Maybe the lumber men thought there was something wrong with them. Maybe they couldn't figure how to get these particular ones out."

"Maybe they weren't here then," Francie said. "Maybe they were puny little baby trees a hundred years ago."

"Maybe," Heke said. "Too small to take then. Maybe."

Francie's reticence disappeared then, and she began scouting for nuts, stuffing them into the pockets of her red corduroy jacket until the stitching began to protest.

"I thought you said you took 'em all," Francie said, after a time had passed when the only sounds had been their feet scrabbling through the ground cover. It was chilly, overcast. Breathing the air was like drinking a glass of cold water.

"I said, Don't *you* take 'em all," Heke said.

Francie laughed and Heke smiled, and when she asked him, "What was that ancient history to do with the Bluitts you were talking about?" Heke waved his hand through the cool air and said, "I'll tell you some other time."

He began seeing a lot of her. At first she was something different to look forward to, but after a little while, it was Francie herself. There was about being around her the same refreshment to be found from breathing the cool, clean air. The day after he'd helped her find the hickories, she brought him a cake baked from the nuts.

"Here," she said, opening the four corners of a piece of white cloth. "Here's what we did with the nuts I took home yesterday."

"Who's we?" Heke said.

"Me and my mama," Francie said. "Mrs. McCready."

Heke was disappointed, though he couldn't have said exactly why until Francie told him, "Be grateful. I'm not that good of a baker"—and he realized he'd wanted her to have done it for him by herself, her and no one else.

"This little cake all you got out of all of them nuts?"

"This little cake's all I brought," Francie said. "You can break me off a tiny piece so I can taste it."

Heke broke the little cake in half, then he offered the two pieces out on his hand.

"A tiny little bit, I said," Francie said.

"Pick," Heke said. "One cuts, the other picks. That's fair."

Francie shrugged and looked at the two pieces on Heke's palm.

"Hey," Heke said. "You took the big one."

"You're fair, I'm smart," Francie said.

The fall progressed. Francie was still in school; sometimes, if Heke wasn't busy with the this-and-that he did to make a living, he went by and waited for her on the road below the school. It was too far for him to be sure which one Francie was as she left the little board schoolhouse. Heke watched until one girl peeled off from the rest and headed down the hill towards him. Watching her seek for him and find him and head in his direction might have been the thing he liked best.

Heke told his father about Francie one night in late November. He and Royl were having supper: bacon and corn bread and the pickled beans they made late every summer, snapping the beans and cramming them into jars, then covering them with curing salt and letting them set down in the cellar to pickle.

"You should open up a restaurant," Heke told him.

Royl, who ate intensely and in silence, looked up. "What?" he said.

"A restaurant," Heke said. "You know, a restaurant? You're a good cook."

"You trying to butter me up for some reason, Hesketh?" Royl said. "Save yourself the tear and wear. What is it?"

"Well," Heke said. "I think I'm getting married."

Royl's mouth was full. He looked at Heke sideways while he went on chewing.

"Well, it's about time," he said when he finally swallowed. "Beginning to worry the Days was going to run out with you. How old are you now again?"

"Twenty-two," Heke said.

"Twenty-two," Royl said. "Well you better hurry up and get married, before you get so old and ugly no one'll have you. When's the happy day?"

"Let you know soon as I ask her," Heke said.

Royl pulled his tobacco pouch closer to him and rolled himself a cigarette. "So. No news is no news," he said.

"I'm not too doubtful about my answer," Heke said. "I just wanted to set a coupla few things with you first."

"Like what?"

"I want to fix over the house a little bit. Buy a coupla few things. Washing machine and whatnot."

"That's right," Royl said. "I did likewise when I married Rudy. Old house. Needs a bit of a spruce." He looked up at the raw beams of the kitchen ceiling, the tin-shaded light fixture hanging down as if that was what he'd start with.

Heke nodded. Royl smoked, then he picked a flake of tobacco off his tongue. "You wanting me to move out?" he said.

"No," Heke said. "You want me to?"

"You take the big bedroom, I'll switch in where you are." Then Royl got up and headed for the chair near the fire in the front room, where he always sat after dinner.

"Bring her for supper sometime," Royl called to Heke, who was still in the kitchen beginning the washing up. "Her and her family. Tell 'em you're takin 'em to a fine restaurant," and he laughed.

Heke began carting things home from the mail order office in town after that, tall brown cardboard boxes that came off the train from Cincinnati, and that he needed help to load onto the wagon. When he got the boxes home he set them in the parlor, where he and Royl dropped things that they meant to get back to—harness leather in the midst of being oiled and mended, nails and screws in Ball jars with the tops rusted, a shirt with too many buttons off to wear, things with use still in them. Heke just slid it all back using the boxes like push brooms.

Francie broke off a twig while Heke was saying what he said about getting married and she peeled it, then flayed the bottom with her thumbnail. Heke talked about the house and Royl and the way things were to be arranged. Francie peeled her stick and nodded and when he finished, she said it all sounded fine to her and she'd like to, and in the second before Heke bent and kissed her, he saw marriage as the bald trade-off of labor he'd just made it sound like and that it partly was—and he had to turn his head just for a second and just breathe. But then he kissed her, and those first observations were lost in the other reasons there were for getting married.

Heke and Francie went home to their own houses that afternoon, where each had what must have been a version of the same conversation. Their families wanted to meet and it was arranged that three days after, Francie and her mother would drive over to the Day house for supper.

Heke came home late that afternoon, out of the chilly pre-Christmas air and into the warmth and light of the kitchen. The table was set and loaded with bowls and platters of food and Heke thought of the day Narciss was married, the dinner Rudy had prepared, the big cake. He hardly ever thought of Narciss anymore.

"Well," Royl said from where he was standing by the stove. "Where is she? Where's my new daughter?"

"Coming on her own," Heke said. "They are."

"You didn't say you'd go out and run them here?"

Heke nodded. "I did. Said they'd like it better getting here their own selves."

"Well, I hope they don't get lost," Royl said.

"They won't get lost. Francie knows her way around."

Heke heard them arrive—he and Royl both did—the stamping of a mule or a horse and the tack jingling.

"I'm'n'a show them where to put the stock," Heke said, and he and Royl both headed to the front door to greet the company, Royl first. They could hear voices outside—talking, laughing—and the tromp of ladies' booted feet up the porch steps. No men; Francie's dad had died some years since, and she hadn't wanted to bring any of her younger brothers and sisters today.

"Francie," Heke said, talking past Royl, who was already at the door. "I don't know why you didn't let me come for you. I wish"—and then he was at the door and there, standing in front of him, was Sal Bluitt.

"Royl," Sal said, and then she said, "Heke? Do you not remember me? I think he's about to pass out," she said to Francie, and she laughed.

Heke didn't answer. Talk and laughter were nearly bursting out of Francie; she looked like a person holding her breath, her cheeks and her lips bubbled with the effort of containment.

"She's not her mother," Royl said. "You never told me." His voice was flat, parched. He turned right around and headed back to the kitchen.

The merriment seeped out of Francie's face; she stood there, plain and pale. Looking at her, Heke could see the care she must have taken to get ready, hair brushed to burnishment and clipped with fancy ribbon barrettes. The fresh, almost spicy smell of the cold air seemed connected to it.

"Heke. Are you asking us in or are you not?" Francie said. Her voice was belligerent, and she looked ready to push her way past Heke if she had to. Sal had on that agonized look Heke remembered and that he couldn't bear; he cast his eyes down at his feet.

"Why didn't you tell me?" he asked Francie.

"I thought you knew."

"You didn't."

Francie looked away from Heke, sideways down the porch. When she opened her mouth to speak, puffs of vapor came out: it was starting to get cold.

"First, I didn't want to jinx it," she said. "And then we thought we'd save it up. Surprise the both of you."

We. Heke remembered her saying that another time and what she'd said when he'd asked her who she meant. Me and my mama. Mrs. McCready.

It still could have been all right. Heke could have apologized for Royl's odd ways, for keeping them standing out there, stepped aside and asked them in, but he didn't. He stood and looked at them. Francie was Sal Bluitt's daughter. It seemed like the biggest trick ever. Francie looked up at him, waiting. In another moment, she turned and headed for the steps.

Heke watched the back of her same red corduroy jacket and he took a step, ready to call her, but Francie reached out right then and linked her arm through her mother's—Sal Bluitt's arm—and he didn't call.

Royl came out from the kitchen, telling Heke to shut the door, he was letting all the cold air in. "I hope they're well gone," he said. "Sal Bluitt. If that don't beat every other thing. I ain't sat down for a meal with a Bluitt yet. Don't plan to in this lifetime."

Behind Royl, the food, heaped in bowls and on platters set out on the kitchen table, steamed mightily. It was like a photograph—the still, empty room in which nothing had happened yet, but in which something would soon.

"Don't worry about it, old son," Royl said. "Plenty of fine girls out there not Bluitts. You best come on. I have got enough food out here to feed the famished, and it's naught but you and me."

18

HEKE NEVER slept that night.

He went into the room that had always been his. Royl was still occupying the front bedroom, though he had begun transferring his lesser belongings into the parlor. It was crowded in there now, with Royl's things and the appliances, still in their huge boxes.

Heke shut the door and he sat down on the side of the bed, the old horsehair mattress crunching. He sat very still, one large hand on each knee, and he thought his way through the situation, or he tried. There was no "through." It was a maze rather than a straightaway and no matter which point he started from or which way he turned, he got stuck. Francie just kept on being Sal Bluitt's daughter. He didn't mean to stumble against that, but he couldn't help it.

Heke heard the arrival of morning rather than saw it, Royl moving around in the kitchen, slamming the cast iron skillets on the stove burners as he prepared to cook breakfast. Heke kept telling himself he'd get up in a minute, go and have some food, but he went on sitting on the side of the bed. He smelled the strong coffee, then the bacon, and Royl came and stood outside his door and called to him—"Hesketh? You want breakfast?"—but when he got no answer, he went away again. Royl ate his own breakfast, then he sat and drank coffee and smoked until he'd had enough of that and Heke felt the cold air slide in underneath his door as Royl went outside and again, a little later, as he came back, going out and in over the course of the morning. He knew what Royl was doing, same as if he was watching him do it. Royl's days were all the same. That might have been what decided Heke. The ongoing sameness. The everyday. The smell of cigarettes flared up every now and again and made Heke want one, but the urge seemed distant, not strong enough to propel him. It was going on for two o'clock by the time Heke left his room.

Royl was at the kitchen table smoking again, as was his habit in between chores. The kitchen smelled of smoke when Heke stepped into it, and loose tobacco and the cool air Royl had brought in with him and, lingeringly, of the ferric odor of the skillets.

"Saved a plate out for you," Royl said. "Don't know how good it is now."

Heke looked at the plate of food on the back of the stove, but he didn't go and get it. He went on standing where he was, behind the kitchen chair that had always been his, then he spoke out as if he was reciting a prepared speech about the prickly history between the Bluitts and the Days.

"You going someplace with this, Hesketh?" Royl said.

"I know Days and Bluitts don't mix is where I'm going," Heke said. "But Francie's different."

Heke felt the relief of something difficult having been settled. His chest expanded, as though it had been crowded before, and his breathing freed up.

"Bluitt girl's not who I had in mind to continue my family name," Royl said. He was leaned back in his chair, one eye slitted against the smoke from his cigarette. His voice sounded friendly, like he wasn't in any doubt of the outcome.

"Days and Bluitts don't mix," Royl said. "Not since the very beginning of being up here."

Heke knew this story as well as Royl. He'd heard it told over and over by Royl and by Royl's father and by his great-grandmother, Mary Flood, who was old and nearly blind and who Heke had been made to sit beside as she lay in the bed in the bedroom that was now Royl's, holding to Heke's elbow with her sharp-clawed bony hand.

"You know what Bluitts done to us, Hesketh. The coal company part

I'm talking about. When the coal company come in here. I have to tell you that?"

Heke knew. Royl told it anyway.

"Kentenia," Royl said. "Called the Kentenia Corporation. Owned by Delanos. Come up into here after the coal. Knew all about it—how much there was of it and where it was located. And right here was the first place they come on account of Lee Day and Bluitt and Jem Skinner had the biggest claim. Near to 200,000 acres. Each had their separate homesteads, but they owned the land together. That Kentenia man—I'm forgetting his name right this minute."

"Davis," Heke said. There wasn't any part of this story he didn't know.

"Davis," Royl said. "Davis, he says to Lee Day, 'I hear you are the one to talk to around here. Everybody listens to you.' Which was true, but, though, Lee Day was too shy to own it."

Royl picked up his coffee cup and wiggled out the last bitter drips with his tongue. It was the cup he always drank from, cream-colored once, stained and stained again by the lifetime of coffee.

"Offered him a pile of money," Royl said, putting the cup back down again. "Not for the land though, for the coal underneath. Said they could keep the land. Lee Day though," Royl said. "He says—'Well, I got to talk to everybody else owns this boundary with me.' "

" 'You think it over, no hurry, you'll hear from me again,' Davis says, and then he rides off. No word come from him though, not for a long little while. Then one day, a Bluitt child come down to here from their house, says won't Lee and Polly come to supper to the Bluitts'. So Lee Day," Royl said. "He walks on up to Bluitt's later on and Jem Skinner's there too, and Bluitt naturally, and you guessed it, Davis, he's there too. They all sit down and Davis is telling his stories and passing compliments around with the salt and finally he tells them how much he's willing to pay them for the coal that's underneath their land that nobody can get at. Good cash money. And the land, the Kentenia

Corporation, they didn't want that, the land would still belong to them, always and always.

"By now Bluitt and Jem also, so I heard it, was starting to grin all over their faces. I mean, there wasn't no way of getting the coal *out* of here then. They was entirely hemmed in here—no roads. The L&N didn't come in for another twenty years. When they first come in here and settled, a lot of them never come out again. No way to. Nobody thought a railroad could ever get all the way to here. It just wasn't something they could of even pictured."

Royl stopped. He got up and turned to the stove and poured himself out more coffee.

Heke hadn't said anything all this time.

"So," Royl said. He planted his arms on the table and scootched his chair in closer to Heke, as if this upcoming part was intimate. "So Lee Day says, 'Maybe I'm stupid, but I don't get it. What's your company supposed to get out of all of this? Nothin?' "

" 'Well,' Davis tells him. 'Nothing now. Nothing till the railroad gets put in.' Lee Day says, 'But that might be never,' and Davis, he says, 'Well, Mr. Day. I'm a patient man. I work for a patient company. And if the day never comes, then you've put a big one over on us. My company can afford to wait on the railroad, that's the bottom line. Everything stays as is for the present—which, by the way,' Davis says, 'includes your land taxes. You'll still be paying those,' and he laughed and everybody did.

"Taxes, that clinched it, it made it seem like the company wasn't stupid, handing over something for nothing. If Davis had told them the company wanted to pay them just for going on living and farming their own land, they wouldn't've believed him. But if they all still had to pay the taxes—" Royl shrugged.

"Well, Lee Day," he continued. "He still said no, just didn't sit right on him. And Jem, he went along with that because, well, I guess he just did. But not Bluitt."

Royl took a deep breath and, as if that reminded him he wasn't smoking, reached for his tobacco again.

"Bluitt," he said. "He took the money. Went behind their backs. And Davis, he only needed one signature for the whole boundary to be signed over, the law said. Bluitt, he sold the land right out from underneath them. Whole hill turned inside out, them deeds said it—coal companies had the right to the coal and the right to do anything they wanted to get to it. And Lee Day and them, they all still had to pay the taxes. There they was, livin on land they didn't know they didn't own, till they built the L&N up to in here. It was Bluitt did that. Bluitt let the coal companies in."

Royl's face was red and his breathing was stentorious. He rolled himself another cigarette, then he stood and lit it off the front stove burner where the flame was turned low under the coffeepot. The first drag he took burned the cigarette nearly all the way to the bottom. Heke waited till he turned around again.

"That was in the long ago," Heke said to his father. "It's naught to do with now. With Francie."

"No such a thing as a good Bluitt," Royl said. "Just pure badness."

"I'm marrying Francie," Heke said. "I made up my mind."

"Not and live here, you're not," Royl said. "No Bluitt child's living in my house."

"She's not a Bluitt," Heke said. "Even if Bluitts were the ones who caused this county's ravagement and ruination, Francie didn't have nothing to do with none of that. She's not even one."

"She's Sal Bluitt's," Royl said. "Who on earth knows who sired her? Could have been anyone."

"McCready," Heke said. "She's Francie McCready, and her mother wasn't even a Bluitt neither. Married one. Not even married to him no more, and he wasn't even Francie's father. Couldn't of been."

"Like I already said, Francie's father could of been a lot of people," Royl said. "Could of been anyone."

"I'm marrying her," Heke said again.

"Well, you go on ahead and do that, old son. But like I said, you'll not be living here."

Heke got up from the table and went back to his bedroom and sat down on his bed again and he stayed there for another long time. He lost track of the sounds of the house, of Royl coming and going, and of the light. When he looked up again, it was night. The room had receded around him, the furniture and his own self resorbed into the darkness.

In the morning, Heke hitched their one mule Jenny to what he and Royl called a wagon, though it was really more of a cart, and he headed out in a westerly direction towards Francie's. It was the kind of trip that would have been impossible in Lee Day's time. There weren't any roads then, you had to travel on foot or, if you had a wagon, bouncing over the creek beds. It was so isolated in here, once they settled, some of those old Days never came out of the hills again in their lifetimes. Heke wouldn't ever have met Francie then, where she lived as far away as the moon.

A loamy smell came at Heke when he first stepped outside, and the strong burst of pine that usually followed a soaking. He looked up at the sky—pearly and unrevealing. He'd been inside a long time and it startled him, as he rode out of the yard behind the stalky-legged mule, that he might have missed significant weather. He breathed and breathed again and the cool air that smelled of cold pumpkins and a little of rotting vegetation was calming. He saw he had been mistaken to keep himself inside for so long.

After he'd tied the mule to the fence that surrounded the small, neat house Francie lived in, Heke headed for the porch. He didn't pause outside the gate of Francie's house as if he was dithering, nor break stride or slow except when the gate, caught by a pile of windfall leaves, would open only so far and he had to stub the leaves away with his foot. After that, he went straight up, like he lived there.

It wasn't the Bluitt house, but it had a shut door, as the Bluitt house had that last time Heke had been there, with glass panes that shivered when he knocked same as that other one had, and a taste came up in the back of Heke's throat and he had to put out his hand and press it hard against the front wall of the house to keep himself there, until Francie came to the door.

But it wasn't Francie who came. It was Sal.

"Heke," she said. "What're you—"

"Come for Francie," Heke said. He'd made up his mind. His distaste for Sal began to recede. Maybe she had her reasons for what she'd done, maybe she didn't, but it was a long time ago. He didn't want to live like his mind was in a bygone time, body in the present. He wanted to live in the here and now. "For Francie," he said again.

"Oh," Sal said. "Well, Francie isn't here."

Heke nodded, he didn't know what else to do. It had not occurred to him that Francie might not be here. When he'd pictured her, she'd been sitting on the side of a bed hour after hour, same as he was. It surprised him to think she'd been moving around.

"Okay," he said. "I'll wait for her then, I can wait. If that'd be all right"—and he raised his chin towards the inside of the house.

"Oh," Sal said again. "Well I'm afraid not, Heke. Francie's gone. She's gone from here. She—isn't intending to be back."

"Well, where's she gone to?" he said. "I've got the wagon"—and he turned to look behind him where he'd hitched the cart and mule to the fence, testament, somehow, to how serious and concrete he was in his purpose.

Sal looked at him. She kept silent, a silence that went on so long, Heke was forced to look up, to make sure she was still there, and it went on even longer than that.

"I'll go get her," he said in case Sal hadn't understood him, and he turned towards the wagon again. How far away could she be?

"I'm sorry for what dad said. That's him, not me," Heke said.

"Well, Heke," Sal said. "That's fine. Only Francie doesn't want to be found." Her face was pinched up with its customary look of grief, and her eyes were moist and pink-rimmed like they always had been, only then, that day, they made a true match with the occasion.

Heke came down off the porch. Imagination failed him; he had pictured himself coming here for Francie, telling her his decision. It hadn't occurred to him that she might make it turn out different.

He went back through the gate to where the mule stood and he untied her bridle from the fence and backed her up a little, leaning into her shoulder.

"Well, we'll just have to go and find her ourselves," he said to the mule. How hard could that be?

He dropped the bridle as if he was going to climb up into the wagon, but he didn't. He walked around the wagon and then he walked around it a second time and he just kept on doing it. The mule stood, patient and forbearant, as Heke walked around again and again and again, as if he couldn't think of any other place to go.

After a while, he climbed up on the wagon and clicked his tongue to get the mule started and steered homeward. He didn't have a single idea where Francie might be found. But moving again through the cool air, the reins loose over his chapped knuckles, his mind cleared. Aimlessness left and purpose overtook him and a series of places he could hunt for Francie began to present itself, each place begetting another, so that he was not despairing at all as he brought the mule up and turned her, heading into town; he was closer to elated.

He started at boardinghouses, going first to the ones he knew of, asking at those for the names of others. When it began to get dark he went home, but he was up again early the next day to continue. He didn't keep the same hours as Royl and so he didn't see him.

Heke went to Francie's school, which was not in town, and he went into shops which were, but Francie didn't turn up, or she didn't reveal herself to him, though Heke went on believing she was nearby.

Sometimes, he had the feeling she was watching him from some concealed place, and he kept turning around, but he never saw her.

Nobody seemed to know anything. None of the girls he stopped and spoke to as they came out of the school knew where she was, though Heke saw their eyes slide and their hands work deep into their jacket pockets when they answered. He thought they must be the same girls he had watched leaving the school with Francie—they were dressed the same, dresses and jackets, books hugged up against their chests, indistinguishable, at a distance, from each other, though Heke didn't know if these were the right girls. He yearned hard towards that time, not long since, when he had watched Francie separate herself from the bundle of girls and head towards him.

Every once in a while, Heke returned to Sal in pursuit of clues, hints—was he warm or cold? Going in the right direction? But Sal just looked at him with her perpetual damp mournfulness and said she hadn't heard from Francie her own self and wasn't even sure where she was.

"She telephoned once or twice," Sal said. "But I never heard from her since," and her eyes moistened up again.

That's when Heke had a telephone installed at his house. Besides himself, Sal Bluitt was the only one who had the number. And she never called.

Days passed and then weeks and everyplace that had seemed it might possibly be harboring Francie took on the opposite aspect—devoid of her, and empty—and then Heke couldn't bear the picture of himself, trawling up and down streets he'd gone up and down innumerable times already, believing he would see her everyplace. He waited each minute for her to pop up right in front of him, glee crowding her wide face, and he held his neck pulled back on his shoulders without knowing it, in anticipation of the anticipation of surprise, but she never did. Days passed. He gave up; he went home, as there was no place else to go, but he couldn't bear it there either. In populated areas, where there were people, he watched for one of them to turn into Francie; at home, there were trees and bushes, the overgrown remains of a kitchen garden, Royl's three empty cabins. There was the possibility of nobody, and still, Heke was on the lookout. He walked up to the old Bluitt house so many times that it ceased to be for him the place he had seen Sal Bluitt and the man, and it became tied, in his mind, to Francie.

He couldn't stand the repetitive sameness of home—the taste of Royl's coffee every morning, the smell of bacon and cigarettes and cold air, smells he could have drafted or transposed or reproduced in another form, if that were possible. He kept his shoes on all the time, even when he lay down on his bed, because he never knew when he'd need to jump up and get out of the house.

He couldn't be near Royl. The way he spoke grated on Heke, the way he rolled his cigarettes, the same the same the same. Heke would bolt, walk up into the hills or drive into town, but he couldn't stand being there either. And then one day he passed the old courthouse that sat like a bosomy matron at the edge of town, and there was a recruiting poster hung up outside, the kind with the spaces left blank for the where and when, and he went into the fly-ridden limestone building, its edges crumbling to chalk, and signed up.

Heke made two promises that day, one to the government of the United States to serve and protect, and the other that he would not entertain thoughts of another woman until, one way or another, he'd made things right with Francie. And he kept both of them.

19

WHEN HEKE had been gone from the county jail for ten days, Mattie went up the hill to his house. It was still early, but already bright and hot, sun cracking across the far side of her windshield.

When he'd been in the jail in town, Heke had not seemed gone to Mattie; he had seemed captive, but here. Between visiting him and running errands and cooking things he did not eat, she hadn't had time to drive up to the house. She didn't want to be going there now, but if she didn't do it, it wouldn't get done. There was no one else.

Mattie's weight pitched against the door as she came around one of the mountain's long centrifugal curves. The sun slid closer to her on the windshield, and the mop and cleaning powders and polishes and sprays she was carrying in a bucket from her own house slid as well.

She got off the highway and onto the byroad that Y-ed out from it, then got off that and took the dirt road in front of Heke's house, all three roads visible from the slight elevation of the porch. Mattie parked in the deep overlapping circles of shade thrown by the tulip poplars and sat in the car for a minute. The windows were rolled up—she'd had the air-conditioning running—and the car went on being cool for a little while. The sunlight, visible beyond the poplars, was soft and slant, not the sun of high summer. It would soon be September, back to school and the frantic busyness she craved now, and knew she would regret craving before long.

Mattie sighed and got out of the car, pulling the mop and the other things from the backseat. The cleaning products clopped against the plastic bucket, a sound that was jarring in the quiet.

Gleams of sun struck here and there inside the house, burnishing the wood with a patina of ancientness, a richness, even, it did not have in any other light. The front room was wider than it was long with planked floors and a raw-beamed wood ceiling. The hearth, made out of rough gray stones, took up almost the whole wall opposite. There was a straight-backed chair beside it, a rocker beside that, which Mattie could claim to have seen four generations—Heke, and Royl before him, and Royl's father Kingston before that, and Mary Flood Day, Heke's great-grandmother—each come to in their turn. She had, at one time, thought she would be one of them, one in a line, the generations continuing.

Royl had lived an unexpectedly long time. He'd caught pneumonia the second winter after Heke joined the army and nobody had held out much hope for him. Mattie had written to Heke in France to let him know.

Royl pulled through though—he'd passed away only six or seven years ago. She had written to Heke in France about Royl's recovery too, and gone on writing to him, but she didn't know if Heke had gotten the letters.

Columns of dust poured in the light from the bedroom window composed of the settle and decay of so old a house as this, and of the slow crumbling of the scores of newspapers Heke had saved for some reason and that were piled everywhere around the room—they made a sort of bench at the foot of the bed, a nightstand beside it. Mattie sat down on the bed. She slid off the beaded Indian moccasins she was wearing and stretched out.

It was Heke's bed, or it had been Heke's most lately. Mattie could feel the impression, the long sack-shaped dip his body must have likewise slid into, a dip he had not created, but had deepened and helped to shape. She extended one leg fully, then the other. His life here was finished. All done. It made her breathing go tight, and she put her hand on her chest as consolation. She hadn't wished or hoped for anything from him for a long time. Even so, she hadn't forgotten wishing and hoping, those parts of her girlhood now finished.

Mattie moved her head from side to side on the pillow. There was a crackling sound at the back of her neck and she thought of the ancestors, hers and Heke's, going all the way back to Lee Day and Polly; of how they had stuffed their pillows with feathers or seed husks or whatever was to hand. She pictured some long-ago woman working on a pillow slip, fingers smart and quick.

Mattie rolled her head again in the pillow's cool trough and the crackling sound came again, although this time it didn't seem to be the sound of seed husks or feathers. She slid her hand underneath and drew out a small, thin, pamphlet-sized calendar book, the kind given away free at card stores at certain times of the year. The book, which said 1970 on its front cover, was five years out of date. It was like Heke not to have thrown it away.

Mattie thumbed through the pages, but there was nothing written in the book, no appointments or events marked down in any of the little boxes. She was about to replace it when the pages with boxes gave way to pages with horizontal lines meant for telephone numbers, empty, empty, empty, until she came to the last one.

Lusa, it said on the first line, with a nine-digit telephone number after the name.

Naneen, it said on the second line and below that—

Cass's sister, Peggy, in Oldhio.

Sylvie had strapped Christopher into the front passenger seat, then she got into the truck. She sat there, leaning all the way forward, her tender chest squeezed up against the wheel as if this—driving—was something she'd forgotten how to do. The rhythm of it. What you did first, and second, and third.

She looked at the baby sitting like an almost empty flour sack, the remaining flour pushed into the middle, the corners of the sack limp. He looked back at her.

"Don't be so worried, Pa," Sylvie said. "I know how to do it"—and she put the truck in gear and backed up.

They hadn't been away from here in, she couldn't remember how long it had been, how many days or weeks. Her life did not happen in days anymore, A.M. or P.M., the ordinary revolutions of time. It was either light out, or not.

It was barely 6:00 A.M. when Sylvie pulled into the driveway behind her sister's car, unbuckled Christopher and lifted his warm, damp weight onto her hip. The strap of her purse slid off her shoulder and the purse banged against her knees as she headed for Naneen's side door, rang the bell, then took a step back and looked up. It was light out. Morning.

There was no answer to her first ring, so Sylvie rang again. They were home, Naneen's car was in the driveway, she'd just parked right behind it.

Why didn't Nan come? She always answered the door right away, or one of the boys pulled it open before she could tell him not to. Where could they all be?

Sylvie took her finger off the bell. It was the kind that played a tune audible deep inside the house, rather than buzzed or chimed. It was not possible to make it sound urgent or insistent.

"Nan," Sylvie called, knocking now, and calling again. "Nan, can you hear me?"—because it began to seem possible, then likely, that something had happened. Someone could have broken in and tied them all up and robbed the place or there could have been a leak of some kind in the furnace or the gas line. What if Naneen and the twins had succumbed to poison gas? They could be upstairs, unconscious, their limbs flaccid, their heads lolling back and forth, eyes too heavy to open.

"Naneen," Sylvie called in a rising voice. "Nan!"

There was a noise behind her and Sylvie turned. The woman who lived in the next-door house on this street of close-set houses was standing outside her own side door.

Sylvie turned back to Nan's door, pressing so close to it she could taste the soot on its painted surface. "Naneen!" she called, her voice raspy. "Nan!"

Nobody came. Sylvie looked at the woman again.

"It's all right," Sylvie said, switching Christopher to her outside hip to show she was harmless—a mother with a baby.

"I—I just forgot something. At my sister's here," and she put her hand flat against Nan's door.

The woman didn't speak. She tipped her head to the side as if she did not believe Sylvie's story, or perhaps to show that she wasn't interested; she'd only come out to collect the milk from her milk box, that was all. The light above the woman's side door was on; the woman was holding her bathrobe closed at the neck.

"Truly," Sylvie said, and then she turned back to the door, knocking and ringing both now, to hell with the woman anyhow. Maybe she should try the ground floor windows? But the door flew open right then and there stood Naneen, in baby doll pajamas, blazing.

"Nan," Sylvie said. "Is that what you sleep in?"

"What is it?" Nan said. "What's wrong? Is it the baby?"

Sylvie peered into Christopher's face, then she said, "Oh. No. I mean, you're all right"—and she fluttered her free hand against her chest. "The boys. Are they okay too?" Sylvie asked, and she leaned into the doorway and sniffed.

Naneen ran her hand through her hair. It stood up in separate hanks over her head like bundled wheat sheaves, her scalp white and chalky underneath.

"Sylvestrie," Nan said. "What is the matter with you, what are you talking about? Do you even know what time it is?"

Sylvie looked at her blankly. "Well, what do you mean? It's morning, isn't it?" she said, and looked up at the sky.

"I have to go grocery shopping," she said. "I thought, if you wouldn't mind watching the baby for me. That's what I'm doing here. Even though I told old whatever-her-name-is I lost something." Sylvie leaned close to Nan and whispered the last part.

Naneen's head went up, she looked past Sylvie. The neighbor was still there, apparently examining her own slippered feet.

"Oh no," Nan said softly. Then she called, "Morning, Mrs. Thomas," and waved.

Mrs. Thomas straightened up.

"Everything's all right, everything's fine, sorry if we bothered you. My sister here needed something."

Naneen put her hand on Sylvie's shoulder and patted it with sisterly affection. Then she pinched the bone hard—"Ow!" Sylvie said—and pulled Sylvie inside.

"Sylvestrie," Naneen hissed at her after she'd closed the door. "It's barely gone six o'clock. You got this whole nosy neighborhood roused awake."

"Oh," Sylvie said. "I—"

"And when're you going to get some maternity clothes on you? I swear to God."

"Why?" Sylvie said. "What do you mean? You can tell?" She smoothed the tight cloth of her dress over her stomach.

"The only one who couldn't tell would be a blind man," Nan said. "And he'd know too, if you happened to bump into him."

Sylvie, Mattie thought. It's that girl's been into this house. That girl, the last to be lying on this bed. I told her not to come near here. I told her not to. Sees it, wants it, takes it. Oh no, you will not. Mattie sprang up from Heke's bed as if it had turned suddenly hot and shoved the little calendar book in her pocket.

Real heat met her as she came crashing through the front door, the air outside distinctly hotter and thicker than it had been inside the house. She moved at a fast walk across the shimmering hot yard. The heat was dense. Bird sounds were intermittent and desultory.

The door to the middle cabin stood open—Mattie thought maybe the girl had run, hearing Heke's door slam, seeing Mattie approach—but the inside of the cabin, as Mattie peered at it from the front porch, did not look like somewhere that had been vacated in haste. Nothing spun or tipped or seemed infused with residual motion. There were no crusts or crumbs or plates left on the table. The lights were off, the chairs neatly pushed in. Some toys sat on the floor near the sink, left when the child was done with them.

"Hello," Mattie called, but her sharp voice brought neither a response nor the sound, someplace inside the cabin, of activity ceasing.

"Hello, hello, hello, hello," she called again.

Her hand was on the door, she was about to open it and go in, write a note, threatening and curt, that she would leave on the table anchored, perhaps, by one of the plastic blocks that were on the floor—she even opened the door a half inch to go and do it, but then she let it close again. It was still trespass. Even if it was justified, even if it was called for, she could not bear to put herself side by side with Sylvie; for the two acts, trespass and trespass, to cancel each other out. She had long since stopped expecting to be a bride in Heke's house but, after all this time, she had not expected it to be another girl either.

Dear Syl,

Here is more money I am sending you. I hope you and the baby do fine. Cass

Dear Syl,

Here is more money, 20 dolars, I will send more soon, Cass. I hope you and the baby's fine

Dear Syl,

Here is a few more dollars I know you can surly use. It rained here today. It has been hot but today it is rainy and cold. I hope the baby and you do fine. Cass.

Since Cass has been gone, Sylvie hasn't spent any money, or needed to. There was enough food in the cabin from their last shopping to last a little while if she wasn't too choosy about what she ate, which she wasn't. And she'd been helping herself some out of Heke's pantry as it didn't seem like he'd be needing it anytime soon and it was a shame to have it go to waste. Anyway, she was keeping track of what she borrowed on the back of one of Cass's letters—canned peaches mostly, she couldn't seem to get enough of them. She'd eaten all Heke had, taking the empty cans and lids with her when she went, to throw away. She ate them with her fingers, standing over the sink so there wouldn't be any drips.

Dear Cass,

Today I went shopping. I left Christopher with Naneen because it is too hard shopping with him because he is too grabby after everything and also wants to be getting out of the push basket all the time as you know. I got to Nan's too early and woke her and everybody and caused a ruckus don't laugh! In the grocery I bought bacon bread ham canned peaches animal crackers and something else I can't remember at this time. The canned peaches are all for me and the animal crackers are all for Christopher. I also bought another box for Naneen's boys. I know you would say this is a waste but it isnot. Naneen helps me out. We saw Turner Ward—you remember him, the one who asked me all the questions at the trial and the one who used to go with my sister Lusa but then they did not get married. He was outside the street at the market. He said to say hey. I hope you are fine as we are fine.

XXXXOOO Sylvestrie

P.S. Milk

20

TURNER WARD hesitated outside the supermarket as the automatic-eye door shut behind Sylvie.

"Well, will you look who's here," he'd said when he first saw her. Gladness crowded up in him; he couldn't have said exactly why.

"Oh. Hey," Sylvie had said, without excitement. "What're you doing prowling around out here?"

She said some other things as well, but Turner got stuck on "prowling," like she'd meant he had no satisfactory lair.

"Prowling?" he said. "I'm out for a walk, I'm often out walking at this hour. To get my head clear. It's cooler," he said, though it wasn't by much.

"I wouldn't call it 'prowling' by any stretch."

Sylvie looked at him as though she had no idea what he was talking about.

He did look rumpled, like he might have been out all night. In fact, he had been home alone. Clothes just didn't fit Turner right, or at least his clothes didn't. He was so big. Beside him, Sylvie didn't look any bigger than a pixie. His upper arms were the size of some other people's thighs, and his thighs were so large they nearly overlapped when he walked, causing the inner seams of his pants to hike up, rub and ripple. The seersucker he'd put on fresh-pressed that morning hid some of the usual puckering, and the fact that he was holding the jacket on one hooked finger over his shoulder had kept it neat. But his shirt had pulled partway out of his waistband, and was stuck to his back where he had sweated.

"Kind of early, isn't it?" Turner said. "How come you're up and out?"

Sylvie shrugged. "Maybe I'm just prowly my own self," she said.

Turner smiled; he shook his head, then he looked away down the street. The sun hadn't risen as high as the buildings yet. It was still shady in front of the market where they were standing, though the sky was a light, lit blue up above, like the top of a gift box.

"Quiet out," Turner said.

Sylvie said, "It's always quiet up where I am. To me, this is a crowd."

Turner's head swung around—had he missed some knot of people down at the other end of the street?—but there wasn't anybody except the two of them. When he looked back at her, Sylvie had a tiny smile on her face.

"Oh," Turner said. "Ohh, you mean"—and he laughed and his finger went back and forth in the air between them. Sylvie tapped the side of her own head to show him he was brainy, and swift.

"You're not nervous up there?" Turner said. "After the shooting and all?"

This time Sylvie laughed. "Why?" she said. "You think Heke's prowling around, thinking to do it again?"

"There," Turner said. "Prowling. You said it again."

Sylvie frowned. "So?" she said. "That word against the law all of the sudden?"

Turner seemed ready to laugh, he'd seemed ready since she began speaking, but he didn't. He looked down at his feet. Brown wingtips that could have used polishing.

"Well," Sylvie said. "I've got to go ahead and do my shopping."

She took a step towards the market, near enough so that the magic-eye door swung open.

"Where's your entourage?" Turner said, coming up behind her.

"What's that?" Sylvie said. She turned to face him again, and there he was, unexpectedly close, almost right on top of her, near enough so she could see water beaded in his hair as if he'd just stepped from the shower, and smell the chalky mint smell of toothpaste on his breath.

"Hey," Sylvie said, and fanned at the insufficient space between them. "You're the one making me nervous."

Turner backed up. "You didn't answer my question," he said, leaning a little across the distance he'd just created between them.

"What did you ask?"

"Where's your entourage?"

"What's that?" Sylvie said.

"Your entourage," he said, a little louder, rotating his arm as if he was mixing batter in a big, big bowl. "Oh you know, people. The people you have around you."

"I don't know who you mean, 'people around me.' Usually I have my baby boy with me, but I left him at my sister Naneen's. I don't know do you remember her?"

Turner shrugged. He didn't want to stand here and talk about her sister.

"And Cass, that's my husband? He's in Oldhio."

"Ohio," Turner said. "What's he, gone on vacation without you?" He was smiling, his voice now its customary boom.

"No," Sylvie said. "He wouldn't do that. What would he do that for?"

Her tone was serious, plain. When he spoke again, Turner's voice was tamer.

"No," Turner said. "Of course he wouldn't." His jacket slid down off his shoulder to the sidewalk. He bent and picked it up and swung it back over his shoulder again. Sylvie pointed at it, then reached out and brushed the sleeve, faintly marked with soot.

"Thank you," Turner said. "I'm afraid I'm always a little less than splendidly turned out."

"He went to find work," Sylvie said.

"And did he?" Turner looked down at her; her head seemed to stop right around the bottom of his rib cage.

"Well he did, yes, a tide-me-over kind of job. When he gets a good job, a permanent, we're all going to move there. Get us a house and whatnot."

"That right?" Turner said. He was suddenly—he did not know what it was: jealous, but not of a person, of a place; a new place that might claim her.

"Won't you miss us?" Turner said, and winced at the coyness of his tone, and so after he spoke, he did not smile.

"Us?" Sylvie asked. "Miss who-do-you-mean?" She raised her eyebrows, which were almost invisibly pale.

"Well, I meant here, really; I meant this place. Home."

"No," Sylvie said. "Well, I don't know. Maybe." She shrugged. "I haven't ever been any other place. I think I'd have to go someplace else to find out if I missed here. Don't you think so?"

Turner didn't answer for a while, long enough so that when he spoke, it sounded like he was addressing some wholly other question.

"There's people," he said, "never leave home. Some people spend their whole lives living in one fine place."

"You calling this a fine place?" Sylvie said.

He smiled. "Maybe."

"You ever lived elsewhere?" Sylvie asked, and Turner said he had. He'd been to college in Lexington, not that that was far. Washington, D.C., for law school. And he'd been in Vietnam.

"Oh," Sylvie said. "Well, that's far."

"That is," Turner said.

"And you like it here best?" Sylvie said.

"Of those places." He'd wanted to come back, after his tour. He'd wanted a place he knew, small and tight around him, where he recognized trees, birds, flora and fauna. He'd moved into a small apartment, not even his family's large estate some miles out of town; a little place, everything within arm's reach. His need for these things had long since passed, though. Now, everything was just small.

"See, I don't know. Maybe I would too. But when Cass gets a job—" She shrugged. "There's just no jobs around here," she said.

"Well, I'll keep my ears open for you," Turner said. "Sometimes I hear about things. Sometimes I'm in a position to—"

Sylvie nodded vaguely; she looked away. "I have to go now," she said. "My sister's watching the baby."

She wrapped her arms around her waist as if she was just noticing the absence of Christopher's weight, but the tightness was uncomfortable and she let go.

"Sure," Turner said. "I'm going down the street, I haven't had my breakfast yet. Living alone's fine, but cooking, that's another thing altogether. Stop on in, I'll treat you to a cup of coffee. When you're done shopping."

"Well, no," Sylvie said. "I don't think I want to do that. Thank you for the offer, just the same."

"That's fine," Turner said. "Offer stands, though. You get thirsty, come on by the luncheonette, I'll be there, I'm not going anywhere." His voice ascended through this last part as the automatic-eye door was closing behind Sylvie.

21

MATTIE HAD left everything up at Heke's—mop, bucket, all her cleaning supplies. She was still on the mountain when the absence of clatter from the backseat made her realize she would have to go back. There was no place to turn around, though, on the narrow road; even if she'd remembered farther up, there was no place to turn around. She would have to go all the way to the bottom, then up again.

"Well, I'm not doing it," she said. She was off the mountain by then, signaling before she made the turn onto the flat road into town, sun glazing her back window.

"Let those other things stay up there," she said. "I'll get myself new ones." She sounded defiant, pleased by the unaccustomed picture of herself as profligate.

Mattie drove into town and found a place to park almost immediately at the easternmost end. Other cars perambulated slowly looking for spaces, but the people moved quickly into and out of the old brick storefronts, the colors of their summer clothes blurring.

Something pricked at Mattie's leg from inside her skirt pocket as she got out of the car—the little calendar book. She turned it over in her hand, then stuck it in the glove compartment. No, she was not going to do any shopping right now, she was going to the luncheonette. It would be empty at this hour—past breakfast and too early for lunch—and she could use a cold lemonade. Or an iced tea. One.

But the luncheonette wasn't empty; it was crowded and clamorous. Mattie squeezed her way in, then stood blinking beside the door while the people at the tables nearest to her looked up. There was one empty stool at the far end of the counter: she headed for it.

"What can I get you?" the counter girl asked.

"Oh. Let me see, what do I want?" Mattie looked up at the menu—white plastic alphabet-soup letters fixed to a black rubber board. It was full of misspellings and gaps.

"Will you look at that," Mattie said. "Sandwich, spelled San Ich. Doesn't that sound like an exotic island you might like to go to? San Ich."

"What kind of sandwich?" the girl said.

"Oh no, I was just—. I'm just going to have a drink," Mattie said. "Isn't this heat awful?"

The girl stood impassive, pencil against pad, and did not answer.

"Now, do I want an iced tea or a lemonade, that is the question," Mattie said, looking up at the menu again. The "o" in the word "donut" was missing.

The girl rolled her eyes and taptaptapped her pencil against the pad.

"Miss Mattie, is that you?" It was Turner Ward, sitting beside her. He'd swiveled his stool around and was leaning towards her.

"Oh. Turner. Yes," Mattie said. "It's me. I'm just trying to figure out what to order here. Just a drink," she said to the girl.

"Now, if you'll allow me, Miss Mattie, you look like a young lady who could use a lemonade. Wouldn't you say so?" he said to the girl behind the counter. The girl smiled, then stopped smiling; opened her mouth to speak, then she didn't.

"A nice cold lemonade for the young lady, think you can handle that for us?" Turner Ward said.

The girl hustled away as if it was a race, her body tilting forward in the narrow lane of space behind the counter. She soon returned with the lemonade.

"Thank you, darlin," Turner said, and touched the girl's forearm with one finger. The girl flushed.

"Thank you, Turner," Mattie said.

"You're very welcome. I wish it wasn't so noisy in here," Turner said, and leaned as close to Mattie as he could without coming off his stool.

"It is noisy in here," Mattie said, swiveling slightly towards him as well. She picked up her glass and sipped from it. Ice cubes slid and rested against the side of her nose and she had to set the glass down and take a napkin and wipe it.

"Let me ask you a question, Turner," Mattie said.

"Uh oh. This isn't going to be some kind of a test, is it?" He threw both hands up in the air and raised his heavy eyebrows and leaned way back on his stool. He waited for her to laugh, but she didn't.

"If somebody was trespassing on somebody else's place," Mattie said. "What could you do about it?"

"Well, me personally, not a thing. Call up the sheriff, he's the one you want."

Mattie nodded. She let there be a pause, then she said, "Well, what if it's not you, exactly? What if you're a third party? A caretaker, so to speak. Watching their place for them while they're gone. And somebody else, a person with no authorization at all, is—"

"I'm sorry. I apologize, Miss Mattie. I'm afraid you lost me. Somebody else and Somebody who?"

Mattie picked up her lemonade, then she set it back down.

"Heke," she said. "Heke Day. You know he's—Well, you know he's 'not at home.' "

Turner picked up his fork and combed the tines across his empty plate. "Yes ma'am," he said quietly. "I know he's not at home. I know exactly where he is."

"Oh no!" Mattie said. "I didn't mean—I'm not accusing you of something, Turner. It's not a complaint. You Did Your Job," she said in the same severe voice in which she offered praise to her students. "I hadn't finished what I meant to say," Mattie said.

Turner raised his arm to signal the counter girl. When she came, he pushed his empty coffee cup towards her, for refilling. Mattie waited till the girl, abashed at having received neither look nor word from Turner this time, stepped away.

"I go up there to do for him, at the house," Mattie said. "As he lives alone. I always have done, years and years." Mattie heard how that sounded as she spoke it: years and years. A little flame of anger shot up inside her startling as a swift pain out of nowhere. Now what was that? you might say after the pain had gone away again.

Turner nodded, hunched over his coffee.

"I hadn't been up there in a while truth to tell, but I was there this morning, and I could tell, things were amiss. Someone's been in there who has no business in that house."

Turner swept the handle of his coffee cup back and forth. "So now," he said. "What you think belongs to you, somebody else thinks belongs to them, is that it?"

"No!" Mattie said. "That's not what I'm saying at all. I'm the caretaker. Somebody's trespassing. I want it stopped."

"It's probably just kids," Turner said. "You probably even know them."

"I certainly do know them," Mattie said. "Her. I know exactly who it is. Not any kids."

"You're sure?" Turner said. "You have proof of some kind?"

"I do," Mattie said. "A little book with telephone numbers written in it I could show you. I found it at Heke's, but it wasn't Heke's book."

"Well, how do you know that?"

"I just do know," Mattie said. "It isn't his handwriting. And the names written in it have nothing to do with—"

She was still speaking and he was already shaking his head. She spoke louder, as if above his disagreement.

"The names were this other person's relatives," she said, her voice sliding upwards. "They had nothing—"

Still, he was shaking his head—

"to do with Heke at all!"

"But you don't know that," Turner said. "Maybe the person gave that book to him to hold for some reason—safekeeping, or an emergency. You or I wouldn't know that."

"I do," Mattie said. The angry flame shot up again. "Believe me, I know."

He was shaking his head again. "You're not privy to his every thought and deed."

"Well, no," Mattie said. "I'm not. But—" She slowed and faltered. She had stopped wanting anything from Heke long since, but maybe it didn't look to other people like she had.

"You need definitive proof," Turner said, standing, pinching his wallet out of his back seersucker pocket. "Something tangible. Or witnessed. Who's the person, anyway?"

"Sylvie," Mattie said. "Heke's been letting them live up there in one of his cabins. In one of his *cabins,*" she said. "Not in the house. Sylvie Pomfret. That's who it is."

Sylvie was outside the cabin, searching the scratched-up ground in front for small stones, then pitching them against the wall. It was so quiet. There wasn't any sound, other than sounds she made herself. In the interval between throwing one pebble and throwing another, the silence thudded back.

Christopher had fallen asleep in the car, drooping over the seat belt, and though Sylvie tried, she had not been able to wake him.

"Lord, Sylvestrie, leave him be, he's naught but a baby," she'd told herself as she carried him inside, but even that was said loudly. So maybe he'd wake up and be company.

She had wanted to get home, out of the noise of the day—the headache and racket of Nan's twins and of town.

"I'm not used to this," she'd said to Nan a number of times. "Up where I am, it's so quiet."

But the one little taste of human jostle and chime she'd had today must have claimed her because now she didn't see how she was to live up here, alone, in all this panicky silence. How had she ever done it?

Sylvie thought about calling Nan, but she had just seen her. She thought about calling Cass, but she had just written him a letter, begging paper, a stamp, an envelope from her sister. She looked towards Heke's house. From where she was standing it was invisible to her.

It was overcast now, the sun gone behind an impenetrable scud of silver, but it wasn't any cooler at all. Sylvie went into the cabin, into the bedroom and lay down beside the sleeping bundle of baby. She was tired from the day, and this had become their regular sleep time, but her eyes wouldn't stay closed. And wasn't it hotter than it had been all the last hot, terrible days? Her whole body was sweat-skimmed and she felt tight inside her own skin as if it were a garment that had shrunk and lost its give.

Sylvie got up again and took off her dress—I do not either need maternity clothes, she said, looking down at the rise of her stomach. She put on the T-shirt of Cass's she had worn—what day was that?—to wash beneath. It was still damp—she had left it balled on top of the bureau rather than spreading it out—and smelled mildewed. She lay back down on the bed, more comfortable in some ways though the smell already bothered her; soon she would find it intolerable.

"God," she said.

And then the phone began to ring in Heke's house. It was a small sound, far away, but with no other noise to obscure it, distinct.

"You hear that?" Sylvie said, and nudged the sleeping baby. She sat up and swung her legs over the side of the bed and listened to make sure she had heard it.

Yes. There it was again.

"Cass," she whispered. "Pa, I believe that must be your daddy calling. I'll be right back, don't worry," and she was up and running towards Heke's.

Cass—as if he were calling in response to the letter she'd just this afternoon written and mailed; Cass, it had to be, who else? the phone ringing and ringing because he knew how far she was; how long it would take her to answer.

22

ONCE HE'D started, Turner couldn't stop picturing Sylvie: Sylvie as she stood outside the supermarket, Sylvie in her tight pink blouse. His conversation in the luncheonette with Mattie had started him off, but the pictures were ready and waiting. It was a distraction, also a purpose, as if Sylvie was the reason he'd come back to live here, it had just taken him until now to know it.

Turner's secretary, Dorothy Rae, was baffled. When she called back to him from her desk opposite the front door, he never answered. She had to get up and go to the door of his office.

"Turner," she said to him one morning. "Did you hear me? You taking a little R&R time I don't know about?"

It had always been Dorothy Rae's private opinion that Turner was too smart for the cases he took on—local matters, mostly small and mundane; that the work was not ambitious enough and did not engage him. Turner was smart in a big way, his work mingy and small. Nevertheless, he turned the light, thin pages of the law books as if each matter he took up was weighty, worthy of notice.

"You know what, Dorothy Rae, you are absolutely right. I do need a little R&R," Turner said. "I think this heat's addling me." He scrubbed at his eyes with the heels of both hands.

"I'm going out, get a little air is what I am going to do," he said, and then he stood and stepped out from behind his desk.

Turner's office was not on the main street but perpendicular to it, a quiet road where there were a few offices and a shop or two on the ground floors of the mostly shabby mostly frame houses, although one or two of them were brick. Across the street there were train tracks, built on a shored-up parapet of earth with a steep drop down the other side. The sidewalk ran out at the end of the street—one step down and you were walking on dirt—as if there were no possible other place to go.

There was an ashy railyard odor to the air, the smell of a train just passing, though these were freight tracks and they hadn't been used in years, not since the last coal boom ended. The sun had heated up the rails, that was all, and it had heated up the wooden ties and the gravel, but the powerful train smell made Turner restless, and he turned around abruptly in the middle of the sidewalk.

"Oh. Oh, Turner. Oh golly," a woman's voice said, and when Turner looked down from the loftiness of his natural height, there was Mattie.

She was smiling, patting at what looked like a shower cap on her head. Marshmallows of cotton stuck out around the outside edges of the cap, and she had on a pink cape that covered her from neck to knee.

"Miss Mattie," Turner said. "What has happened to you? What's wrong?" He sounded stricken—was she in the midst of a treatment of some kind, something medical and severe? She gave off a strong chemical smell. He tried not to take a step back.

"Miss Mattie," Turner said again. "Can I do anything for you?" His voice was gentle and he bent his knees so he could see into her face. "Do you need to be taken somewhere?"

"I was at the *hairdresser,*" Mattie finally said, and hitched a shoulder at the splintery, two-story house a few doors down that stood behind a patch of lawn the color and bristliness of coir.

"I still am. It was too hot inside, and those chemicals." She fanned at the air in front of her.

"I just came out to get a breath," Mattie said. "I did not expect to run into anyone." She closed her eyes and put her fingers up to her temples where they were thwarted by the rolled-up wads of cotton.

"Yes," Turner said. "I believe the chemicals they use are very toxic."

"Well," Mattie said. "I don't know about that. They smell bad, though. Especially those permanent waves."

"Oh," Turner said. "Ohhh. I thought you meant—permanent waves! Well, you had me scared sick the other minute—" but he was looking over Mattie's head now, as if he'd lost interest even while he was still speaking.

"Yes, well, I'm going back in now," Mattie said, and when Turner didn't answer, she just turned and walked off.

"Oh, Miss Mattie. Wait a minute please. I've been meaning to ask you—" he was coming towards her, big leather shoes slapping the sidewalk. "Was there any resolution to that little problem we discussed a couple of few days ago?" he said.

Mattie stopped and turned and waited for him to catch up, though she clearly didn't want to. Her mouth was tight and she had her arms tightly crossed underneath the cape so that it folded around her. She looked like a big soft bird, the kind that was earthbound.

"What was that?" she said. "A few days ago when?" Hair dye was beginning to seep down her neck, but she didn't move her hands to touch the wadded cotton.

Turner stopped before her. He tipped his head back and looked up at the overcast sky.

"Do you think it might rain?" he said. "Lord in heaven hear our prayers."

"Turner! It is imperative that I get out of here right now. Right this very minute."

Mattie's face had gone pink, now she was pink all over, and pretty near to sobbing.

Turner frowned. "Well then, don't let me keep you," he said. "I was just asking after you. Just making sure everything was all right."

"What?" Mattie said. "Turner? What could you be talking about?"

"That trespassing incident you were upset about?" he said. "I just wanted to find out what all ever transpired with that."

Mattie tucked at the cotton again—it was spongy and wet.

"I'm not any further along than I was," she said. "I've called Heke's phone a time or two but nobody answers."

She had let the phone ring and ring, sure Sylvie was there, too sly to pick it up.

"Well," Turner said. "I thought I might take a drive up over to there, see what I could find out myself. I just wanted to ask what you might think about that."

Mattie was stalking towards the beauty shop now, holding her head stiffly as if she were carrying a full glass of water on it.

"Well, thank you, Turner. Thank you. That's thoughtful of you," she called, but she didn't stop.

"See what all's going on. Check it out," Turner called back. "I'll call you later, let you know."

"Uh huh, well thank you," Mattie called. By this time she was practically running.

"A little drive," Turner said, out loud to himself. "A little drive," he said again and took off walking, though he wasn't heading home, where his car was, he was going in the opposite direction, towards Main Street, and the luncheonette.

It was practically empty, and cool. When Turner came in, the chrome legs of the chairs and the stems of the counter stools picked up his reflection in miniature and when he walked, the whole room seemed set in motion.

"There he is," Turner called out. "The very man I am looking for."

"What brings you out at this hour?" the sheriff said, as Turner took the seat beside him at the counter.

"Can I get an iced tea, darlin?" Turner called to the waitress.

"Dorothy Rae kicked me out of the office," Turner told him. "Said to get a little R&R. 'Turner, you are gettin addlepated,' she told me. I think she thinks I'm crackin up; hell, I know she thinks that."

"Why's that?" Junior said.

Turner shrugged, looking down at the bleary countertop between his elbows. "Not enough to keep me busy," he said. "Or that's how she'd put it. But anyhow, I thought I'd drive up in the hills a little bit this afternoon, cool off, thought you might want to come along."

If he was surprised that Turner was inviting him someplace when he'd never asked him anyplace before, Junior didn't say so.

"Obliged," is what he said. "But Dorothy Rae isn't paying me for no R&R time. Today's a workaday for me. I'm working."

"Thank you, darlin," Turner said as the girl set his iced tea down on the counter.

"Actually, this is work," Turner said. "I thought I'd go on up to the Day place, look around a little bit."

"Well, why?" Junior said, swiveling to look at him. "Why would you want to do that?"

"Miss Mattie thought there might be some trespassers up there," Turner said.

"Why's she think that?" Junior said.

"Not sure," Turner said. "Not certain."

"I have got enough to do without bounding around after trespassers," Junior said.

"Well, you don't have to. I'll do it," Turner said. "That's what I'm telling you. I'm taking a drive, I'll head up that way, stick my nose in and just see what's what. I'll play scout."

Junior gave him a sideways look. "You got even half an idea where the Day place is located?" he said. "I'm guessing probably you don't."

Turner shrugged. "It couldn't be that far. Mountain's only so high. How far could it be?"

Junior turned front again. "I'll put it to you this way: God himself'd get lost if he had to find this place without some kind of guidance. It isn't just up, it's in."

"Why I came looking for you, sheriff," Turner said. "Get you to draw me a map. Or maybe you should just go too then. Miss Mattie did report it."

"Due respect," Junior said. "But she did not report it to me. Far as I'm concerned, that's the same as it doesn't exist." He stood and began rumbling his pants pocket after money to pay for what he'd had.

"On me," Turner said, standing too.

"Yeah?" Junior said. "Shucks. If I'd of known, I would've had a whole lot more to eat."

"Doesn't look like you need a whole lot more to eat," Turner said and they both laughed, a sound like a paper bag crumpling in the otherwise quiet.

They headed outside together, walking into the slap of heat on the other side of the door. Junior stopped. He looked first one way down the almost empty street, then the other.

"So," he said after a minute. "Think there's anything to this trespassing business?"

Turner shrugged. "I wouldn't know," he said. "Thought I might just as well check it out as not. I won't though, if you're telling me not to."

"I'm not telling you nothin, Turner. You can go where you like. It's a free country."

"You know, when I was little," Turner said. "I thought that meant you didn't have to pay for anything."

"Yeah, no," Junior said. "One way or another, everything's paid for. You going?"

"I am," Turner said. "Now all you got to do is head me in the right direction."

23

TURNER GOT lost anyway, though the sheriff had drawn him a map on a napkin from the luncheonette. It sat on his dashboard as he drove, fluttering up in the rush of air from the opened windows, a sketch of three long-boned fingers of road emerging from the wrist of the highway—first you take this, then this one, then this other, the sheriff had said—but Turner kept looking at it long past when it had anything new to tell him.

The map made the way seem straightforward, but it wasn't. The joints of the fingers—the diverging roads—were invisible; the places where they left the main artery and went off in other directions, invisible too. The map had prepared Turner only for the road's roughness; for its pocks and erosions—coin-sized, plate-sized, the size, in some places, of a mattress—as the surface of the napkin was bumpy.

It was almost dark by the time Turner got there, the darkness creeping towards him from below. Leaving the last road, he had finally seen how the three did fan out side by side as if they were three hanks of hair waiting to be braided, but it was visible to him only at the end of the trip, when he no longer cared. His back was stiff by that time, and the grit from the highway had mixed with the oils and sweat on his face, and all he wanted to do was turn around and drive home.

He stopped, though, in the dark dip of the tulip poplars in front of Heke's—the dirt road was the third strand of the braid—and got out of the car into air sticky with the smell of pine. The joints of his knees and his hips ached as they always did if he spent too much time driving. He was too big to sit comfortably in a car. He drove a Cadillac, but even so.

In the light that was left, Turner could just make out the three cabins farther up the road, dusky and uniform in color so that they appeared to be blue. He'd seen Heke's house first, large and looming up the rise before him, but when he looked for it now in the near darkness, it was gone, as if the ground had opened, and the house sunk slowly under.

Turner shut the car door softly, with just enough force to put out the interior light. After the click of the door, there wasn't any sound besides the faint, occasional whistle of his own breath. There were no bird or insect noises, although he sensed birds and insects; no sounds of small animals in the underbrush. It was the most complete quiet he'd ever been in, tangible and encroaching, like the dark, but more carnivorous.

He looked in the direction of the highway. It had been there a minute ago, but now he couldn't see it, he couldn't even see his own hand. In the minutes he had been standing here, the darkness had thickened and coarsened and cohered around him, and he had disappeared. The night had taken on the taint of devilment and mischief. The pine smell seemed sharper.

Turner's breath was coming fast, and he hunted for the car door handle, but it wasn't there. The car, yes, the engine still ticking, or was that his pulse battering the taut stretched skin of his hand, but not the door. Turner had known a boy once who'd gotten lost in the mountains. He'd been found the next day, but been forced to spend the night in a darkness so complete, eyes open or shut it didn't make a difference, and Turner pounded at the car now, the metal rebounding.

And then something glinted out of the primeval dark, shone in the curved black surface of the glass of the car window. It was a tiny scoop of light, a pinpoint, not nearly enough to see by, although the act of seeing at all calmed Turner. He located the door, yanked at it, then stood near it, putting first one hand then the other into the weak sun of the car's interior light.

The gleam was coming from the house, and when his heart had

come back to normal and he was breathing easier again, Turner began to move towards it, as anybody would, alone in pitch darkness. He left the car door open behind him so he'd be able to find his way back, and kept his eye on the lit house window as he neared it.

And then, there in the window, was Sylvie.

She was visible only from the waist up, dressed in a garment—was it a dress?—of gray gauzy stuff the same color and quality of steamed glass. He did not know what he was doing here. He could not look away.

Sylvie held perfectly still. The air did not stir; it was heavy, dense and becalmed. For two days, since the day she'd gone into town for the groceries, she'd been unsettled and nervous. The air frisked with static; her hair, when she ran a hand across it, crackled as if it were about to catch on fire. She kept expecting a storm, but no storm came. Now she stood at Heke's bedroom window and looked out.

And saw what? Turner knew she sensed something, she was poised, her whole self listening—a shoulder, the lift and angle of her rib cage. It was the way an animal listened, flesh pricked up, though it didn't necessarily face the source of the disturbance.

Could she see the car light? Turner wanted to look behind him—was it visible from here, that tiny man-made star? But he did not look, did not turn his head, as if he were afraid she might hear his neck creaking or the beating of his heart or—there it went again—the stealthy inward whistle of his breath.

If he had stood where Sylvie was standing he would have known she couldn't see it. The small, weak, interior car light would not breach such a distance nor show through the shadows of the tulip poplars, and even if she had somehow seen it, Sylvie would not have thought "car," but "raccoon" or "bear," the steady watchful eye of some animal.

She thought that anyway, although she did not see the light: a presence out there. She wasn't afraid, but had planned to go out and sit on the top porch step for a little bit, and now she wouldn't do it.

"Who's out there?" she said.

She put both hands against the old screen covering the window, and she pushed.

There was a change in the flavor of the air, a rustiness from the old stiff metal screen. Turner tasted it, a cold tang, and he began to back away from the house.

Dry grass stung his ankles as he moved and when he turned, scanning for the car light, not finding it—heart, heart—finding it then, grass pricked at his flesh through the fabric of his socks and broke off and fell into his pants cuffs. When he was back home, pacing the house with his head down as was his custom, the chaff would drop out and he would kick it and, as he continued to pace, it would skate across the wood and under the various loose rugs. Later, years after Turner was gone from this house, bits of dried grass would still turn up from time to time in the corners.

Sylvie stepped from the window back into the kitchen. In the sink were the two empty cans from the peaches she had already eaten that day. She kept telling herself to wait, eat them more slowly so they'd last, but she couldn't, was opening a new can even while she remonstrated with herself, panting after the silky coolness of the fruit.

She broke the top off the can and put it inside one of the empties in the sink, and then she dipped out the peach slices one after another and leaned over the sink and ate them.

Christopher's bottles were lined up on the back of the sink underneath the window, the remaining cans of peaches crowded up on the wood countertop to the right. She put her own things only in corners and unused inches of space. Every day she brought their dirty clothes, hers and Christopher's, and the empty peach cans back to the cabin. Nothing piled up.

When she'd finished the peaches, Sylvie wandered back into the bedroom where she leaned against the doorway and looked at the baby asleep on the bed, then at the telephone. Why didn't Cass call her? He never had since the time the phone had rung over and over and she had run up here from the cabin, but still missed it. Stood with the receiver in her hand for a long time because it seemed impossible that he had chosen that same exact moment to hang up. She'd hardly left Heke's house since, but Cass hadn't called again. And Sylvie couldn't call him, she had no way to reach him. Her little telephone book with Peggy's number in it was missing.

She picked up the packet of letters, tied together with twine, that she'd found underneath the mattress the first time she'd hunted for the lost book. They were addressed to Heke, some foreign address, ink faded to brown. Sylvie thumbed the packet to see if her telephone book was stuck in between letters, though she'd done it before and it wasn't. She put them down again, and came around the bed and reached, gently, underneath the pillow where Christopher was sleeping, for perhaps the twentieth time.

It'll turn up, Sylvestrie, she told herself, and pushed against the mattress and stood up.

I should've just memorized that number anyhow. Just so's I'd have it. Stupid, stupid, dumb, dumb, dumb.

She hadn't memorized it on purpose, afraid knowing the number would make Cass's absence more concrete. But she had been wrong. The absence of the number made Cass seem not just far away, but like he had disappeared altogether.

24

TURNER WAS unable to sleep. Not just the night he'd seen Sylvie up at the Day place, but after that, night after night, he slept almost not at all. By 10:00 he was often unable to stay on his feet and would go and lie down, though he wouldn't remember lying down until he woke to find himself splayed across the bed on the diagonal. Often he was fully dressed, sometimes still with his shoes tied and with an imprint at his waist, wildly red, from his belt. This was always in the middle of the night. By one in the morning, he was up.

A restlessness had seized him, he thought it must be a symptom of something, he thought he must be sick. His heart beat too fast, causing him to stop what he was doing and put his hand over it many times a day, his fingers creeping between the buttons of his shirt. His blood sped and he sometimes shook with cold, as if the weather had changed, or as if he had ague or a fever. The possibility that he might be sick was a comfort to him—something concrete with a potential antidote—though he could not prove illness.

He tried. Went out one afternoon and bought a thermometer, examining the package in the pharmacy to see if there were restrictions on the weight or height of the user, but no; the instructions were the same for a child over the age of six and a man his size; the temperature was taken for the same duration. This seemed impossible to Turner and during the day, the two or three or four times he took the thermometer from his desk drawer and put it in his mouth, he left it there for twice the time the package called for.

He didn't have a fever. This made him variously distrust the thermometer and suspect he might have picked something up, some semitropical parasite causing an elusive temperature.

"Dorothy Rae?" Turner said, coming to stand in front of her desk. "Can you tell me the symptoms of malaria?"

Dorothy Rae didn't answer, although when she looked up Turner could see the variety of answers she might have given play across her face—

Do you want me to look it up?

Or, Well, that's one my kids must've missed.

Or, Is that a legal term, Turner?

Or, What is it we need this information for?

But she didn't say these things.

Turner went back to the drugstore where he'd bought the thermometer and consulted the pharmacist on over-the-counter sleeping medications.

("But, why are there different dosages based upon body size when a thermometer's used the same amount of time on everyone?" Turner said. "What kind of sense does that make?" The pharmacist just looked at him.)

Ultimately, Turner bought two types: a cold medication (Do Not Operate Heavy Machinery While Using, which sounded promising to him, industrial grade, as if he might be bulldozed or steamrollered into sleep) and one the pharmacist recommended—Sleepys? Dozees?—that Turner took out of politeness though it sounded too soft to do the job.

But the effect of the pills was the reverse of sleep. He felt more alert after he took them, although the colors and outlines of objects blurred. He paced more quickly through the rooms of his house, ducking at the doorways, telling himself over and over it was unlikely he would die of a faulty heart, with no predisposition or family history, at the age of thirty-eight.

"Turner? Mattie's on the line."

Dorothy Rae stood at the door to Turner's office. She did not come all the way in, wary of whatever was afflicting him, whatever it was that had turned all the shadows and hollows of his face blue, though she spoke in her usual snappy way.

"Turner?" she said. "Hear me?"

"I'll call her back," he said. "Please tell her I'm tied up. I cannot talk to her right now."

"It's the third time she's tried this week," Dorothy Rae said. "Couldn't you just—"

But he didn't look up, eyes on the papers before him though the case was small, dull, involving the disposal of trash. His concentration, of late, had improved, perhaps as a result of the medicines.

"Tell her I don't have any news for her yet," Turner said, still without raising his head. "Tell her I'll get back to her the minute there's something to tell. She'll know what you're talking about."

Mattie put down the phone. She'd been trying to reach Turner for days, since the morning following the day he'd told her outside the beauty shop that he was going up to Heke's, see what Sylvie was up to. He'd said he would call her, and she had been sure—securely, almost triumphantly sure—that he would, as amends for the discomfort he'd caused her. He'd made her stand out on the street, a sodden mess, while hair dye ran loosely down her neck, darkening her hair so that now it was too dark, an overburnished color, like tarnished brass.

He had not called. Mattie—reluctantly at first, but then less reluctantly—telephoned him.

"He's out," Dorothy Rae told her, or she said he was in but could not be interrupted.

Mattie frowned. Lately, she did not like Dorothy Rae.

She set her glass down, one of two juice glasses left from her mother's set that had come in three graduated sizes, each size with its own motif around the rim—oranges for the juice glasses, tomatoes for the middle-sized ones and for the tallest, grapes, as if you were meant to drink wine from them, wine by the tumblerful. Mattie remembered the almost unpleasant sensation of drinking from these glasses when she was a child; the way the painted fruit felt underneath her lip, as if a bit of paper were caught there. She had turned and turned the glasses, looking for a comfortable spot. Now the paint had almost entirely chipped off.

Mattie could see the outline of herself in the window beyond the table, or sections of herself in their delineating colors: the blue of her shorts, the poppy orange of her blouse, the brass-colored smudge of hair.

"You," she said. "Are going out. You are going to go and pay the man a visit. You are owed an explanation, is all there is to it."

If he had taken the trouble to speak to her. If he had come to the phone, been gracious and polite—"Miss Mattie, I haven't made it up there yet, strange as that might sound. As soon as I find out anything, you will be the first to know it"—Mattie would have believed him, but he said nothing.

Outside, Mattie hesitated, deciding whether or not to drive to Turner's office, rocking back and forth between the street and the car in the driveway.

"You'll walk," she told herself, saved, once again, by professional dispassion. "You're walking."

Turner's office was on a street that ran parallel to hers, trees on both sides, big ones, leafed out. It was unlikely she'd meet anyone. She'd have the whole shady way to herself.

25

MATTIE WENT right past Dorothy Rae. She didn't say hello and she didn't stop, just headed straight back to Turner's office, her chin raised and her hands pumping. Dorothy Rae stood up behind her desk, but slowly, like someone who'd been standing a long time and, just a minute ago, had her first chance to sit down.

"Mattie?" she said. "Mattie? Mattie?"—her voice forbearant and tired, a voice that made you remember Dorothy Rae had children. "If you're looking for Turner, he isn't here."

Mattie had seen this for herself by then, the door to Turner's office standing open, although she stayed where she was, boldness having deserted her at the portal, and scanned the room: the two windows behind the desk, the other door on the far wall.

"Is that a closet, Dorothy Rae?" she said, pointing at the door.

Dorothy Rae looked where Mattie meant her to, then she looked away. She smoothed the front of her skirt. She adjusted the matching fabric belt so that the buckle was centered.

"No," Mattie said. "I didn't think so. Did Turner see me coming and take off?"

"No!" Dorothy Rae said, an answer she could give with truth and, therefore, forcefulness. She was looking right at Mattie now.

"He didn't," she said.

But the room had the air of a place recently, hastily, vacated. There were papers on the desk, some turned up, some turned over; a pair of glasses; an uncapped fountain pen; a seersucker jacket on the back of the chair.

"Dorothy Rae. I think we both know that is not true."

The two women faced each other, Dorothy Rae in the shirtwaist dress that was striped teal blue and the color of nickels. The dress was both old and old-fashioned but it had been ironed to vehement crispness; in it, Dorothy Rae looked trim.

"Dorothy Rae. Why will Turner not take my calls? Why will he not get back to me? It would just be so much simpler. Less harsh."

"Mattie. Just between us, Turner hasn't been himself lately," Dorothy Rae said. The blood had come up in her face and turned her skin dusky.

"I don't know what it is, truly I don't. He's always taking his temperature," she said, and went over to Turner's desk and slid open the center drawer.

"Here you go," she said. "See?" She held the thermometer towards Mattie then snatched it away again as if the sense of compensatory justice Mattie was owed had quickly burned up in the face of her much stronger loyalty to Turner. Dorothy Rae stayed at Turner's desk, straightening papers, after she'd put the thermometer back in the drawer.

"Dorothy Rae," Mattie said. "What have I done to the man? Can you please tell me that?"

"Nothing. Oh Mattie, this doesn't, none of this, have one single thing to do with you."

Mattie turned her head away; she was looking, now, at the wall to her right, where there were cases holding law books. The law books were black and red down the spines, or black and green with gold leaf lettering. They did not look like real books to Mattie.

"I didn't mean that the way it came out," Dorothy Rae said. "I mean, he's going through some—thing. Some—I don't know what it is. Keeps asking me do I know the symptoms of exotic diseases.

"If you want to know my opinion, I think the man hasn't got enough to keep him busy, to keep his mind occupied, so he's open for mischief. I'll tell you the truth," Dorothy Rae said. "I don't even know where he is right now myself. I didn't even know he'd gone out till I came looking for him. He used that door there," she said and pointed at the door Mattie had asked her about.

"You know when anybody's used that door? Never."

They were silent for a moment, both looking at the door.

"I apologize," Mattie said. "Dorothy Rae? I owe you an apology. I shouldn't have thought it was you, shielding him."

Dorothy Rae's eyebrows went up. She hadn't known Mattie did think that.

"Maybe he is ill," Mattie said.

"Maybe. Or maybe he just hasn't got enough to fill his mind. Sharp as he is, he should be practicing the law in some big city someplace. I don't even know what he's doing here."

"Or the heat," Mattie said. "This heat's got us all a bit addled."

Dorothy Rae was capping Turner's fountain pen, which had bled a thumbprint of ink onto the blotter. The cap clicked.

"It's funny you should say that," she said. "Put it that way. That's just what Turner said."

Turner had bolted from the office through the back door that no one ever used but, in spite of how it looked, he had not seen Mattie. No one approaching his office was visible to him unless they came through the strip of scrub woods behind, and even then he would not have seen them as he sat with his back to the windows.

He had been working. He had opened the folder with the label on it Dorothy Rae had neatly typed; he'd thought he was reading, but he hadn't read. His eyes traveled the sentences, and when he came to the end of one page, turned it face down and moved on to the next, but he was accumulating only mileage; he couldn't have said what the papers were about.

Turner stood up. He stretched his arms and he stretched his long spine, laying his palms flat against the ceiling, which he could do without reaching. He was tired, he was jumpy, but he wasn't intending to go anywhere. Stood there with his damp palms marking the ceiling and threw his head back, and it was too far and too fast and he got dizzy. The room heaved, the floor slopping up one wall then up the other.

He had to get out, take a walk maybe, move around. He could not face Dorothy Rae, who he would have to pass in the outer office where she sat typing, who he would have to explain himself to, so he went to the back door. It stuck, it protested as he pulled on it, hard and repeatedly, until the continuous skin of paint that covered the door and the outside wall of the building loosened and released.

"I'll be back," he said to the empty room, to the shut door of his office, to no one. And then he was gone.

Dorothy Rae stepped into Turner's office again after Mattie left. She straightened the two stacks of papers—read and unread—and the stapler and the leather cup that had pencils in it Turner never used. Busywork.

He'd gone out the back door. She'd heard its protesting, sucking sound, although she hadn't known what the sound was at the time, never having heard it before. When she went back to see, Turner was gone. He hadn't even told her he was leaving.

Turner walked with his head down, as if into a hard wind. His heart was going as quick and heavy as it had, on and off, the last few weeks, but now he did not regard it. He walked fast, his long legs covering ground. Anyone seeing him wouldn't have called hello.

Turner's got some kind of important business to attend to, anyone seeing him would have said. His mind's occupied.

No one did call to him though, not that Turner would have answered. He walked without looking up and without breaking stride, as if he'd known, all this time, where he was going.

26

SYLVIE WAS trying to walk the big box into the center of the room. She feinted around and around it, as if she was missing the angle or side best for grasping, but the box went on being taller and wider and bigger and heavier than she was, and she couldn't get a hold.

"This is like trying to make a tipsy man get up and walk straight," she said to Christopher, who sat on the floor at her feet, but the box did not fight her as the man might have.

Sylvie had been cleaning out the front parlor of Heke's house, weeding through layers of calcified junk. She'd found old shirts in need of mending, hardened now into something other than cloth, and clattering broken tools and broken chairs and, back near the window, plates with dinner forks left soldered to them and soda cans somebody had snipped into the shapes of Stutz Bearcats and tiny airplanes with tiny moveable propellers and wheels, things that were toylike though they were too sharp-edged to be toys.

But mostly there were stacks and piles of old newspapers. Their edges went straight to powder in Sylvie's hands, shedding as she carried them by the moldy armful across the porch and down the front steps and over the distance to where the pickup truck was parked in front of her cabin, the paper bits scattering over the yard as if they were a trail she'd left to make sure she could find her way back. When she and Christopher drove a load out to the dump, the paper bits flew out behind them so dense, Sylvie raised herself out of the seat and leaned close to the rearview mirror and said, "What is that? Is that snow?"

The parlor now had a visible floor. The long wood planks, laid when the house was first built, had emerged dark and dry after years of woodsmoke and neglect, but intact and clear enough for Sylvie to set Christopher safely down and know he would be neither injured nor avalanched nor lost. She moved on to what she'd been after all along: the boxes.

There were three of them, clustered breast to breast like hens. Dust lay as thick as tablecloths across their tops. One box held a range and one a refrigerator—these things Sylvie could not even budge and had no interest in anyway—but the third box held a washing machine.

"I have got a real use for that," she told Christopher when she paused in her dancing struggle with the box to wipe the sweat out of her eyes or rub at her waist where the strain of the tussle was sometimes apparent.

Turner had to go home to get his car. He refused to carry the keys to work in his pocket, which would have been like giving himself permission to use them. There was a gauntlet of his own devising he had to get through if he wanted the car and he meant it to be difficult, the car the grail he both withheld from himself and promised. He relied on pride and his own willpower as deterrents, and on that shocked look of Dorothy Rae's and, if these things weren't enough, on the fact that he'd told himself he could go, if he had to, at night (when he didn't want to make the drive) or on the weekend, when who knew what people might be up there. And it had all worked, until today.

Until today, when none of it had worked. When he had leapt some invisible boundary, pulled and pulled on the back door of the office until the painted skin of the door had pulled away from the frame and he had tumbled out, large grafts of paint the size of outstretched palms hanging from the door frame. And when he was outside, forehead puckered against the relentless sun, bounding away from the office, Turner wondered, in a part of his mind that was small and removed from the bulk of his thoughts as a handkerchief is small and set apart in a pocket, whether Dorothy Rae would even be there when he got back.

That was only part of his mind, enough to distract him as he slapped along the pavement, but not enough to make him stop.

The car keys were in the bedroom, in the top drawer underneath his socks, not, as they usually were, on the tray on top of the dresser where, at night, he dumped the day's change from his pockets and his fountain pen and the keys.

As if he'd asked someone to hide them, as a precaution. As if they were contraband, or unsafe.

In the top drawer, underneath the socks, another trick he had used on himself that had worked, so long as he'd believed in its make-believe strength and inviolability. Now, he opened the drawer, flipped through the socks—black pellets folded in on themselves bouncing away across the floor—and plucked out the keys. He didn't even pause to see if he could find the map the sheriff had drawn for him.

Which, as it turned out, he did not need.

Turner parked farther from the house than he had the first time he'd been up here, but except for this discretion, he had given up stealth. He didn't want to seem like the kind of man who hid in the bushes in daylight.

He raised his head after unfolding himself from the car, a process that required him to push back on the steering wheel, swing his legs sideways and burst his large self outward.

Now, he stood breathing the air that was hot and dry and made the inside of his nose prickle. It was very quiet, though daylight. The quiet was no less intense than it had been in the dark, but it was different, less watchful now, and more active. There was a lush undercarpet of sound that had been absent when he'd been here at night, an insect sound that was constant and audible only as one sound, a powerful whir of white noise, like a running machine. The air was full of tiny jigging particles of heat.

Turner was in no hurry now, as if being here was what he'd craved and proximity was calming. He lingered beside the car, stamping gently until the pins-and-needles he sometimes got when he drove went away.

"Maybe I'll build a house myself, right here," he said softly, a peaceful idea that settled him further, as if it was only the place that had drawn him.

"Maybe I'll see about buying some of this land," he said.

He turned his head towards the highway where single cars passed at intervals, sun streaks that could be seen but not heard from where he was standing. Ten minutes ago, he'd been one of them.

And then a brief high-pitched shriek punched the air, a great rending, as of cloth. The insect noise stopped. Turner's shoulder jerked and his hands rose hip height but otherwise he didn't move, waiting for the sound to repeat so he would know what it was, where it had come from.

The sound came again, and though Turner still didn't know what it was—it was clear, this time, it had come from the house—he took off that way, plunging through the low-hanging tree whips that flailed at his face as he ran. Gangs of midges hung, unmoving, in the air, and the tall thin grass there was no one to cut twisted around his ankles.

Snakes, he thought, and he moved faster, pulling his feet free of the long twisty stalks.

The sound came again. Turner was close enough now to see Sylvie, standing in the room to the left of the front door. She was moving in and out of the frames around the windows but slowly, he could see her revolving, or she was backing up, backing away. Turner slowed; he stopped, his chest moving in short hikes with his short, sharp breaths, and watched her. The piercing shriek repeated, but Sylvie continued her slow-motion backward walk, she never stopped moving at all. From time to time her head tipped back, then it tipped forward and Turner thought it again—snakes—it was a snake she was backing away from, stalking her ever so slowly.

He flew up the porch steps, his feet drumming, searching for something—a gun, a rake—he could use against the snake. Nothing; a broom, and he reached for that.

"Are you all right?" he called. His breath ratcheted again and he was sweating hard, sweat pouring down his back and the sides of his neck, rolling from him and spotting the porch floor. He held still, waiting for an answer, but there was no sound now, and Sylvie had disappeared from the window.

Turner stood listening for what might be happening inside, focused only on that, but the sweat dripped, stinging one eye then the other, and he reached, blindly, for his shirt cuff and dropped the broom. There was the broomstick's brief clatter and then an undecided silence, and then Sylvie's voice—"What is it?"—deeper than Turner remembered. He unrolled one shirt sleeve and wiped at his whole face with it.

Sylvie came out on the porch. The door creaked as it opened, then smacked shut. With the hand that was not holding Christopher underneath the bunched-up skin of his thigh, she was working to untwist his fingers from her hair.

"Ow," she said, and leaned down to ease the baby's strong hold.

"Oh. It's you. I thought I heard something," Sylvie said, and just then the baby let go. Sylvie sighed. She kissed his fingers, then held them tucked inside her palm. She looked calm and powdery dry, not like someone who has just had an encounter with a snake.

"Everything all right?" Turner said, re-rolling his shirt sleeves. "Well, it is, that's obvious, you're fine, you look fine. I thought I heard—"

Sylvie frowned up at him as if she was trying to make out what language he was speaking. Turner looked away, out, again, towards the highway. He needed to not be looking at her.

"What?" Sylvie said. "Thought you heard?"

"Well. Nothing. Screaming?" Turner said. "I thought I heard—"

"Oh, that was this little guy. We were just dancing," Sylvie said, as if Turner had gotten the verb wrong.

"We were just dancing, weren't we Pa?" and she smiled at the baby and did a few backwards gliding steps.

Turner nodded. Dancing. He wanted to dance with her. Tiny little thing. "Oh," he said. "Well then. Long as everything's all right," and he moved towards the edge of the porch.

"Hey. You know what? Could you maybe just help me out a minute in here?" Sylvie said, looking behind her towards the house.

"I have been trying and trying to get this machine in there to budge, but the two of us, we're at a standstill. It is giving me a terrible time."

She stepped to the door, held it open with her back, the door bisecting her from her head to the top of her buttocks. Her skirt moved a little bit against her knees.

Turner didn't follow, as if he was unsure whether it was him Sylvie was inviting in, or where the invitation tended. The porch was shaded, a little dark. Maybe she thought he was somebody else.

"Um. It's Turner Ward?" he said finally.

Sylvie stayed where she was, with her back against the open door. A fly went inside. It was large and stayed near the porch floor as if it was too heavy to loft.

"Is that a yes or a no?" Sylvie said.

Still Turner hesitated. Sylvie sighed and rolled her eyes and he moved then, lumbering in like the heavy, freighted fly.

"Here, this way," Sylvie said and stepped in front of him, heading towards the parlor. Turner followed. She hadn't once sounded surprised it was him.

27

MATTIE SAW Turner go by. She did not know, at first, it was Turner, her eye caught only by the big silver Cadillac, or the glare that slid along its flank as it moved. The car had stopped at the light, the driver visible to her only as a bulky shape, dark green and pulsing to her sun-tripped eyes. He seemed to take up a good deal of the front seat, breadth and height, his head flush with the car roof. And then the light changed and the car pulled away, and after that Mattie knew it had been Turner, though she didn't know where he was going, of course, or not then.

Her house was dark when she came in. The living room had a dim, bedroom-type light, the tasseled shades pulled down as they always were, to keep the sun from fading the large birds and large flowers on the sofa upholstery, the pale blue upholstered chairs.

Mattie went from her front door through the kitchen and straight out the back door without stopping. The sun was just beginning to reach the backyard, one narrow white stripe down its eastern length as she stepped out onto the little slated porch outside the back door. She stopped there.

The garden was very large. It took up most of the yard, all but the very back where it was too dark to grow things, the dirt bald and trashy with fallen twigs and small branches that came down in storms, pom-poms of leaves still attached. That part of the yard smelled of the spray from feral cats.

"All right. Now," Mattie said to herself. "You can do this." But still, she didn't move from where she was standing. The tin cans of various sizes and empty mayonnaise jars and aluminum pie plates she had set at the ends of each row to scare the intruding animal glinted sharply in the sun. What if it was out here, its head raised, stealthy and quiet since she had come out of the house? She had believed it to be nocturnal, but what if it was not? She almost allowed herself to go back into the house, her breath easing with the anticipated permission but "No," she said, sharp, firm. "Go."

Her commanding voice got her down the steps, the slap of her sandals causing a squirrel to stop foraging momentarily. It shifted back onto its haunches, all articulation gone underneath the skirt of fat that spilled around it as if it sat stuffed into a can.

Mattie kept to the perimeter of the garden. Weeds had overtaken it, lush when they should have been sere from lack of water, and the squash leaves, since the last time Mattie had looked, had grown to the size of science-fiction experiments, some of them three feet across.

The lettuces were pale green and frothy from a distance—the thing must not like lettuces—but when Mattie got close she could see they had bolted; they would be bitter, not good to eat. She passed them; passed the peas, their vines twisted thickly around on themselves, as impenetrable as steel chains, and the tomatoes she'd meant to cage but hadn't. The tomatoes grew in the center of the garden, and she had more or less abandoned them. The plants drooped steadily downwards, but they bore despite their posture, the tumbled fruits flattening under the bushes like breasts beneath a sleeping body.

Mattie's eyes fanned the garden again. This time they were hooked by the pushed-up stalks of the rhubarb all the way at the back. She wouldn't have to step inside to reach them—and rhubarb was poisonous, raw. It would not have been touched.

"A cobbler," Mattie said, as if it was what she'd had in mind all along, and she headed for the back of the yard. The leaves of the plant were the crinkled green of old spinach, pocked with little worm bites, its stalks celery-like, except for the color, a deep pink, like worn velvet.

Mattie carried the rhubarb up from the garden, its butt end crumbed with dirt. It had a sharp, fresh, vegetal smell and she held it out, a little away from and in front of her. In the kitchen, she laid the rhubarb in the sink and turned the cold water on it—white porcelain, bright magenta stalks, the chocolate brown of the dirt washing away down the drain, a little mesmerized by it—and then her head snapped up and she said, "Well. I know where he was going," and it was Turner she was talking about.

He had been driving north, towards the mountains, Heke's house. She could picture the long silver thread of that silver car flashing, dipping and rising like a breaching fish. He was driving up to Heke's, as he'd told her he would; he would call her when he got back, maybe later, most likely in the morning. He was going to stop by and tell her, "Finally, Miss Mattie, I have got some news for you—" and she'd say, "And I've got something for you too, Turner. Cobbler. Rhubarb. What do you think of that?"

28

BY DUSK, Turner was gone. The air had begun to turn blue as he drove back down the mountain, the blue altering the color of the hills and the dun, parched grass as he passed, softening them. One house and then, a long way after, another house and in between, that darkening, settling blue again, but the lights from the houses themselves shone white or gold and they did not seem lonely.

When he got home, Turner poured himself the last of the milk, drank it, then went into the bedroom. He emptied his pockets onto the dresser and took off his clothes and folded them onto the chair beside the dresser and then he lay down on his bed, although it was a boy's bedtime, not yet fully dark. Outside, bats swooped, black and tatty against the darkening blue sky. Turner watched them for a minute, not long; soon he was asleep.

When Turner woke in the morning, the peacefulness that had displaced frenzy up on the mountain the day before was still with him. He kept checking for it, expecting it to dissipate as he went about his business—showered, dressed, loaded his pockets with his wallet, clean handkerchief, change, car keys—but it was always there, present and intact, as if being in Sylvie's presence had cured him of that same need; Sylvie her own antidote.

Dorothy Rae was already in the office when Turner arrived. He hadn't expected to see her.

"Dorothy Rae, what on earth you doing in here so early? You run away from home, girl? Your husband know where you are?"

Dorothy Rae looked at him tentatively. Turner sounded like his old self this morning, crazy new Turner didn't seem to be with him, but who could tell? She shifted from foot to foot. She cleared her throat. "I made muffins," she said.

"You did not. You a mind reader now?" and Turner went over to the table against the far wall where there was a coffee urn Dorothy Rae kept filled and going all day and a jar of powdered creamer and sugar packets and stirrers and today, a tinfoil-covered plate. Turner stooped down and delicately raised the foil, making noises of gluttony and pleasure, not because he wanted a muffin (nor, truth be told, any of Dorothy Rae's ponderous baked offerings) but because he owed her these signs of his gratitude.

"Thank you, darlin. Mmm. I am going to take this sweet thing inside. The amount of work I have got to do—" and Turner headed to his office.

Dorothy Rae exhaled. Her knobbed Olive Oyl shoulders dropped inside the thin cotton shoulders of her dress as if she had been holding her breath. She went to her desk and took the plastic dust cover off her typewriter.

They worked companionably through the morning, although so little noise came from Turner, Dorothy Rae stopped typing from time to time and listened to see if he was still there. She had called a painter about the door, but, of course, he had not come yet.

By mid-afternoon, though, Turner was finished. Calm fled, agitation, inattentiveness rising in him as the heat of the day also rose.

He tried. Forced himself to stay in his office, to stay put in his chair, sometimes gripping the armrests to keep himself from rising, and when he couldn't, when he finally came out to the front and stood beside Dorothy Rae's desk, forced himself to sound like his old self, as if there were some question he was coming out to ask her, or some job he needed her to get done.

"Whew," he said, perching on the edge of her desk. "Isn't this heat wave something awful? Could anyone ever believe it would last this long?"

Dorothy Rae looked up at Turner, her fingers still poised on the keyboard. She waited for him to say something else.

"Well yes," she said when he didn't. "It is a very long hot spell. Unusually so. I was just thinking that myself."

"I don't know about you, but I am so uncomfortable, I just do not know what to do with myself," Turner said, and there was a sinking-down inside Dorothy Rae because this was going someplace she could not predict, and because she didn't know what to do with him either.

"It's because of your height, Turner. I believe I read someplace how it's harder for very tall people to cool off," Dorothy Rae said.

"You don't say," Turner said. "Well, I have no doubt you are exactly right. But now, this is what I thought we might do about it. Close," he said.

Dorothy Rae blinked—"clothes" is what she heard. "Yes," she said. "But I'm already wearing my coolest—"

"Close," Turner said, drawing the word out. "As in shut. Be not open." And he showed her what he meant with his hands, shutting.

"Close," Dorothy Rae said. "You mean forever?" Her fingers jumped on the keyboard and typed an inadvertent letter. She put her hands in her lap.

"Forever? Dorothy Rae, I have got a pile of work this high on my desk—forever! Course not. Until the heat breaks. That's all. We'll take a vacation," Turner said, then pointed at her. "We still have that sign? That vacation one? I was just remembering that. We still have it?"

Dorothy Rae had shut off her typewriter by this time and was standing beside her desk, repeatedly smoothing down the skirt of her dress.

"Ye-es," she said slowly. "I guess we've got it someplace. We've never used it, of course, but I am sure I didn't throw it out," and she began to edge towards the front closet where office supplies were stored and where they hung their coats, when they wore coats, and she put her galoshes in wet weather.

"Yes," she said, from deep inside the closet. "I've got it. Here it is."

The sign, now hanging on the shut front door of the office, was a drawing someone had once made for Turner, a cartoon man lying beside a river, fishing pole stuck in the bank, fishing hat pulled down over his eyes.

"Closed for Vacation," the sign said. Underneath the hat, the man was smiling. Mattie stood and stared at the sign, as if she kept expecting it to say something different.

It was afternoon. She had waited to come to Turner's office until the business portion of the day was mostly over. His absence had not occurred to her. Vacation? She stood on the pavement looking at the sign, reading it again and again, the paper shopping bag holding the cobbler looped over her wrist.

The sheriff stopped short as he came around the corner. There stood Mattie, right in his path, staring intently at the closed door to Turner's office. He probably could have gotten away, half of him wanted to. The other half was pleased. He hadn't seen her in a while, not since they'd moved Heke.

"Miss Mattie," he said. "Something going on I ought to know about?" He was behind her, close to her shoulder.

"Is that supposed to be Turner?" Junior said. "I didn't even know he even fished, son of a gun," and he leaned past Mattie to peer at the sign. A scent rose off her, a freshness, and he left his head there a little bit longer than needed.

Mattie blinked. The air had begun to bunch up, tiny hopping particles darkening her vision.

"Closed for Vacation," Junior read and stepped back, and right then, Mattie knew she didn't believe it. Turner was not "on vacation." Dorothy Rae had never said word one about the office closing the last time Mattie had been here. Dorothy Rae would have said.

"Here, Junior, you might as well have this," Mattie said. She handed him the shopping bag with the cobbler in it.

"Well, now, what might this be?" Junior said.

"It's a cobbler," Mattie said. "I made it. Do you like cobbler?"

"I like everything you cook," Junior said. "How about I get us some coffee and you come back to the office and we enjoy this cobbler together?"

Mattie barely heard him. She was studying the sign. "Vacation," she said, turning to the sheriff. "Please. Who believes that?"

"Uh oh," Junior said. He grinned, trying to get her to change course, but she didn't grin back. He put his hands in his pockets and looked away, towards the sidewalk that ended, the trees beyond.

"I want to file a report," Mattie burst out. "I want to make a complaint." Her face was bright, her blue eyes watery and vivid.

"Lord have mercy," Junior said. "What?"

"There is a girl living in a house does not belong to her. She's trespassing," Mattie said—all those sibilant s's.

"Miss Mattie," Junior said, a conciliatory officer-of-the-peace voice.

"And," Mattie said.

"Miss Mattie. Do you want to know what I think? Come on and let me buy you that cup of coffee. Or a lemonade. Something cool?"

"*And,*" Mattie said. "Furthermore. Turner said he was going on up there to see about the situation. Dissuade her from trespassing. I know for a fact—"

"You do not know for any fact—"

"for a fact," Mattie said, her face beefy and puffed so that the word itself seemed factual.

"He has been up there before—twice—but never reported one single word to me about it. *Twice* he told me he was going."

"Miss Mattie—"

"—at least twice, and that he'd call me,"

"Miss Mattie—"

"when he came down again. Both times he said that. Swore. And I have waited and waited."

"Maybe he hasn't gone yet," Junior said. "Maybe he meant to but he didn't. This heat. Maybe he went—on vacation," he said, pointing at the sign. But if Turner hadn't gone up the mountain, he'd at least intended to. He'd asked Junior to draw him that map.

"He's up there right now," Mattie said. "Go on up and see if you don't believe me. He's there this very minute."

"Miss Mattie," Junior said. "I know all about that. But so what if he is? That's not against any laws."

"Trespassing," Mattie said. "Trespassing! They both are!"

"Shhh," Junior said. "Miss Mattie, please. Don't excite yourself. It isn't necessary for you to get yourself so worked up. You need to put your concentration elsewhere." He put his hands, one on each of Mattie's shoulders, and leaned down towards her, close enough so she could see the pores in his skin, the reddish color his beard would be. The color a wife would wake up to. "Lemonade?" he said.

"No," Mattie said. "You are not seeing what I mean. This girl, she is already married and she has a baby and Turner—. She is *trespassing* up there. Moving herself into Heke's house. She thinks she can just have everything."

29

Mattie turned away from the sheriff—he called to her, but she didn't answer—her face hot, a prickly-heat sensation peppering the back of her neck. She had not slept at all last night. She had gone ahead and baked the rhubarb cobbler for Turner, but baking had been a mistake. The heat of the oven swelled and mixed with the already oppressive weather until the small house was unbearable, stuffed with heat. Mattie left the back door open when she went to bed, but the creature was out in her garden at night, and the screen door did not latch properly. She pictured herself waking in the middle of the night to find it sitting on her bed, its eyes red as stoplights in the dark. She could not close her eyes.

And then she'd heard something—was that the tin cans outside clattering?—and she bolted up; she ran to the kitchen and shut the door, then came back to bed. But the heat was so dense she couldn't sleep: it was like breathing through straw. She'd thought about buying an air conditioner on and off, but it was so rarely hot like this, and she got a nice cross-breeze if the back door was left open, which now, of course, she could not do. And still it would have been all right, she could have tolerated the night, if Turner had called in the morning with news of his trip up the mountain, but Turner had not called.

Heading home, Mattie crossed the street to the side where the sidewalk didn't end and continued down it. She could feel the sheriff's eyes on her, walking away, even when it was impossible that he might still see her. He hadn't offered her a ride home today. She noticed, but then the notice faded.

Mattie went up the front steps to her house, and into and across the darkened living room to the console table against the far wall of the house that was still frantically hot from last night's baking.

Once, Mattie and her mother had gone up to visit the Days. Bad weather caught them that afternoon, just when they would have been starting for home, rain so fierce and so fast, the mud on the hilltops turned to slip and skinned down the slopes. There were hardly any trees to stop it. Mud squeezed downwards like a spill of melted chocolate.

They'd spent the night in what had been Heke's room, then, Heke gone to sleep elsewhere. The room shared the hearth wall and Mattie had slept close against it, the waning heat like a warm hand on her back.

Her car keys were in a bowl on the console table, where she always set them. Mattie picked them up and left the house again right away, banging the front door shut so that the curtains in the dark and silent living room stirred at the bottom. And then she was driving up the mountain.

It was not dark, true night several hours away, but the light, as Mattie drove, became flatter and deeper, the shadows of things more pronounced than the things themselves.

She kept a lookout for Turner's Cadillac from the off-road as she approached Heke's, that long silver car she had seen in town, and she did see a car finally, up near the house, although she wasn't sure it was the one she was hunting. It didn't look silver now, it looked gray, no longer sparky with sun, and Mattie pushed herself closer to the windshield several times to get a better look, her foot going down heavy on the gas so her own car stuttered forward.

He had parked in the deep watery shade of the tulip poplars in front of Heke's, the place where Mattie herself always parked, and a charged-up feeling rushed through her, as if all her faculties—blood, blood pressure, the quick quick beating of her heart—were now working past peak. She bumped onto the dirt road and parked at a distance from the house, the car on a slant because the ground there was uneven.

Mattie stood beside her car for a moment and looked around as if adjusting her vision to the proportions and colors of the late afternoon. She smelled the dried-out ground and dry grass and always, underneath everything, the faint tinge of coal that gritted the air up here. She closed the car door quietly just as, the other night, Turner had done.

A breeze came, a weak one that tried to lift the heavy cotton of Mattie's skirt, failed and was gone. Mattie stopped and touched her fingers to her forehead as if she didn't know what it was, the breeze that had just fluttered up and quickly died away again. Then she went on crossing the field towards the house.

Turner was standing in the clump of scrub where he'd stood the first night he'd come up here. Mattie saw him—who would not have seen him?—sheltering behind the gangly sticks and short batons of scrub growth like a child who, hiding, thinks he is invisible, and she was relieved because he was not in the house, he was outside, apparently scouting, just as he'd told her he was going to.

Mattie waved her arm over her head to let Turner know she was here too, and grateful for his vigilance though he was turned away and didn't see her.

"Turner," she was about to shout, but at the moment of calling to him something stopped her from calling, her hand in the air.

What was he looking at? *Looking,* not scouting.

Gratitude, relief slipped away from Mattie as, a minute ago, the breeze had slipped away. She didn't call, and when she resumed walking, she changed course, veering out in a broad arc so she would approach him from the side instead of from behind.

The air stirred again, a little gust that, this time, flattened the thin fabric of Mattie's blouse against her and made Turner look around. Mattie held still, poised and alert, seeing, now, how exposed she was out here in the middle of the field, as out in the open as a rowboat in a calm sea. But Turner didn't see her, and when the breeze died down, he turned front again, shedding the tension of movement for the different tension of watching.

His hand was on one of the scrub trees, palm to the scabby bark, holding to it in the same absent way children in a bunch all touch, as if each arm, each leg, was a shared thing belonging to all of them.

Mattie blinked, then she began to move again, positioning herself on the same tangent as Turner, though she was still too far downhill to see what he was looking at.

No sound from Mattie reached Turner, or he heard no sound that was not part of the soft gathering of wind that came up from time to time behind him and made the leaves clatter, and combed the grasses flat. He might not have heard it if there was anything to hear, so intent was his watching, so necessary to him. He did not know why this little girl had such a powerful draw for him, but she did. It felt significant.

Turner could see the house from where he stood, the parlor. The light there wasn't on nor did any light shine from the house, but his eyes had adjusted long since and he knew what he was seeing.

Sylvie was hanging up wash, gliding into the room then from it again. The slight whitenesses of the pieces she snapped and shook out and hung glowed a little, enough so he could see her before she slipped, once more, behind them.

Mattie crested the rise, puffing some, and she could now see the house, but the windows looked only dark to her, the house empty. She took another step forward. The grass here was almost knee-height and dry and sharp as broken quills. One pricked at the tip of her finger, her hands hanging down, and she jerked the hand up, and squeezed at the fingertip, waiting for the blood to bubble there, sucking at it when it did, and when she looked at the house again, a light had come on.

Sylvie leapt clearly into Turner's view. In the sudden brightness inside, Turner saw that the room was hung with wet sheets and miniature shirts and with dresses, all of them with the semi-transparent gloss of waxed paper, porous to the light. His heart picked up, and he didn't move his eyes from the window, and he didn't blink.

Sylvie stretched to hang something and light filled the garment she had on, something thin and sheer and fully revealing, not of particulars, but of the solidness of her female self underneath it. Turner could see her complete, her breasts elongating upwards as her arms went above her head and the slope of her stomach, the fabric skinned tight across it, and how, everywhere, her skin was rosy.

"Pregnant," was the first thing Mattie thought, the first she was conscious of thought, though so many things crowded her head, at that minute, that one didn't have to be the first.

"Trespasser, intruder, liar, you said you were up here to—

"Wanton, shameless—"

But pregnant was the first that stuck. The slip Sylvie had on was taut across her belly, the slippery divided petals of its top full like plastic bags filled with water.

"She's pregnant and she is living in Heke's house. Just came in here and took, took, took."

Mattie began to advance. She felt light-headed, a cousin to faint but with her faculties sharpened instead of falling away. The grasses poked and whipped at her, releasing their stored-up dry smell.

"Miss Mattie. Miss Mattie?" It was Turner—she strode to him, then past him—he sounded surprised, as if they were running into one another at the luncheonette.

"Miss Mattie. What on earth are you doing here?"

But *she* belonged here. Out of the three of them, she was the only one who did.

Turner reached for her as Mattie stalked by him, but his fingers only breezed against her arm.

"Don't you touch me, Turner Ward. You touched enough people

around this place. Don't you ever dare touch me," and she turned and took off across the dry bald patch before the house where all growth had been worn away.

"What? Miss Mattie?" Turner called. "What?" He took a few steps after her, then held up, as if he was not permitted to follow; as if Sylvie and Mattie were bonded in some kind of female rite in a place off-limits to him.

Mattie was yelling now. She was near the porch, then up on it, her footsteps aclatter, her voice high and oddly pitched.

"You," she kept saying. "You—" but nothing followed.

Turner looked up, as if some other thing was making the sound. Bats kited across the open space above him—the sky again that darkening blue—but he counted only two or three, and they were silent.

Sylvie froze. She held a dress in her hands, lifted to lay across the rope she had rigged, end to end, across the parlor. She'd found the rope, S-coiled in a box in the mudroom, but no useful clothespins and she had not felt the dollar-some-aught they cost was an expense she could justify. She was flopping things up and over the rope which she had nailed, accidentally, just a bit past her own comfortable reach. She carried them in, a piece at a time, from the kitchen where they'd hooked up the washing machine, she and Turner.

He had muscled the machine, still in its box, one slow shove at a time, from the parlor then across the less even floor of the front room and into the kitchen where he then had to stop and back up and lift one end so Sylvie could uncurl the tacky strip of linoleum the box had torn up and dragged with it.

"Can you hook it up?" Sylvie had said, and Turner nodded but went on drinking the second of what would be five fast glasses of water, the faucet blasting out water cold enough to make the tap sweat.

"I love this so much," Sylvie said when the washer was hooked up and running. It stood in the middle of the kitchen—there was no other place for it—and Sylvie half lay across its top, the vibrations pressing up into her at spots—under her arms, at the hip.

"Oh," she said, pushing off the machine. "That felt funny."

She'd bought detergent, although not pins, and when she heard Mattie's voice now—*a* voice, before she knew whose—she matched the shoulders of the dress she was holding seam to seam and folded it over her arm. The dress was cool and damp and Sylvie lowered her head and laid her cheek against it—not long, just for a moment—breathing in the detergent's clean, sharp, lemony scent.

30

MATTIE KNEW where every light switch was. She knew the location and order of the rooms, their relation to each other, where the floors rose or dipped or skewed a little to one side. No part of the Day house was unfamiliar to her, nor the stories of who had built the house and lived in it and lived in it next, things Sylvie did not—could not possibly—know. Things only Mattie knew, and would never tell her.

Odd sounds, consonantless and incoherent, came from Mattie as she crossed the darkening yard and then the apron of dirt that circled the house below the porch, rouged in the light from the parlor window. But the sounds stopped as she got close to the house, and her footsteps slowed as if what was ahead of her required silence and concentration.

It was still inside. The door to Heke's bedroom, to the right of where Mattie stopped, was shut, the kitchen straight ahead of her dark, the only light came from the parlor and Mattie did not go there as if, in a room so lit up, hiding was unlikely. She headed for the kitchen, walking on the outside edges of her feet, turning on the other lights as she passed them.

Sylvie was not in the kitchen. She was not in the room where Mattie had slept close to the hearth wall that long-ago day of the flood, and she was not behind the closed door of Heke's bedroom, where a little boy slept in the middle of the bed, a small flung bundle walled by the bed pillows.

Sylvie was where she had been all along, between rows of the colorless wash. It had turned the air humid and gray, and the room, as she stood there, seemed both bright and dull like the blank screen of a black-and-white television.

"Don't you move. You stay right where you are," Mattie called.

Sylvie made a fast scan up and down the rows of wash because she was not dressed, she had on a slip and nothing else. Everything else was wet, she had washed everything. The dress she'd been about to hang up before Mattie's arrival was still over her arm, wet too, but Sylvie put it on anyway. It stuck to her, the hem twirling up inside the bodice in back, and she tried for it with one hand, then the other, the fabric just out of her reach. The lemon detergent smell surrounded her, a chemical odor, no longer pleasant.

"Show yourself," Mattie called to her again, and Sylvie did, pushed a hanging pillowcase aside and stepped from between the pieces of wet wash to the entrance of the parlor.

"I'm here," she said and smiled and went on tugging at the hem of the wet dress that clung in ungainly and revealing ways to her slip and to her skin, a state of undress that would have brought a sharp comment, had Mattie been looking at her.

But Mattie had stepped back and back again and was looking over Sylvie's head, at the wash as limp as battered flags and bunting hung on a day with no breeze, and at the floor of the room, which appeared to have been emptied.

"What have you done here?" Mattie said. "What have you done? Where are all his things?"

Her face, flushed to begin with, deepened in color until she was a red Sylvie had never seen on a person before, as if little feeder veins had swelled up and burst under her skin.

"You ought to calm down a little," Sylvie said. "You'll get the blood pressure. My dad had that. Can I get you a chair or something? You want to sit?"

"You know what I want?" Mattie said. "You know what would make me feel so much better?"

Sylvie's head bounced up and down as Mattie spoke, waiting for instructions—a chair, a glass of water—ready to fetch what was needed.

"For you to get right out of here," Mattie said, and her voice rose again, shrill and high-pitched. "That is what I want. Get yourself decent, and get out."

Footsteps boomed up the porch steps then across it, and Turner bounded inside, flinging the screen door back so hard it slapped against the outer wall of the house and, springless, stayed. He strode into the room, then just stood there, gargantuan in the small house, his head almost touching the ceiling. They could not have built a house this size, the first Days, if Turner had been among them.

The shouting of the moment before had stopped. The two women stood and looked at Turner, mute, joined together in their looking.

Turner put his hands in his pockets, then he took them out again and rested his palms against the ceiling that was the color of creosote and so low, his arms stayed bent at the elbows.

"So," Turner said, finally. "You girls want to tell me what's going on here? I heard a ruckus." He spoke in a booming and jollying voice, too loud in the room's heavy quiet.

Sylvie and Mattie did not answer. It was as if, in Turner's presence, they had moved towards each other in alliance against him.

"What? Something private going on in here?" Turner said and laughed, expecting them to laugh too—the noise that had come from the house just a minute ago had been anything but private—but they neither laughed nor answered. Turner looked from Sylvie to Mattie, then back at Sylvie again. She had changed, she had put on a dress. It was a waxy gray color, and did not seem to fit her too well.

"You want to shut that door?" Sylvie said finally. "Flies."

Turner took his hands down from the ceiling and looked behind him at the door. Moths the colors of muslin and cream and cream spotted with coffee walked in ditsy patterns across the screen. There weren't any flies.

"I'd like to know what is going on here," Turner said in his big voice. "If that's not too much to ask."

"Can't you at least be a little quiet?" Sylvie said. "My baby boy's sleeping in the other room."

"I don't want to impose myself where I am not needed or wanted," Turner said, in what was almost a whisper, obliging Sylvie to look at him, though he did not look back.

"I only want to know, is everything all right? Miss Mattie?" he said, in the tone of a teacher, calling on the one student who could be depended upon for the true and proper answer.

Mattie looked at him. She was slightly mollified, slightly less red, given a little more time, she might have answered, but Turner didn't give it to her.

"Sylvie?" he said. "Everything all right?"

And there was no more alliance, not between the two women, not between Turner and Mattie. There was a shift in the air of the room.

"Both of you," Mattie said evenly. "Had better get right straight out of here." Her voice broke.

"Miss Mattie," Turner said, his voice slow and bright, his face shining. "There is no need for you to be—"

Mattie closed her eyes. She was that precipitate magenta color again, her lips, two thin bands of milky white.

"It's the blood pressure," Sylvie said. "Same as my dad."

"What have you done here?" Mattie said, turning on Sylvie. "What have you done to this house?"

"No, no," Sylvie said, softly, almost smiling, as if now she saw the trouble: Mattie hadn't seen things properly and now was Sylvie's chance to explain.

"It's improvements," Sylvie said. "Really. Look—" and she turned away and headed towards the kitchen, then stopped to see if Mattie was following her.

"You have to see," Sylvie said, and beckoned to her. "It's grand. Turner helped me."

"Oh yes," Mattie said, and her eyes narrowed. "I know what Turner's done."

"The washing machine," Sylvie said.

"You are a liar, Turner Ward," Mattie said. "The things you promised," and she shook her head and her fists clenched and then she went for him, barreling across the room, swinging before she got there, one fist catching him below the shoulder.

"Miss Mattie," he said. "Please. I know you do not want to be doing this." He was so tall, he didn't need to step back to be out of her reach, he just leaned away.

"No?" Mattie said. "Why? It against the law? Like trespassing?"—and she tried for him again.

Turner had recovered himself by then, and he caught her swinging hand and held it as gently as he could, and reached for the other one, but Mattie didn't stand still for it.

She tore away from him, pivoted, and she headed for Sylvie.

Sylvie never moved, she just went on standing where she was as if she could not see what Mattie intended, or maybe she thought Mattie was just honoring her request to step through and have a look at the kitchen after all, to see how she'd rescued the washing machine and made it useful.

"Whoa," Turner said, as soon as he saw Mattie move, and in two steps he was between them.

Mattie ducked around him, trying to reach Sylvie. "What have you done?" she said, her head bobbing around the left side of Turner's torso, then the right.

"On whose say-so are you in this house? On whose say-so are you touching anything?"

"I just fixed it up a little," Sylvie said, folding her arms in at the elbows so she was narrower, harder to reach.

"Threw out some papers is all. It's *improvements,*" she said again, as if Mattie had missed this word, as if it was the key to everything.

"This place has stood here for more than one hundred years," Mattie said. "It has withstood years and years and years of life just fine without your help."

"Is that a good thing?" Sylvie said. "For a place to just sit, not doing anybody any good?"

"You've done wrong here," Mattie shouted. "Can't you see that? Not everything's yours just because you want it to be. You don't have any right here and you don't have any business. Criminal trespass," she said, her voice rising. "Turner, I want this girl arrested."

"I'm not doing anything," Sylvie said. "It's improvements."

"Whose improvements?" Mattie said. "Who for?"

"Miss Mattie. First of all, I am not anybody who can arrest anybody. And I don't see that harm's been done." Turner's voice was avuncular, calming.

"Why don't we just hear her out?" he said.

Mattie held up her hand. "No," she said. "Oh no. I will not."

She spun around again, into the clear space behind her. Her heel skidded as she turned and the buckle of the sandal bit hard into her flesh, making her hop once and suck in her breath, but she didn't stop.

Heke had protected this place against intrusion, against threat; that was all he had done. He could not be faulted for that.

"Shut the door will you?" she heard Sylvie say to Turner behind her. "There'll be a plague of flies in this house before you know it."

It took Mattie a while to reach the sanctuary of her car. She couldn't maintain the speed with which she'd left the house and crossed the yard, it was too dark and she had only the headlights of occasional vehicles up on the highway and a burr of orange light from someplace that shone in her hubcaps to navigate by.

But when she finally got there, her fury was as fierce as it had been inside the house, and she couldn't drive. She paced back and forth. Pieces of the tall, dry, hollow grass snapped off and stuck under her heels and trailed behind her. But the walking had no permanent effect, a calm minute followed by one in which the specter of Sylvie and Turner together inside the house rose, and she was no longer calm.

Mattie took deep breaths. She used on herself the tactics she used on upset children in school—agreement, soothing words, touch—wrapping her arms around her own waist, but she was no comfort to herself, there was no comfort here.

Inside the car, Mattie leaned over and popped the glove compartment where she kept things—things that might be necessary in an emergency, that might mean the difference between life and—

Say she was caught by a blizzard, a mud slide. Say she had a flat tire on a quiet road at night and she was alone—

A flashlight, a road map, flares, gloves, socks, bandages.

Her fingers touched these things—someplace there was a flask with brandy in it—she was her own rescue dog. Something fell out, bounced off her knee then to the car floor. And she remembered now, or she heard, as if his words had taken all day to travel and reach her, Junior, asking to buy her a lemonade, a coffee, something to drink with the cobbler. She hadn't even heard him, she'd been so caught up in this, and now she yearned hard for it, something behind her growing smaller, in the distance; another thing over, finished, done, past.

Turner stood beside Sylvie on the porch of the house, as if they'd come outside to watch a guest depart. Far away, the interior light of Mattie's car winked on.

He was aware of Sylvie's nearness, and of the lit-up rooms behind them, and when a sound came from inside—Christopher, coughing—it seemed natural to him to say, "He all right? You want me to go in and have a look?"

Sylvie looked at him for a long moment, puzzled, as if she hadn't known anyone was standing there.

"What?" she said. "No." Her voice came out soft; she cleared her throat before she spoke again.

"You should go," she said. "What are you even doing here?"

Mattie leaned over sideways to grab what had fallen, now that she had opened the door and could see what she was doing in the car's overhead light. It was the little paper phone book she'd taken from under the pillow at Heke's some time ago. Sylvie's book, the one with Cass's sister's telephone number in it. That's what it was.

31

CASS JUMPED when Peggy's telephone rang. He bolted upright on the couch, the newspaper sliding in single sheets through his fingers. The phone hardly ever rang here. One morning Peggy's usual ride to work—another woman in a uniform the shape and color of a cardboard box—had called to say her car wouldn't start. Cass heard the kick of frustration in the woman's voice from where he sat at the table smoking, the plate with the eggs and toast and ham he'd just finished still in front of him.

Cass was lying on his back on the sofa as he did most nights once Peggy and Steve had gone to bed, soothing his cricked spine after a day of bending over envelopes, the smoke from his cigarettes crowding the air above him. Sometimes he listened to the portable radio that sat on the windowsill near the kitchen table, but mostly he stayed on the couch and smoked and read the old newspapers he took from the pile in the basement. The secretary girl was still searching the Help Wanteds. Each day, before he opened to that page, Cass was hopeful there'd be no ads circled because she'd found herself a job.

"Phone," Cass called to the shut bedroom door after the third or fourth ring, but neither Peggy nor Steve came out to answer.

The phone rang on and on. Cass kept hoping each ring would be the last, but it never was. He didn't want to knock on the bedroom door, in case they were sleeping, and he didn't want to pick up the phone himself, which Steve would probably take as one more example of Cass overstepping, but finally, he answered.

"Yes?" Cass said.

"Hello? Is this the number for Peggy?" a woman said. One of the girls, Cass figured, from Peg's car pool.

"It is," Cass said. "But she can't come to the phone right now. I'm afraid she's sleeping." He paused, expecting the woman to say she surely knew how that was and how she hated to be calling at this hour except she wanted to let Peggy know as soon as possible that she couldn't be driving her to work in the morning, something to do with her car. But the woman didn't say any of those things.

"Okay. I'll tell her you, um," Cass said, and trailed off.

"Well, that's all right. I'm really calling to speak to Cass," the woman said. "Peggy's brother. Is he there by any chance?"

Cass didn't answer. Him? Why? Had he won something?—a lottery ticket Peg had bought in his name? Or maybe he'd done something wrong without knowing it, violated some building or city ordinance, though the only things he could think of had to do with envelope stuffing or with the newspapers he took from the basement and they were just trash and he always put them back the next day—

"I put them back, if that's what this is about," Cass said. "I always do. I'm not doing anything to them."

"Would this be Cass to whom I'm speaking?"

Cass hesitated. His father used to say, "Never sign anything, then nobody's got nothing on you." This felt, somehow, the same.

"This is Miss Mattie Wheeler?" Mattie said and then she paused as if waiting to hear the effect her name had upon him.

"Who?" Cass said.

"Mattie Wheeler," she said again. "Hesketh Day's cousin, who rents you out that cabin. I was just up there at the Day house today and—"

She inhaled, then let the breath out slowly; it made Cass want a cigarette, but his pack was over by the sofa, too far to reach. In the silence, Cass heard a clock ticking, though he didn't know if it was coming from Mattie Wheeler's house or here.

"I have something to tell you that concerns your wife, Cass. Some unpleasant news," Mattie said, although there was nothing of unpleasantness in her voice.

"I hope you won't mind my calling?"—and she paused.

"'Unpleasant?'" Cass said. "What does that mean?" It was a borderline word—something good on its way to going bad—turned milk or skanky clothes.

"What're you talking about?" Cass said.

"It's your wife," Mattie said. "Sylvie."

The noise of the clock stopped; Cass could no longer hear it. His ears, his whole head, were filled with a rushing sound like harsh running water.

"What's wrong?" he said, his voice rising. "What are you talking about? She hurt or sick or what is it?"

Mattie had not turned on the light in her kitchen—the lamp in the living room gave off enough light to see by—but the kitchen now seemed to be darkening at the edges, the darkness crowding inwards. Mattie opened her mouth to speak, but she could not, and she could not go on standing. She reached for a chair from the kitchen table and pulled it closer to the phone and sat down. She should not have made this call, set things in motion. She had a strong urge to hang up.

"What're you trying to tell me?" Cass yelled, his voice exploding suddenly through the phone. Mattie jumped where she sat, the bones in her backside hitting the seat of the wooden captain's chair.

"What're you talking about?"

"Oh," Mattie said weakly. "No, I—"

The story was too long, she couldn't get through it. Maybe she could just say everything was fine, and hang up. She could say Sylvie had asked her to contact him since the cabin didn't have a phone—

The cabin didn't, but Heke's house did. And Mattie saw again the way Sylvie had taken over, changing things that were not hers to change, hanging up her wash while the little boy slept on Heke's bed. The memory was invigorating. Creeping paralysis fled and the darkness backed up again to the edges of the room. When she spoke this time, Mattie's voice was different, crisp and sure.

"Sylvie's just fine," Mattie said, leaning over to turn on the kitchen light.

"Rest assured. She was fine when I left there today. But I am not about to lie to you. I've been concerned. I thought you ought to know what she's been up to. Who she's been keeping company with."

Cass leaned against the wall. He could hear Mattie palavering on, but he wasn't following, she had left him at "fine." Sylvie was fine; she was walking around up at the cabin, Christopher riding her hip, both fine, just how he pictured them, just how Sylvie said they were in her letters.

"Okay then," he said, when Mattie paused. "Well you told me. I'm glad to know she's all right."

"Oh well, she must be"—Mattie's voice came thin and insinuating through the receiver Cass had already begun moving away from his ear.

"She's moved herself into Heke Day's house, moved herself in lock, stock, and barrel," Mattie said. "She's up there using his things right this minute, living in that house like it belongs to her, completely uninvited."

"No," Cass said. "What? No she isn't."

"Oh yes," Mattie said. "I can assure you. I've just come from there, she is. And she is keeping steady company with Turner Ward, that's another thing you might want to know about," Mattie said.

"And pregnant on top of it all. I guess she's fine, for somebody so busy."

Steve's car was a twelve-year-old blue Plymouth Duster with more than 180,000 miles on it. A skirt of rust ran around the undercarriage and the car had no working heat, no working radio and one door that had come from some other, junked Duster, and that was a different color blue.

Steve treated the car as if it were an aged and slightly invalided parent, asking of it only the minimum, promising tender-handed care in return. He drove it to work and he drove it back home again. When it was necessary, when one or the other of the maids who rode Peggy to her job couldn't make it, Steve and the Duster were backup and sometimes, when the weather was nice and Peg said she was dying for a breath of air, they took the car out for what Steve called "a little run."

In return, Steve gave the Duster his Saturday afternoons. Peggy did the household chores, Steve took care of the car, gassing it up, checking the oil and the spark plugs and the radiator fluid. He took it to an indoor car wash in the cold and battering months, washed it himself in warm weather with a bucket of soapy water and clean soft cloths, the portable radio from upstairs tuned to a ball game and set on the hood.

"Steve's more married to that car than to me," Peggy had told Cass more than once. Sometimes she laughed when she said it, sometimes she didn't.

The breeze through the open kitchen window reached Cass where he was standing by the phone, or standing again. He had gone for a cigarette after he'd hung up, then come back. The lit cigarette was still between his fingers burned all the way down, the ash long and delicate. He was feeling his way through Mattie Wheeler's story. None of it sounded credible to him, or it wouldn't have if Turner Ward's name hadn't been in it. His name had come up in Sylvie's letters, too.

Cass lay the cigarette down gently in the ashtray, watching to see if the ash broke or didn't. He was aware of sounds from the bedroom again, sounds that had not gone away but that he had been deaf to or forgotten—and he leaned near the door and held his breath, trying to make out if Peggy was awake.

He couldn't hear a thing though, other than the laughter from the TV with its repetitive rise, plateau and falling away, and finally Cass went back to sit on the sofa. It was hotter there, the sofa set against the wall farthest from the windows. Underneath it, the boxes filled with unstuffed envelopes and with stuffed ones ready to be sealed and sealed ones ready to be stamped and mailed and the other boxes filled with pieces of flat white paper he hadn't gotten to yet, pushed against his heels.

Cass twitched and shifted and then he stood and went to the table again, and sat in the chair where he sat for meals, his back to the bedroom. The TV noise rose and dipped and droned behind him like a mosquito, and he couldn't stand it nor the breeze either, which made the curtains tongue in and out, and which ruffled the same spot just above his elbow over and over, and he got up and went to sit on the other side of the table where the sound was diminished, if not altogether gone.

Cass sat for a long time, lighting one cigarette after another, smoking them down to the damp, yellowed filters. He sat with his head on the hand that did not have the cigarette in it. He must have dozed off. When he lifted his head, the noise from the TV had stopped.

He got up and went to the boxes underneath the sofa. He took a piece of paper from the thick thick stack of clean, white, sharp, unfolded sheets and he wrote a note on the back.

"Peg," the note said. "The telephone rang I don't know did you hear it probably you did not. It was for me anyhow. There is some kind of trouble at home with Sylvie in it but I do not know what. I had to go. I could not wait I know you will understand. You know where to find me. Thanks for everything. Your brother, Cass. And I am sorry I had to borrow the car there was not any other way but do not worry I will drive it careful and keep it good and I will return it and I will take good care of it. Promise."

Cass picked up the paper sack he'd carried his clothes here in, and where Peggy put them again, clean and folded, after she did a wash. He took four packs of Steve's Tareytons from the refrigerator where Steve kept the cartons for freshness, then picked up the keys to the Duster from the little stand in the vestibule. He came back to the dining table again, fished in his pocket, and set five dollar bills beside the note.

"Money is for smokes," he wrote. He went to the refrigerator again and took one more pack of Tareytons, and he added "Sorry" to the paper, then he was gone. It was almost 4:30 in the morning. This long night was nearly over, and he was in a hurry to get home.

32

CASS MADE the drive without stopping except to buy cup after cup of black coffee, and then to pee. He got the coffee in takeout containers, packets of sugar on the side, which he saved to take home. Sometimes there were only a few, sometimes many, and at those times his face lit up as if it was money in the bag, instead of sugar.

He had no idea of the time. The Duster had no working dashboard clock or radio, and Cass didn't have a watch; he noted the time in the cafes and gas stations where he made stops, and guessed how long it was in between, but he wasn't ever right. His mind was on other things and he could not tell if minutes passed, or hours. He kept squinting up at the sky, but it remained a steady steely color and didn't have much to tell him.

As he drove, Cass ran through the morning with Steve and Peggy, living their unvaried daily routine along with them. He watched them sit down to breakfast—silent, because Steve did not like talking at meals—then saw Peggy clear the plates and wash them and wipe down the table and the sugar bowl and the salt-and-pepper shakers and the plastic honeycombed napkin holder grouped on it.

He heard the baseboard cupboard below the sink open and the double "shwft shwft" of an aerosol spray, and then Peggy came out of the kitchen with her dust cloth at the ready and went for the surfaces of wood, metal and glass. She was dressed in her maid's outfit, everything except the apron.

Soon they would leave the apartment and go to work. If he were there, Cass would be sitting down at the table again with his boxes of envelopes, and he lifted his right palm from the steering wheel and ran his thumb down the paper cuts that lined the insides of his fingers like basting stitches.

Steve was the first to leave in the morning, picking up his car keys as he headed for the door—"No, hey, back up," Cass told himself. "What about the cigarettes?"

Steve took a fresh pack from the refrigerator each morning, he would have noticed five whole packs gone before he even made it to the car keys. He would have straightened up from the refrigerator, his face an apoplectic red.

"Son of a bitch stole my smokes!"

"Who?" Peggy would have said, her face coloring, as if she was the one Steve had accused.

"Who? Son of a bitch brother of yours, who do you think? I told you he was a no good, goddamn—"

Here, Cass had to backtrack once again as he remembered the note he had left on the table. They would have seen that before anything else, before the missing car keys or the cigarettes. Peggy would have seen the note as she came in to set the table for breakfast. She would have read it, looked over at the sofa to see if Cass was really gone, then out the window as she tried to figure out how long she could keep from showing it to Steve.

"Shit," Cass said, and scrubbed his knuckles hard across his scalp.

"Cass," Steve would be saying.

"Fucking skinny-assed motherfucker son of a bitch fuck stole my motherfucking car!"

Would Steve call the police? Cass knew he would. Peg would try to stop him, hovering close by while Steve dialed, trying to get Steve to listen:

"He is not bad, he's a good person. He wouldn't have done this if he hadn't of had to."

"Emergency," Peggy might say, hunting Cass's note for the word, finding it, holding it up so Steve could see it.

"Son of a bitch been leeching off of me two months. Two months I have been carrying his sorry ass."

Peggy did not say—"us, not you." She did not say, "he's my baby brother," or "I'd do the same for your folks, if you had any folks you still spoke to." When the police showed up, Peggy would have just gone into the bedroom and shut the door.

Steve would have called them, Cass was sure of that. The only question was, would the police chase after a car that might not even make it the three hundred miles it had to go?

No, Cass thought. Probably not.

It took Cass almost ten hours to get home, more than twice as long as it should have. The route was tricky, but it wasn't the first time he'd made the trip, he and Sylvie had gone to visit Peg before Christopher was born. Had he been looking out for where US60 diverged from I-64 and, a hundred miles later, after a series of go-here's and go-there's merged back again, Cass would have been home by eleven, noon at the latest, but he was pondering what the police would do, and living out the rest of Peg and Steve's day. (Steve riding to work in Peggy's car pool, bulky and unyielding in the backseat, forcing Peg and the other box-brown women to sit with their arms folded inwards, like shut umbrellas. He would insist on smoking in the crowded car.)

Had he arrived in good time, Cass would have found Sylvie and Christopher outside the cabin, Sylvie sitting on the bottom porch step while the little boy splashed in the washtub. She'd raise her head as the Duster came up the dirt road towards her, then stand, knotting and unknotting her fingers because she was here alone and didn't recognize the car. When she saw it was Cass, her face would smooth out, gladness chasing the worry.

But Cass didn't make it home till after three. And though he did drive slowly up the dirt road and park beside the cabin next to the pick-up, what he saw when he got there was something different altogether.

Cass got out of the car and went over to the cabin and he stood there, one foot on the bottom porch step, looking up at the door. It stayed shut. No hint of movement or commotion came from inside. It was hot and dry out, and the air smelled like straw. Every second that passed, that Sylvie continued not to be here, his anger heated up.

"Where are you?" he said, but he knew—Mattie Wheeler had told him where Sylvie was.

Cass kicked at the bottom step of the porch—the cabin seemed to vibrate, to shimmer in the hot air—then he took off for Heke's place. He turned and looked back once or twice, willing to let the whole thing rest if Sylvie would just be there.

He was halfway across the yard when he saw Turner Ward, standing in the scrub at a distance from the house, too far from the dirt road to have heard the Duster. Cass was only able to see him because the land peaked up where the cabins were, a little higher there than elsewhere.

"Sylvie," Cass yelled, but he kept his eyes on Turner Ward, wanting to see the reaction his voice might provoke.

"Syl," he called louder.

Turner just went on standing in the same spot, like he hadn't heard anything, or was convinced he could not be seen.

"Syl," Cass bellowed.

Inside the house, Sylvie froze. The sound of Cass's voice, the prospect of the nearness of his physical self rang in her and she couldn't breathe, tugged at the top of her dress as if it was the fault of the tightness of the cloth, or the baby inside her, or the weather.

"Syl," the voice called.

"Cass," Sylvie said, and closed her eyes in case it was not; in case she had conjured the voice out of her plain, strong need to hear it. But the next time he called, she was sure—Cass!—and she ran to the door and then he called again, and what she heard this time, in the voice and in the swift, hard footsteps, was fury.

"Syl," Cass yelled, one more time.

There was a silence, then Sylvie's voice came from above him: "Well, what?"

She was standing on Heke's porch, the screen door propped open with her foot, fingernails digging into the door frame to keep herself from running down to him because she wouldn't run to any man who called to her that way, even Cass.

Cass looked at her, then he shook his head and looked away. "Christopher?" he said, and Sylvie said, "Christopher's fine, if that's your question. Asleep. Or he was, before you came hollerin around."

"In there?"

"It's coolest," Sylvie said. "It has been God Almighty hot." She sounded uppity and defiant, as if the heat had been Cass's doing.

"I'm'n'a need to call Peggy," Cass said. "You got her number, right?"

"If I can find it," Sylvie said, and she stepped inside Heke's door.

"What's it be doing in there?" Cass said, calling her back. "Why isn't it over to our house?"

"The phone's here," Sylvie said. "We don't have one, in case you never noticed. I kept thinking I was gonna call you."

Her face went hot and she looked down, as if she had told him more than she meant to; as if she was a girl waiting for a boy she liked to come and get her. Her bare, knuckly feet were powdered a cinnamon color from the dry ground, even though she had cleaned them that morning, stepping into the washtub to lift out the slick and shiny baby.

Cass wasn't looking her way though; he was turned towards the scrub where he had seen Turner, though he couldn't see him now because of the pitch of the ground. Sylvie came down the porch steps and stood beside him.

"What?" Sylvie said. "What are you looking at?"

Cass lifted his chin. "Him. Out there. Turner Ward."

"Again?" Sylvie said. "Man's always prowling around here."

"Always?" Cass said. "What's that mean?" He was trying hard not to hear Mattie Wheeler's voice in his head, although at least half of what she'd told him—that Sylvie was staying at Heke's—was clearly true.

"I don't know," Sylvie said. "He's been up here prowling around four times maybe. Maybe three. More than once."

"He's been up here?" Cass said. "How come? You asked him to pay you a visit or something?"—his voice was drawling and sarcastic, he couldn't seem to help it.

"Ask him?" Sylvie said. "That look to you like a man asked someplace? You see him sitting up here on my porch, drinking iced tea?"

Cass looked behind him at the porch, then away again. "This isn't your porch, Syl," he said. "Nor your house neither."

"I know that, Cass, God! I know whose house it is, what do you think, I turned stupid?"

"I just expected to find you at the cabin," Cass said.

"Well, you found me here instead. But you still found me."

They stood side by side, both facing towards the scrub, near each other but not touching. The quiet stretched out. The air was hot and motionless.

"Well, I don't see a thing," Sylvie said finally, and moved as she spoke, hitching her shoulder sideways, a tiny movement that was enough to disrupt the stasis of the moment before.

"You sure you didn't mirage him?"

"He's here," Cass said. "See? Over there," and he raised his arm and sighted down it to where Turner's car was parked, chrome or mirror flashing now and then as light hit it.

"Son of a bitch," Cass said.

Sylvie put her hand on his arm. "Cass," she said. "It's naught but a nuisance," but he shook her off and headed in the direction of Turner's car.

Sylvie watched him for a minute, then she turned and went slowly back up the porch steps and into the house. She sat down on the side of the bed next to Christopher, his fists and his small face bunched in the vigor of sleep, and ran her finger across the telephone receiver. For a long time, this phone had been her connection to Cass. Even if they hadn't called each other it seemed reserved only for them and for that one purpose. She never thought about the time she had used the phone, the day she called an ambulance for that photographer. She thought about how they—she and Cass—had not used it.

In a little while Cass would come walking in here, sweaty, his face and his hands streaked with dirt.

"You might want to maybe use that," he'd say, and point at the telephone. "You might want to call up an ambulance or something like that."

"No!" Sylvie said, and she stood up and went to the door of the bedroom although she stopped there, she didn't go out. She hadn't even touched Cass yet; he hadn't even touched her.

"Oh God," she said.

The front door was open, the bright yard and the tulip poplars framed by the wood of the doorway, but Sylvie didn't see them. All she saw was Cass.

And then she heard the sound—a smart spank across the air that made her jump, even though she'd been expecting that very sound. Christopher flung himself again, but Sylvie did not wait to see if he'd woken. She ran from the room, past the false brightness cast by the hanging wash, out the door and across the porch. She had to slow at the top of the steps, turn her feet sideways on the narrow treads and jut her front outward like a chicken's poitrine, for balance, but when she reached the yard she took off running again, even though her body was swollen and tight and her breasts heaved up and down as her feet hit the ground.

Turner's car was a long way off, and Sylvie was hampered by discomfort and by breathlessness. The heat was worse now than it had been, the air had stopped moving altogether, and halfway across the field she couldn't do it anymore and slowed to an urgent, stiff-legged walk, patting her chest and drawing quick breaths.

And then there was a flash, the hazy sky lightening briefly right where she was heading, and Sylvie drew a deep breath as if she were preparing to dive into water and she ran again. She knew what that flash was, and that it went with the noise she had heard from the house, carrying all that way in the hot, dead air.

Turner's car was parked slightly aslant, the long grass frilling up around the wheels as if it had been here for weeks instead of hours. Sylvie saw Cass who stood facing the Cadillac, his back to her, but she didn't see Turner, and she stopped and put out her hand as if she could no longer stand without some kind of support, and when there was nothing to grab onto, she bent over and put her hands on her knees and breathed into the scoop of her body. Her leg muscles twitched and adrenaline pumped through her. She was sure she was going to be sick and shut her eyes.

She saw things anyway, though—the powdery dirt from that other morning, how it was wetted down under where the photographer lay, not red but a darker, Dr Pepper color that seemed lifeful as it spread across the dirt. She saw the photographer struggling to raise his head and to stand, like a deer fallen where injured, kicking out, eyes rolled to whiteness. It strained to raise its muscular neck, couldn't, then lay it back down again where it looked limp, no longer muscular, like a scarf upon the ground.

That noise cracked the air again. Sylvie, still with her hands on her knees, looked up.

Not a gunshot. Thunder.

Cass had reached Turner as he was opening the car door. It was locked. Cass saw him fumbling with the keys.

"You're not afraid to steal away my wife, but you're scared somebody's gonna come and take your car while you're doin it?" Cass yelled. "Who do you think's gonna do that? Sylvie? Who all else you seen around here old enough to drive?"

Turner looked up, then down at the car door again.

"You got your car all locked up nice and tight against thieverousness, but you don't have no problem thieving against me?

"You wanna know what scares me? Not car thiefs. You. You are what I'm scared of," Cass yelled, but he didn't sound scared, nor look it. He'd stopped on the other side of Turner's car, his face red and distorted, his hands grabbed tight at his sides.

"Man who'd go after another man's wife."

Turner had unlocked the driver's side door by then. It stood open, but he didn't get into the car. He spoke first.

"You're right," he said.

"I'm right," Cass said. "What is it I'm right about?"

"All of it, mostly, I guess," Turner said. "Except the car theft, I just always lock my car. But I guess I was trying to steal away your wife." He put up his hand, palm out, forestalling Cass in case he was planning to charge.

"I didn't exactly know that's what I was doing," Turner said. "I didn't have a plan or an idea or anything. But that's what it comes down to. Must be something about the women in that family. She told you I dated her sister back in high school?"

"Naneen?" Cass said. He'd been standing turned slightly away, as if that's all of his attention he was willing to give Turner, but now he faced him.

"Nan*een?*" he said again.

"Not Naneen," Turner said. "The other one. Lusa."

"Well, Lusa's gone," Cass said. "Lusa don't live around here anymore. She's gone to—"

He stopped as if he'd just heard himself, making conversation on a shared point of interest. He shook his head.

"Well anyhow," Turner said. "I'm just trying to tell you, it was me, it wasn't ever Sylvie. She never gave me so much as the time of day. That's the truth. She never did one single thing."

"I know that," Cass said. "Shit. You telling me something I don't know about my own wife?"

"No," Turner said. "I'm just going on the record. I'm—"

Turner stopped. There was Sylvie. She had straightened up and now he saw her.

"Well," he said. "There she is," and he raised his chin towards Sylvie. "Ask her yourself."

Cass turned and looked over his shoulder. The light was behind Sylvie; it shone through her hair and the back of her dress. Against the brightness, the leaf print of her dress disappeared. Cass could see now that she was pregnant. He looked at her, Sylvie looked back, but they didn't speak.

"Go on and ask her," Turner said.

"I don't need to ask her nothing," Cass said. "And I don't need advice from you about it either."

Thunder cracked again—the three of them looked up. The sky had darkened, over to the right. Tarnish-colored clouds were moving fast in their direction. They were bottom heavy, in the way that Sylvie was.

"If it's all right with you, I think I'll be off," Turner said. "See can I beat this thing down the mountain."

They all stood for another minute. The air was still and calm between them, as if they were friends telling each other good-bye; as if Turner Ward had been their guest and Sylvie and Cass had come down from the house to see him off. Turner got into his car the way he always did—butt first, swinging his long legs in after. His need to be down the mountain before the storm came seemed bigger than anything else at the moment, bigger than any interest he'd taken in Sylvie. It felt gone, though who knew if that was true.

The big, slow-moving Cadillac rocked up onto the dirt road, then headed towards the highway. Turner's elbow rested on the rolled-down window and he lifted his hand in departure. Cass didn't wave back.

"Let's go," he said to Sylvie, but when he turned around, she wasn't there.

Christopher had woken with a start at the first break of thunder, an inward suck of breath followed by a wail of fright and lonesomeness Sylvie heard all the way across the yard and the field, and she braced her arms around her breasts—one over, one under—and ran.

Cass hiked back up the field, veering away to his left, towards the cabin. The pickup was parked there, and Steve's car, and the metal washtub filled with water sat on the dirt below the porch, grit silted over the bottom. The water, when he touched it, was as warm as his hand.

Cass tipped the tub until it emptied, then walked it behind the cabin where he leaned it in its usual spot against the back wall. A silverfish skittered out, then another. Cass put his finger to the spot. The wood was as fragile as paper, and splintered where he touched it.

He had forgotten how much he hated it here.

Cass patted his shirt pocket and pulled out the pack of Steve's Tarrytons. A matchbook was slid in behind the cellophane and he pushed it out and lit the cigarette. He'd left Peggy's with his hands full of cigarettes but no matches. On one of his coffee stops there'd been a box filled with matchbooks on top of the cash register.

"Okay if I take some of these?" Cass had asked the waitress who'd fixed his coffee for him—black, with the sugars on the side.

"Help yourself," she said without looking up and Cass grabbed a handful of the matchbooks, then another, since she didn't seem to care. His shirt pocket bulged with them. It was elating, a windfall, something he didn't have to pay for.

He'd felt the same way about the cabin when they'd first come up here—how it was free, or almost, and how the minimal rent would take some of the burden off until he found work. He'd been wrong though. You paid for everything. Everything cost something. Without sugar, coffee tasted bitter. The cost of living here, was living here. And then he crushed the filter of the smoked-down cigarette under his boot and went to find his wife.

33

THE SKY darkened to a sulfurous green, soupy and dim. No breeze skimmed the dry grass or the treetops—not here, and not in the distance. The chatter of insects heightened in speed and pitch, though it would soon stop.

Sylvie stood outside, Christopher on her hip, rubbing an eye with his fist. Cass came striding quickly towards them, but he didn't put out his arms for Christopher when he got there, nor ask Sylvie to hand him over.

"Hey, little boy," Cass said softly, and he touched the baby's shoulder at the place where his vaccination mark bubbled the skin.

"I've been gone a long little while, haven't I?" Cass said.

Christopher leaned away from him a little, but Cass didn't seem to notice.

"This heat ever going to quit?" Sylvie said, and fanned at herself with her free hand. She swung back and forth, making a little breeze that lifted the delicate hair from Christopher's forehead.

"I need a wash," Cass said.

"Now?" Sylvie stopped swinging.

"I'm hot, Syl. I'm just off of I don't know how long, driving."

He was sweaty, his clothes bunched with wrinkles, his face greasy when he wiped it with the bottom of his shirt.

"I'm just asking," Sylvie said. "You can have it up here in the bathroom, or you can go on back to the cabin and have a stand-up wash in the washtub. Your choice." Her voice was defiant, as was the tilt of her head.

Cass didn't rise to it though. He looked at the damp hairs on Sylvie's neck wisping out of the scant ponytail that quivered when she moved.

Christopher reached out just then and put his sticky, padded hand on Cass's shoulder. After a minute, Cass raised the hand to his mouth, kissed it, then laid it back down on his shoulder again.

"So," he said. "I guess we're having another one."

Sylvie frowned. "Noo," she said. "You think so?"

Cass took out his pack of cigarettes again.

"No need to be testy," he said as he lit one. "I'm just making conversation."

Lightning flared over to the west, but this time, no thunder. The air was listless, heavy as a blanket, still.

Cass blew smoke towards the sky, then he went on looking up.

"Syl," he said after a little while. "You know what? Let's get out of here."

Sylvie nodded, she pointed up at the house. "You want me to run a tub for you?" she said.

"No," Cass said. "I mean. Let's get out of here, out of this place, altogether." He described a large circle with his hand, like he meant more than the house, the yard, the hilltop.

"What?" Sylvie said. "Now? It's about to pour buckets in about another minute."

"I don't care," Cass said. "I just, I don't know, some itchy feeling come over me. I think we need to leave here. Now." He dropped his cigarette and stepped on it, though it wasn't even half smoked.

Sylvie had her lips pursed, but when Cass finished speaking she didn't argue with him. "Having a feeling" was something she took seriously, and was prepared to honor. Cass wouldn't have said such a thing for no reason.

"Okay well," she said. "Let me just go pack a couple of few things." She handed Christopher over to Cass, then went up the porch steps. Christopher watched her go, but he didn't fuss to go with her.

"You sure you don't want to just get cleaned up a little first?" Sylvie called once she was inside. "While I'm getting myself together? You'll feel better."

"I'm fine," Cass called back. "Maybe I'll just stand here till the rain comes and gets me all pretty again, right little man?"

Cass bounced Christopher up and down on his hip. Christopher went on looking up at the house behind him where Sylvie was moving around in the parlor, a dim gliding shape that appeared and disappeared as she traveled up and down the rows of laundry. Some of it she took down and some of it she left.

"Syl," Cass called.

"What?"

"Just hurry."

She was outside again in five minutes, two loaded brown paper grocery bags in her arms.

"What're you taking these for?" Cass said, and pushed a can of Sylvie's cling peaches further into one of the bags that was otherwise soft, stuffed with clothes.

"Quit it, Cass. Heavy enough without you dragging all down on it."

"Well here, then, hand 'em over, you take him," Cass said, and he swung Christopher out on his arm towards Sylvie.

"The pickup's naught but ten steps," Sylvie said and she turned and marched forward, one bag on each hip, her belly jutting in between them.

"I thought you was in such a blessed hurry," she said, turning to Cass, still behind her. "Come on."

They made it to the pickup as the first drops fell, hot and stinging.

"I'm not gonna put these in the back. They'll get soaked," Cass said, taking the bags from Sylvie. He'd set Christopher on the hood of the pickup and Sylvie stood in front of him, a steadying hand against his back, watching the drops of rain spot the truck.

"Well, leave me some foot room," she said. "I'm not riding with my feet all hanging out the window."

Cass leaned into the cab again, to stuff the bags as far as they'd go underneath the dashboard.

"Cass?" Sylvie said. "Whose car is that?"

"What?" Cass said.

"That blue car over there. Whose is it?"

"Peg's. Steve's. Borrowed it," Cass said.

"Steve know about it?"

"Well, he does now."

"You planning on givin it back to him?"

"I am," Cass said.

"Oh yeah? How?"

"Don't have that part 100 percent figured out yet," Cass said.

They got into the pickup. Sylvie settled Christopher so he sat straddling her lap, face in, a position in which he was contented.

"Okay?" Cass said. "Everybody ready?"

"Ready as I can be with less than five minutes of notice. Where we goin, anyhow? Ow, baby boy. Don't grab me like that." Sylvie untangled Christopher's fingers from her hair, then she brought his fingers to her mouth and kissed them, as Cass had before.

"Out, away," Cass said. "We'll figure out the where part later. You got any money?"

Sylvie tapped her bra. "I took what I had, left over from what you sent us," she said. "Not gonna get too far on it though. You?"

Cass was backing up so he could turn around and head out on the dirt road. "Nope," he said. "I haven't got a single dime."

It took the rain a while to get going, those first few drops as Cass and Sylvie were getting into the truck just teasers.

"That can't be it," Sylvie had said, leaning sideways to look up at the heavy, smoke-colored sky.

When the rain truly began there was no way to mistake it. Water rushed down in a sheet so dense and so nearly solid, they couldn't see through it. It was a wall of rain, no space between the drops that were hard and cold now, as the temperature swiftly dropped.

"Syl," Cass said. "I'm'n'a pull off." He was shouting, the din of the rain hammering the roof of the pickup was so loud.

"What?" Sylvie shouted back at him. "What'd you say?"

"I'm'n'a pull off," Cass shouted. "I can't see one inch in front of me." He was leaning all the way in towards the windshield, steering with his chest. Sylvie clutched Christopher tighter and tighter against her, until the little boy whimpered.

They were both relieved to be away from the highway, where speeding trucks might be a danger, but it wasn't any easier going once they were off it. The rain was so fast and so strong, nothing else was visible. There was no road, no house, no cars parked in driveways, no bushes or trees, as if the entire landscape had been washed away.

"Cass," Sylvie said. "Where are we?"

They'd come off the highway at the first exit down the mountain, close to Naneen's, so they headed for her house. It took over an hour to cover a distance that usually took no more than three minutes. They crept, the next thing to not moving at all.

"It has to ease up soon," Sylvie kept saying, but it didn't. The rain continued with the force of a bucket of water overturned from a height. The insides of the pickup's windows fogged over. Cass rolled his down and drove with his head and shoulders out to see the road, ducking inside the cab again to catch his breath. He wanted to stop altogether, wait it out a little, but Sylvie wouldn't let him. Her own breathing was shallow and quick, although Cass couldn't hear her over the incessant downward drumming of the rain. The windshield wipers were going, but useless.

They got soaked to the bone just crossing from the driveway to Nan's side door, and when she opened it to them, she burst into tears.

"What's wrong?" Sylvie said. "What happened?"

"You were driving in this?"

"That's why you're crying? We didn't know it was going to pour like this," Sylvie said. "And Nan, you didn't even know we were out in it until now, and now we're not."

Sylvie let herself be hugged although she was wet through. The force of the rain had pulled the rubber band out of her hair. Her dress stuck to her like no dress.

"I know it now," Nan said. "You ever seen rain like this? God Almighty."

Cass turned and looked out the side door. The rain was as solid and impenetrable as a curtain made out of fiberglass.

"How long you think it'll last?" Nan said, and looked at her watch.

Something crashed outside. Everybody flinched and one of Naneen's little boys shrieked, then shrieked again. Cass scooped him up. Naneen stood with her hands pressed against her cheeks.

"Oh Lord, I wish Tucker was home," she said.

Cass said, "Your electric go out?"

Nan, still with her palms to her face, nodded.

"I think that's your garbage cans blowing," Cass said. "Here—" and he handed the boy to Naneen—"I'll go out and get 'em."

"No!" Naneen said, and grabbed at him.

"I'll be right back," Cass said.

"Please," Nan said. "Don't go outside. I'm begging you."

Cass took her by the wrist and moved her hand. "Nan," he said. "It's all right. They might maybe cause an accident out there, break a window or something. I'll be fine," he said. "I'm already wet anyhow."

"It's okay," Sylvie said, stepping nearer to her sister. She'd forgotten how much Nan hated storms of any kind, demonstrations of the fierce capriciousness of nature.

"What makes you so fearless?" Nan said, and Sylvie said, "Dry land."

They stood for a minute watching the rain through the living room's front picture window. The houses across the street, or what was visible of them, looked bland, as if the people inside weren't finding the storm that bad.

"Nan," Sylvie said. "Could you let me borrow something dry please? Our stuff's all out in the pickup."

She had to say it a few times—"Nan? Nan?"—until her sister pulled her eyes away from the window and looked at her.

"You heard me?" Sylvie said.

"What?"

"Something dry to put on please? Our clothes're all out in the truck."

Nan nodded, and headed for the stairs. She went up slowly, a step at a time, as if she had something breakable balanced on her head. When she came back, she had a towel robe for Sylvie and a T-shirt and shorts for Christopher.

"Oh," Sylvie said. "These are cute."

She spread the little clothes on the living room floor and knelt beside them, Christopher still on her hip.

"Can I put him down?" she said.

"Of course you can put him down, Sylvestrie," Nan said. "What kind of a question is that?"

"I meant on your rug. He's pretty wet."

Nan rolled her eyes. She plucked Christopher from Sylvie, set him down on the rug and began peeling the wet things off him.

"Mine're too big for these clothes," she said. "One minute they fit, the next minute they didn't."

"I'll return them," Sylvie said. She was watching Nan dress Christopher, one hand out to take him away if Nan was too rough.

"Return them? I just said they were outgrown. It's not like they'll fit into them after this. And what do you mean, all your clothes are out in the pickup?" Nan said. "You on your way to the Laundromat when this started?"

Sylvie laughed.

"What's funny?" Naneen said, frowning.

"No, nothing," Sylvie said quickly. She touched her sister's arm.

"It's just I never do clothes at the Laundromat, fact I can't even remember the last time I was in it. We're just going," Sylvie said. "Leaving out of here. Or that's what we were doing till we got caught in all this."

"Sneaking out of town?" Nan said.

"Well, no," Sylvie said. "We weren't sneaking."

"You weren't saying any good-byes either, that I could hear. When were you planning to tell me?"

"God, Nan," Sylvie said. "I didn't know myself till about five seconds ago! You make it sound like I'm running away from you or something."

"Aren't you?"

Sylvie sighed and rolled her eyes. "No," she said. "No. Nan!"

Naneen got up and went back to the window; in a minute, Sylvie joined her. The wind had picked up, forcing the trees outside to bend at their tops and the rain parallel to the street. It made the dryness and safety of indoors seem temporary.

"I hate this," Naneen said.

"I know. I know you do."

They were quiet, both looking out the window. Christopher was happy on the rug behind them; Nan's little boys were in the kitchen. Cass had come in through the back door a minute ago, Sylvie heard him, but she stayed where she was.

"Where you planning to go to?" Nan said. "Leaving for?"

"I don't know," Sylvie said. "Just away for starters. Cass said he had a feeling we had to get out, and you know what that's like. I mean you've got to credit it when somebody says they have a feeling, least when Cass says it, he so hardly ever does. And blah, blah, blah," Sylvie said, and laughed.

"What do you mean he had 'a feeling'?" Nan said. "What about, that it was going to storm? Everybody knew it was going to storm, Sylvestrie."

Sylvie sighed: Nan was exhausting. She switched emotions too fast, it was hard to keep up with her, and her range was narrow—sarcastic to supercilious, angry to aggrieved and now, with the storm, frightened.

"I don't know what it was," Sylvie said. "A feeling. That's all he told me."

Naneen went over to the television set in the corner. She turned it on but when there wasn't any picture, turned it off again.

"You want to leave?" she said. "Go away?"

Sylvie shrugged. "I'm fine with it," she said. "I would've liked more than four minutes to pack, but— It's not like things have been so wonderful here."

"So now I'll be the only one left," Nan said.

"What do you mean?"

"The only one of our family left in our home place, that's what I mean, like it's so hard to figure out," Nan said, in that aggrieved and bitter voice.

"Mama and daddy's passed. Lusa's gone. Now you."

"Cass needs a job, Nan, you got one to give him? 'Cause if you don't, you better quit trying to make me feel guilty. Nobody's leaving you. This isn't about you. I got to feed my son, same as you do. And now there's about to be four of us."

"I know that," Nan said. "I don't mean it like that. It's just, we're not going to continue, all of us. Not in the place where we started. One day, there won't be a bitty trace of us."

"Well, so what?" Sylvie said. "I mean, if you're gone, you're gone, what do you care? There'll be somebody else. People make a place go on, it doesn't matter who. Anyway, I'm gonna move, not die, Nan. I expect I'll have a telephone one of these days. You can call and visit us and everything."

Nan shrugged. "Lusa's got a telephone. When was the last time you heard from her?"

"Well, you'll hear from me. I promise. Soon as we get where we're going, I will call you. I promise."

"Just make me one promise at a time," Nan said. "First swear you won't go anyplace till this rain's stopped."

"That I do swear," Sylvie said. "I promise you that. Not till it stops."

But it didn't stop, not for days.

34

THE PRISON had a natural gloom, a shut-offedness of light from outside so that looking up and out the small oblong window, what Heke, what any of them, saw was daylight once removed, a bright parcel just out of reach. But the darkness now, with the rain, was something else, the gloom impenetrable, almost completely undisturbed by the dim yellow puddles thrown by the overhead lights. The darkness pressed down. It had a physical weight and each day the rain continued, the weight pushed a little harder.

The sound of the rain, when it started, had been like pellets hitting the concrete yard outside, and men tried chinning up the window bars to see what it was. But they couldn't see out or down, and at first nobody could tell what was causing the noise—some kind of attack? There was yelling and a roll of panic that passed from cell to cell until the guards came and said, "It's *rain.* It's just *rain.*"

The rain continued. Wetness permeated the prison's interior, seeping through the seams between the wall stones and trickling down. The skim of moss that had been on the walls of Heke's cell when he arrived, a scant green beard, spread. Mushrooms appeared, their stems hovering milky white out of the gloom. When the cells were vacated for meals, and at other times, a detail of guards went around with buckets of hot water that contained a disproportion of ammonia. They dragged the cots to the middle of the floor and threw the ammonia at the walls to kill the moss and the mushrooms. The buckets smoked, the ammonia fumes curling away from the surface of the water.

They didn't do Heke's cell, didn't try. Heke wouldn't get off his cot; he had to be half-dragged, half-carried to anyplace and finally, they just left him where he was. He lay on his cot and fingered the spongy pads of moss. It was cold.

It was cold out then, in the long ago. Ground used to come up sugared with ice in mid-fall, and steam came rising off the distant Cumberland peaks like some big hand up there was ironing.

When he was young, fourteen, fifteen, he'd had a team of Missouri mules, big and hardworking. He'd driven them up into the hills, carrying food from the Wholesale for the little stores spread out up there. They were his, those mules, not Royl's; his, bought and paid for. Boss and Jenny.

Heke made a sound.

"What was that? What was that, Mr. Day?" McGee said, his voice sparky with eagerness. Was Heke finally going to conversate with him? Finally, finally.

McGee jumped off his own cot and crabbed over to Heke's and bent over him, stubby cheeks flushed, eyes aglitter. "You cold? You hungry? You want something to eat?"

Heke sat up, swung his legs over the edge of the cot, something he hadn't done in a long time. His large hands rested quiet on his knees. He looked up at McGee, or he seemed to; McGee wasn't sure.

"I got to see to 'em," Heke said. "Food and water."

"Food and water, Mr. Day?" McGee said. "I can see that you get some."

"Food and water," Heke said. "For those mules." And then he lay back down again. And that was all.

35

STREETS FLOODED. Straight walls of water hurled down the mountain then onto the highway then down again onto the streets, where bubbles the size of ping-pong balls barreled and chased one another through the gutters.

More rain fell in half an hour than had ever fallen in half an hour before, then more in a day, then two days. The streets became rivers, fast-moving while the rain fell, sluggish in the aftermath. Children stood in them calling—"Look at me" and "Take a picture"—measuring themselves against the water which sank slowly as the days passed, from thigh to knee to shin, and down which they attempted to sail makeshift rafts and inflatable pool toys.

Other things went down the flooded streets as well: rats alive and paddling and the bloated torsos of various small creatures—chipmunks, voles, moles—washed down from higher elevations. Rotting plant matter, torn out by the root ends, spun on the top of the water, and nail-studded boards yanked free from houses slid down the streets like floats in a quick parade. An occasional small tree shot by as swift and sure as an arrow. The rushing water pulled snakes out of their coils and spilled them into hurricane cellars where they stayed, seeking out raised places to dry off.

After forty-eight hours the rain stopped, although the sky remained a soggy, leaking gray, and people kept going to their windows and looking up. The water stayed at its highest peak for a few days, then it began to seep away into drains and backyards and fields and parking lots, slow but measurable. Feathered water lines were visible on the sides of buildings, marking the various levels of the flood. The sun came out eventually, and it and the brisk little clouds bumping across the blue were reflected in the brackish water left below.

Three counties were declared disaster areas and visited by the governor, who helicoptered in and toured around in waders and a black rain slicker with a silver stripe across the back. He talked about the federal money he had been promised, as well as help from disaster relief workers, but neither materialized. People either dug themselves out, shoveling the putrid mud and dumping it elsewhere, and hosing down their cars and shed walls and the foundations of their houses as well as any outdoor furniture, bicycles and children's toys that hadn't washed away—or they didn't. The mud was everywhere. Some people just gave up, packed and moved.

Turner Ward went down to Washington to find out about the holdup with the promised money. He visited with the state's delegation—one senator was a distant cousin of his, and two of the elected members of the House of Representatives were old family friends—and when he returned, it was with assurances the aid would be forthcoming and with a bigger purpose, discovered and declared.

Turner moved out of his little, cramped rented place when he got back—one of the things that was now too small—and into his ancestral home, about twenty miles outside of town. No one had lived there for generations. Turner would not have thought of living in it either, had it not been suggested to him as a good idea by the senator who was his cousin. The house had been in need of repairs and so it was now always full of workmen and complicated scaffolds, but it had avoided flood damage as it sat up a long drive and up again on a kind of pinnacle, like a fort. Turner was busy—meetings and coffees and checking in on the restoration of the house, which was large and had property. He didn't have time for some of the things he'd been doing before.

People said it looked like Turner was running for office. People said he'd win.

Cass and Sylvie were still at Nan's house. The question of when they were leaving hung in the air, though nobody ever seemed to speak it out loud, Nan because she didn't want to remind them, Sylvie because she didn't want to antagonize Nan and Cass, because the rain had brought him a certain amount of good fortune, and he didn't want to jinx it. Cass was now working at the textile mill where Nan's husband Tucker worked. There'd been mud and water damage at the mill too, and they needed extra hands.

Sylvie and Nan were at the kitchen table mid-morning, several weeks after the rain. Nan was twirling her coffee mug by its handle, Sylvie sitting heavily with her feet up on another chair, waiting for Nan to notice and make her take them down. She had just finished doing the breakfast dishes, droplets of water still beaded on her wrists. Cass and Tucker had long since left for the mill. Nan's two little boys and Christopher sat in a row on the sofa in the jumpy mesmerizing light of the TV.

"God bless the babysitter," Nan said, and raised her coffee cup towards the living room.

Sylvie, puzzled, looked towards it. "Oh, the TV you mean?"

"Yes and amen," Nan said. "See how quiet they all are? That is my idea of heaven."

Sylvie looked at the kitchen window above the sink. The light glowed whitely through it, as if there was no mud outside. She missed Christopher, used to having him nearby all the time, but now he did what his cousins did, sleeping upstairs in their bedroom and plunked beside them in front of the TV a good part of each day.

"You don't miss those little guys around you though?" Sylvie said. She didn't look directly at her sister when she spoke, lest Nan take offense.

"Well, no I do not," Nan said. "That'd be like saying I miss them tearing around the place and undoing everything I just got done. Only time I get a little peace and quiet around here's when that TV's on."

Sylvie laughed and looked at her sister, but Nan bristled.

"What is so funny about that, Sylvestrie?" she said.

"Nothing," Sylvie said. "I just thought you were joking, about how it's quiet when it isn't."

"It is so, too, quiet," Nan said. "You hear anything?"

Sylvie did. There was the sound of the TV and the radio on top of the refrigerator, which got clicked on first thing in the morning, then went on playing, whether or not anyone was there to hear it. Outside there was the ruckus of chain saws and trucks moving in and out as long as the daylight lasted and often way past it, the clean-up work continuing in the yellow light of Coleman lanterns. There were always hoses running and the scraping of shovels and rakes as people dug out, moving the mud from place to place as if it were a commodity that should be saved for some future use, and the high penetrating voices of children. Clocks ticked, appliances racketed and underneath everything, there was an audible electrical hum.

Sylvie wasn't used to it. She had come to be at home up at Heke's, where the quiet was as plunging and deep as a cold-water lake, the darkness at night as encompassing as the quiet was. She listened for it, under everything.

But it was never quiet here, as it was never dark. There were streetlights on at night and the houses pressed so close together. The shadows of tree branches picked and waved at each other across Nan's living room ceiling as Sylvie lay on her back on the floor, beside the overripe mud smell Cass bore that never seemed to leave him no matter how clean he was, and in the absence of the breathing of her boy.

Cass had been making the hour-long drive to the mill with Tucker since the second morning after the rain stopped, and driving home with him again, but he was a day-jobber, not a permanent employee, as he was a guest in Tucker's house, there at the pleasure of his host.

He never stopped being conscious that Tucker could take these things away, even though Tucker showed no signs at all of wanting to. Still, Cass was deferential, or tried to be, same as with Steve back in Ohio. He waited for Tucker before he stepped out the door of the house in the morning, and if Tucker ran into a neighbor and stopped to speak with him on their way home in the late afternoon, Cass stood outside with him. Most often, it was John Lawrence Fraser from down the street who stopped them. It seemed to be John Lawrence's self-appointed mission to make sure Tucker was caught up on neighborhood doings.

"Hey," John Lawrence called one day, waving his arm over his head. Tucker stopped and put his hand up to shade his eyes and looked in the direction of the voice, as if he wasn't sure who was calling. Cass bit the inside of his cheek and looked away.

"Hey John Lawrence," Tucker called, and he waited on the sidewalk for John Lawrence to reach him. Cass waited too, staring at Tucker's front door. He didn't much care for John Lawrence, whose reports of neighbors' bad luck and misfortune seemed to give him just a little too much pleasure.

John Lawrence, crossing the street and heading towards them, had the appearance of a man who was really parts of two men, put together wrong. His torso was normal-sized, but his legs were a funny kind of short, as if they belonged to someone else. Pants didn't fit him. The cuffs were deeply hemmed and the pockets went too far down so that his change and keys and whatever made a racket as he walked, bouncing close to his knees.

"You heard the latest?" John Lawrence called, clanking his way across to where Tucker and Cass also stood and waited. He had on tall black rubber boots with his pants legs rolled on top of them. From a distance he looked like a ringmaster, except that the boots were mud-caked.

"Can't even stand to wait until he gets here," Cass said. "Whole world's got to hear every word to come out of his mouth."

"What's that?" Tucker said, and he leaned his ear closer to Cass.

Cass shook his head. "No, nothing," he said. "Just talking to myself out loud."

"There's three families ready to roll on out of here," John Lawrence called. "Can you believe it?"

"No. Three? But who'd want to leave here?" Tucker said, as if the place wasn't half underwater and mud-logged. Cass looked at Tucker to see if he was joking, but he wasn't. Tucker saw good in everything. He was the only kind of man who could have been happy with Nan.

"So who is it?" Tucker said to John Lawrence. "Who all's moving?"

John Lawrence had finally reached them.

"Whew, I am puffed," he said and tapped at his chest with a closed hand.

"Talking and walking," Cass said, but Tucker spoke at the same moment—"Slow down, John Lawrence. Just take your time"—and they didn't hear Cass.

John Lawrence turned on the pavement and jabbed a finger at one, two, three houses. They were all on the other side of the street, where the elevation was lowest and the mud worst. At two of the houses, cars were packed up—one with a U-Haul hitched behind it, the other with its over-jammed trunk roped shut, bedding and the cheeks and ears of stuffed animals mashed against the backseat windows.

"Why?" Tucker said.

John Lawrence shrugged.

"Where they going to?" Tucker said.

"Ohio," John Lawrence said. "I believe I was told that."

"No work in Ohio," Cass said. "I just been."

It was the first thing he'd ever said to John Lawrence in these outdoor conversations that looked triangular from a distance, but weren't. John Lawrence eyed Cass—not unfriendly, but curious, as if he'd made up his mind some time ago that Cass never spoke and didn't know what to make of him, now that he was.

"Anyhow, they got jobs someplace, or people to go to who can find them jobs," he said. "Something like that."

"In a part of the country where nothin bad could ever happen," Cass said.

"How do you mean?" Tucker said.

Cass looked down at the sidewalk and shook his head.

"At least they've got something to go to," Tucker said. "Family of some kind, I imagine."

"I imagine it's more like something to go from, Tuck," John Lawrence said. "As in, Get me outta here! The mud! The mud!" John Lawrence laughed, the sound cracking the muted afternoon air.

"I don't know if I credit that, John Lawrence," Tucker said. "Must be some other reason, some bigger one."

"Oh, you know I don't mean anything by it," John Lawrence said. "Man's gotta do what a man's gotta do, that's what I believe. Must've probably been considering a move anyhow, mud maybe give 'em that little extra push, that's all I meant."

"Or maybe they got family to go to," Tucker said again. "They might have been missing them, seemed like now was a good time to go. You're sure they're moving? Not just going for a visit?"

"Moving," John Lawrence said. "That's what I heard. They're gone." He stood with his hands in his pockets, tipping back and forth on his too short legs. The boots were too big on him. Cass could see the empty space out beyond his toes flattening as John Lawrence rocked.

"John Lawrence, I'm gonna have to say bye now, and I will see you later," Tucker said. "I have got to go and wash this workday offa me."

"I hear you," John Lawrence said. "Don't let me stop you, just wanted to bring you up-to-date." He patted Tucker's shoulder and nodded at Cass, then he headed back across the street, his short legs kicking out in front of him like bean bags tossed out, over and over.

Cass had started up the side path to the house when Tucker stopped him.

"Wait," Tucker said. "Hold up a minute. You thinking what I am?"

"No idea," Cass said. "What would that be?" He had to work to keep his voice steady so Tucker wouldn't know how ticked off Cass was starting to be.

"Well, I'm thinking you should see can you rent one of them three houses across to over there."

"How do you mean?" Cass said.

"Them three houses're gonna most probably stand empty if all those people are really moving and not just going for a visit someplace. And if they are moving, they all can't have had time to rent them houses out, which anyway might not be so easy right at the moment. Not too many folks probably have a strong need to live in a place that's mud-bound. I mean, besides you and me," and he grinned at Cass.

"I don't have a job though either," Cass said. "I'm one of those ones planning on moving myself, remember?"

"You have a job," Tucker said.

"Temporary."

Tucker shrugged. "Maybe," he said. "Maybe with all these other ones taking off, they'll be hiring. I don't know. Most everybody around here works at the mill. Thing is, you could probably make yourself a pretty good deal on a house. I mean think about it from their point of view. A little bit of rent's got to be better to them than nothing. Plus, you'd clean up the place, take care of it, case they ever did want to come back."

"A little bit of rent," Cass said. "How little you think anybody's gonna take for a whole nice house?" He sounded sarcastic, but his heart was going quick, quick, quick.

"Well, I don't know Cass, I can't really say. But it's likely to be more than the nothin I'm pretty sure they're getting right now. See what I'm saying?"

"I do," Cass said. "I do," he said again, as the plan became clearer to him.

"You and me ought to maybe go on across there after dinner and see," Tucker said. "Ring some doorbells, talk to some people. Let's just see what happens."

36

THE SHERIFF had gotten a call with the news of Heke's death. He called Turner, who rang him back a few days later. ("He's out of town. Washington," Dorothy Rae had said over the phone, her voice inflated with the importance those brand-new words conveyed.)

"Why you calling me?" Turner said, when he returned the sheriff's call.

"Where are you at?" Junior said, raising his voice as if the ambient background noises he could hear through the phone were coming from his end. "What is all of that racket?"

"Repairs," Turner said. "I'm up at the Ward house." His voice was laconic and lilted up at the end, and he said "the Ward house" like it needed no explanation. Junior didn't recall him speaking like that before.

"Sheriff," Turner said. "I am a wee bit busy. So if you could tell me the nature of the business you were calling about."

"Heke Day," Junior said. "Dead."

"Oh my," Turner said. There was a brief pause, a moment of silence, before his voice returned to briskness.

"I am sorry to hear that. So, you askin me to be the one to go out there and tell Mattie?"

"No," Junior said. "She knows. I thought you might maybe send Dorothy Rae, just to see if she's all right. Tell her about the will and whatnot. She's his next of kin. Tell her come by here, pick up the key."

"Well, okay," Turner said. "I'll send Dorothy Rae on over. Instead of one of us two blundering idiots making a mess of things, that what you trying to say?"

He laughed, then went on laughing, waiting for Junior to do likewise, but Junior felt more allied to Mattie than he did to Turner, and he didn't.

"All right then," Turner said, and hung up.

Dorothy Rae rang Mattie's doorbell, then she took a step back and looked at the door while she smoothed down the front of her skirt. The doorbell light flickered on and off like a jumpy nerve.

"Why, Dorothy Rae," Mattie said when she got there. "Come in, won't you please? Can I offer you something?"

Dorothy Rae stepped from the outside Welcome mat made of slightly shredded rubber, onto a square of carpet cut from and laid over the wall-to-wall covering the living room floor.

"No thank you, Mattie. I'm fine," Dorothy Rae said. "Or maybe just a glass of water, if it's not too much trouble."

Mattie had already turned and started for the kitchen. Dorothy Rae followed, walking tiptoe so her shoes touched the clean beige carpet as little as possible. She laid the leather portfolio she was carrying down on the table.

"Why that's a lovely bag," Mattie said. "It looks brand-new."

Dorothy Rae did not answer, bustling some papers out of the leather binder. The portfolio was new—brown leather so highly polished she could see herself in it. Her initials were stenciled in gold on the outside, although both leaves were open at the moment, the monogram hidden.

"Mattie," Dorothy Rae said, turning to face her. "Why don't you sit—"

"Don't you look nice altogether," Mattie said. There was something different about Dorothy Rae; she seemed taller, crisper somehow.

"Is that a new outfit?"

Dorothy Rae smoothed the front of the skirt again, as she had while waiting for Mattie to come to the door.

Preening is what it was, Mattie thought. Self-satisfied.

"Well, it is a new skirt," Dorothy Rae said, then paused as if she were unsure how much she wanted to reveal.

"It's a new everything actually," she said finally. "Thank you for noticing. Turner gave me a raise, to go along with all the big doings."

"Wonderful," Mattie said. "No one deserves it more than you do," and she raised her eyebrows, and Dorothy Rae blushed, maybe remembering what she was there for right then, and that it was not to talk about her own good fortune.

"Mattie, would you sit down here for me please?" she said. She pointed to the chair beside her, as brisk and detached as a dental hygienist. Mattie pulled out the chair and sat down.

"Dorothy Rae, are you trying to tell me Heke's passed?" Mattie said. "Because I know about that already."

"You do? Turner said you—. What a relief. Not that he's passed on, you know I didn't mean that, Mattie. I just—"

Mattie reached over and touched her hand. "It's all right, Dorothy Rae. I know what you meant."

"How did you find out, though? Turner said—"

"Well, it's a funny thing," Mattie said. She'd called the sheriff herself, the afternoon of the morning it had happened. She'd just known—a feeling had come over her, some change in the atmosphere. And she had been right.

"The sheriff was very kind," Mattie said.

"He was? Well, that's good."

Mattie hadn't known how to proceed, what arrangements she needed to make. She'd been unsure whether, even in death, Heke would be released from prison. The coffin arrived at the cemetery in a plain white paneled van, like an unmarked ice cream truck, accompanied by the sheriff.

"Just you?" he said when he saw Mattie.

"Just me."

She thought Junior would get back in his cruiser and take off, but he had stayed beside her the whole time, his sleeve brushing her arm.

"The last of the Days," he had said, and Mattie had nodded and kept silent. The last of the Days, that was true. But right then and for quite a while after, she'd been thinking more about Junior's kindness than about Heke.

"Yes," Mattie said. "The sheriff was truly kind."

"Well, I am glad to hear it," Dorothy Rae said, her voice pungent, as if she'd never heard mention of any positive attributes of Junior's.

"Truly," Mattie said again.

Dorothy Rae paused in the act of sitting down, then resumed. She perched on the edge of the chair with her back so straight it seemed incapable of flexing.

"Do you know about the will, then, Mattie? That everything comes to you? I don't know what all there is besides the house up there, but that's yours."

"Yes," Mattie said. "Not that I know what to do with it."

"Sell it," Dorothy Rae said. "Or live there yourself, if you care to. It could be your country house."

Mattie nodded. "Yes," she said. "Maybe."

"Well, I'm sure you'll figure out something, Mattie. Now, I am supposed to turn over the key to you."

Dorothy Rae slid her fingers into the inside pocket of the portfolio that was too tight and too flat to have anything in it but papers, then began rummaging in her handbag.

"You know what, come to think of it, I don't think I ever got that key. Turner said the sheriff would be dropping them to me, but I don't think he ever did. I have just been so busy lately. The move and everything, the number of people going in and out. I flat out can't remember a thing these days, I swear it." Dorothy Rae sighed the way busy people do, and shook her head.

"That's fine," Mattie said. "A move can be very distracting. Your boys must be getting big, Dorothy Rae. I imagine they're outgrowing your old house."

"Oh no," Dorothy Rae said and gave a feathery little laugh.

"It's not the house we're moving out of, our house is fine, it's the office. It's too small and too out of the way and—well, it's just not adequate for our needs anymore. Turner—. Well, things are different."

"I have heard he might be running for something. Governor? Senator?"

"Well, Mattie, let's not be getting ahead of ourselves. No *announcements* have been made as yet. You heard about our little barbecue we're throwing, out at the Ward house? Something might be said then, but that is all I can say." Dorothy Rae was smug and, again, self-satisfied as she had been before about the changes in her wardrobe, and though Mattie could see that perhaps Dorothy Rae had earned the right to a certain degree of smugness, she suddenly needed to have Dorothy Rae gone, out of the house.

She stood up. "You'll excuse me, Dorothy Rae, I'm sure," Mattie said. "I'm still not myself. The news and everything—" and she waved her hand as if the air was cobwebbed with her mourning.

Dorothy Rae frowned, either because she now saw herself to have been insensitive or because she was not yet ready to leave, Mattie didn't know.

"I'll stop by the sheriff's on my way and just run that key by for you," Dorothy Rae said to Mattie's back, sweeping together the papers, the portfolio and her large, white, commodious purse, the kind favored by great-aunts and nuns.

"Oh, you don't need to bother," Mattie said.

"Yes I do. It's my job. I should have checked to see that I had them in the first place. I've just been so—"

"It's fine," Mattie said again. "Let me save you the bother. I need to stop in to see the sheriff anyway. On another matter." She stopped beside the door and watched Dorothy Rae packing up.

"Well, if you're sure it's not a bother," Dorothy Rae said. "It would be one little thing off my mind."

"I'm sure," Mattie said.

"Well, thank you, Mattie," Dorothy Rae said. She'd straightened up, and was looking around Mattie's table, making sure she had everything.

"Don't forget our little barbecue get-together, a week from now," she said. "I hope you'll be able to make it. Now I hope I didn't leave anything. I just have too many things crowding my mind these days. You have no idea."

37

MATTIE RETURNED to the kitchen after seeing Dorothy Rae out, and she sat staring at the triangle of floor—back door, sink, table—she had muddied going in and out during the storm. The floor was clean now, scoured of mud, although she had missed a crust under the lip of the sink and it was still there, as hard and dark as a pumpernickel rind.

How many times had she pictured herself arriving at Heke's house, or in the midst of a daily life there, the latest of brides in a long line of brides, the latest of mothers? But she and Heke had skipped those parts—the beginning, the middle. The house had come to her, but not the rest.

After a while, Mattie took her car keys and drove into town. She parked in the lot shared by the supermarket and the Quonset hut that was the sheriff's office. The sheriff stood up when Mattie came in, and it struck her as a gesture so kind, her throat tightened for a moment and a kind of pridefulness came over her—this kindness, for her—and she put her hand against her chest and patted it.

"Miss Mattie," Junior said. "How are you? You all right?"

"I'm fine," Mattie said. "I thought I'd—"

"I know. You came for the key," he said. "Got it for you right here." He opened his desk drawer and took out a sealed envelope and squeezed the bottom to make sure the key was in it.

"Here you go," he said.

"Oh," Mattie said. "Thank you." The pridefulness, the consciousness of kindness, fled. Business. Only. She bounced the envelope on her palm at its weighted bottom.

"Miss Mattie," Junior said, and she noticed that 'Miss,' something you call your old teacher.

"You don't need to call me 'Miss' Mattie, Junior," she said. "I'm not all that old. Mattie's fine."

He looked uncomfortable, as if she'd encouraged him to take a step closer to her than he wanted.

"Mattie, then," he said. "Mattie. Would you care to have a cup of coffee with me?"

"Oh," she said, and had no reaction, not having expected to hear anything like this. "Yes," she said. "That would be fine. When?"

"Now? I know that's a little short notice."

"No," she said. "I mean, now would be fine. And I wanted to ask you, too, if you'd let me invite you to dinner. So I could thank you for all of your kindness."

"No thanks needed," Junior said, and she thought, if he says "Just doing my job," I'll know. But what he said was "I wouldn't say no to your fine food for any reason."

Mattie was returning to her car later on, after what turned out to be several cups of coffee, and was passing the rickety wooden stairway that led to the apartment where Bruce and his family lived, when there was Bruce, as if her thoughts had conjured him.

"Miz Wheeler?" he said.

"Bruce," Mattie said, as if between noticing him and meeting him, she had forgotten he was there.

"I thought that was you," Bruce said. He came closer and looked up at her face. "You all right?" he said.

"Of course. Fine," Mattie said. "What do you mean?" She put her hands up to pat her hair.

Bruce shrugged. "You look just—not so smooth, like you usually do."

Mattie smiled. She liked the picture of herself as being not so smooth, but that wasn't what she was going to say to Bruce. "Well, Bruce," she said. "I guess you have caught me. I have to confess I have not been sleeping very well of late. Something comes into my garden at night and—it's very disturbing."

She'd thought it was gone—drowned or driven away by the storm—but last night and the night before last she had heard it; it had returned.

"What is it?" Bruce said.

"Don't know." Mattie rolled her eyes and grimaced and shook her head at herself.

"Well, is it a walking thing, or is it a snake or something?"

Mattie shuddered. "Four-legged," she said. "I'm sure it's not a snake."

"You need to trap it," Bruce said.

Mattie shook her head. She pressed her fingertips into her eyes. "No, no," she said. "I don't want to kill anything." But the truth was, she'd thought about it, pictured the thing dead and immobile and not without a certain degree of righteous satisfaction.

"Get a Hav-a-Heart," Bruce said. "They don't kill them, just box them up, like. Then you carry them someplace else and let them go."

"How do you know so much about it, Bruce? A city child like you." Mattie remembered Heke and Narciss calling her that, although she'd lived only down the hill from them and, to her, this was not a city.

"Well, we didn't used to live here," Bruce said. "When we had dad."

"Oh," Mattie said. "Oh. I didn't know that."

Bruce nodded. "I can trap him for you."

"Well, Bruce, I have already tried."

"With a Hav-a-Heart?"

"No," Mattie said. She thought of her early warning devices—the cans and jars and pie tins.

"No," she said again. "Something else."

"I'll get you one if you want," Bruce said. "I mean, if you let me have the money. I'll set it up for you and everything. I know how."

"Bruce," Mattie said. "Are you sure you wouldn't mind doing all that?"

"Yes ma'am. I mean, no, I wouldn't mind." He looked solemn, as if he were making a vow of some kind.

"Leave it to me," he said. "We'll get him."

Mattie shut the back door that night before she went to bed. Bruce had set up the trap that afternoon and baited it; now he said they just had to wait for whatever it was to find its way into it. Mattie was afraid she wouldn't hear the thing with the door shut, and afraid she would.

She didn't think she would sleep again, for a third night running, but exhaustion ambushed her, and she did. She woke to sound—scrabbling claws through dirt is what she thought she heard—and lay rigid, straining to make it out. But it was her system, the jars and tins banging together; that thing must be walking right over them.

A voice called—"Hey, hey"—low and urgent, and Mattie got up and went to the back door. She was afraid to open it and stood there, looking at the panes of glass, dark enough to be reflective. It seemed like the middle of the night.

"Miz Wheeler," she heard then. Was it Bruce? Had he been here all night?

"Bruce," she said, opening the door.

"Lookit," Bruce said. "We got him!"

It was lighter out when Mattie opened the door than she was expecting it to be. She could see Bruce and that the trap he was lifting towards her was heavy, even from that distance, and though the light was not yet clear or brightening, she could see the narrow wire of his arm shaking.

"Bruce," she called. "Put it down."

"We got him," Bruce called back.

"What did we get? What is it?" Mattie said. Their disembodied voices flew back and forth across the yard like shuttlecocks.

"Raccoon," Bruce said. "Thought so."

Mattie shuddered. "Put it down," she said again, and turned sideways, her back against the door frame, so that she would not see—or imagine she was seeing—the dark, heaped-up flesh of the raccoon, moving inside the trap. She bit the inside of her cheek, trying to distract herself from an outrushing of hate for the raccoon—a thing, an animal—that had slipped into her life.

"Now we have to drive it someplace," Bruce said, coming towards Mattie.

"You don't still have it in your hand, do you?"

"No. I left it back—"

"Drive it someplace," Mattie said. "Why? Where?"

"You let him go around here, he'll just come back again," Bruce said. "He likes it here."

Bruce had come up the porch steps by this time, his features emerging out of the early, blurred light. "Good eats I guess," he said.

"Where would we take it?" Mattie said.

Bruce shrugged. He turned and looked behind him. "Up the hill a ways? We could put him in the trunk of your car. I'll do it. You want to see him? He's a big one."

"No," Mattie said, and shuddered again. "I do not need to see him."

She stood for another moment, then said, "All right. We'll drive him up the hill when it gets light. I'll make us some breakfast first, then we'll go." She held the door open.

Bruce took a step into the kitchen then hesitated, as if he was not sure Mattie meant him to come inside.

"In here?" he said.

"In here," Mattie said. "Where else?"

The drive up the mountain was unnerving. Mattie could hear the trap sliding back and forth inside the trunk, the raccoon shrieking, or thought she was hearing it; Bruce, beside her in the front seat, didn't seem to notice. Mattie felt trapped herself, inside the car. She wanted to get out and let the raccoon go just anyplace, but there was no place to stop and turn around. She was sweating by the time they reached Heke's, in spite of the car's air-conditioning.

Another vehicle was standing on the dirt road in front of Heke's house, an old pickup hard to see in the shade beneath the tulip poplars. Mattie parked nose-to-nose with it, like a bull and a matador. She didn't know who it belonged to, until she saw Sylvie standing on the front porch, looking up at the house.

"Oh no you don't," Mattie said under her breath. "Not again."

"What are you doing here?" Mattie called. "What on earth are you doing here again?" and she took off fast, her heels drumming sharply.

"What about the raccoon?" Bruce called after her.

"Keys are in the ignition," Mattie called back, but she didn't turn around.

Sylvie watched Mattie approach from the porch, as she had done another time. Stuffed brown paper bags sat, like short posts, around her on the porch floor.

"You better answer me," Mattie said. "I am waiting for an answer."

"I'm not not answering you," Sylvie said. "I just don't see any need to go hollerin."

Mattie pressed her lips together and worked them. "Snip," she said. "If you think you're moving in here, that now's your chance, you can just think again. This place is mine now. Legally. I have the authority to—"

"Who's that?" Sylvie said, and lifted her chin at Bruce, small in the distance, on his way to the field on the other side of the road. He was lugging the trap, holding it up in his hands and using his thigh to push it forward every other step.

"If that's the sheriff's posse, he's kinda little," Sylvie said.

"Don't you be wise with me," Mattie said, turning again to face her. "Don't you even dare try being wise."

"I'm collecting my things," Sylvie said. "I'm moving them out, not in."

"How do I know that's true?" Mattie said.

" 'Cause I just told you. Anyway, we're gone from here. We got a little house across from my sister, down the hill. My husband wouldn't live up here for money. You could ask him yourself only that he's away, returning his sister's car that he borrowed to Oldhio."

"He wouldn't live up here," she said again.

"But you would," Mattie said. "And we both know that is true."

"I would," Sylvie said. "What's so bad about that? Doesn't mean I'm movin into some house didn't belong to me."

Some of the things piled on one of the overstuffed bags spilled over. Sylvie picked them up, then tried to stuff them in another bag.

"Why not?" Mattie said. "It's not like you haven't done it before."

"I was never moving in here," Sylvie said. She was pushing down on the bag while she spoke, which made rhythmical stresses on every other word.

"I kept trying to tell you, but you didn't want to listen. I was only just staying in here 'cause it was coolest. I didn't do any harm. Nobody was even home. Anyway, I'm done, place is all yours. You can move yourself right in behind me."

But Mattie was not going to live here. It was too isolated, too lonely, too far to come with nobody in it to come to. And in spite of the fact that the place was hers, legally, she didn't feel entitled. It was hers by default, because there was nobody else. Nobody had ever said, Mattie this place is yours. I want you to have it. Heke had never said that.

"I have to figure out what I'm going to do it with," Mattie said.

"What do you mean?" Sylvie said. "You're not going to live in it?"

"I have a house," Mattie said. "My house suits me. Not that I have to explain myself to you."

Neither of them spoke for a minute. Insects made the air in the yard vibrate with sound.

"Can I ask you something?" Sylvie said.

Mattie unstuck her gaze from the brightness beyond the porch and looked at Sylvie.

"If you're not going to live here, why'd you throw hissy fits when you thought I was?"

"It's not your house," Mattie said. "No one invited you. You can't just walk in and say, hmm, this place looks nice, think I'll take it, just because you want to. Even if nobody's home."

"I wasn't," Sylvie said.

"Well, it sure looked like you were to me."

"I can't help what it looked like. What it looks like isn't always what it is."

Mattie looked out again, over the hot yard, to the tulip poplars that made the road dark where they stood, and almost always muddy. She'd come here as a young girl, and she'd come here as a young woman. Now, those parts of her life were over.

"This house has stood here over one hundred fifty years, built and occupied by Days," Mattie said. "There's a lot of history here."

"I don't get it," Sylvie said. "How come all anybody's ever interested in is history, preserving things. Not me. I'm interested in presentory: making things the best for the people here now. The rest of it's just stories, brung along."

"I like the stories," Mattie said. "The stories are important."

"You can't eat stories," Sylvie said. "And you can't live in them either."

They stood quiet for another minute. Bruce had made it to the field across the road. They could see him kneeling there.

"What's he doing?" Sylvie said.

"Letting something go," Mattie said.

"Speaking of going, I'm done," Sylvie said. "Just let me check inside one more time, see did I leave anything." She waited for Mattie to nod before she went back into the house.

She was out again in a minute. "Look," she said, holding something out towards Mattie. "I found these, they had your name on them. Thought you might want to have them. Talk about history."

"Found them?" Mattie said. "Or hunted for them, maybe?"

"Hunting something else," Sylvie said. "You wouldn't of seen this little book of mine. Bitty thing? Telephone numbers in it?"

Mattie turned her head.

"Well, so, here," Sylvie said, and she touched Mattie's shoulder with what she was holding.

It was a packet of letters, three or four, bundled together with twine. They were addressed to Heke in France. Mattie recognized the handwriting as hers, or what hers had looked like long ago, when she'd had more time and reason to be careful. The ink had faded to brown, though she knew she had used blue ink.

"Oh," Mattie said. "Where did you find these?"

"Underneath the mattress," Sylvie said. "In the bedroom. I figured they might be important. That's a kind of place you put things if you don't want to lose them."

Heke had kept her letters. He had carried them with him through France and not lost them and brought them home. Here they were, the twine sharp in her palm. Whatever had happened or not happened between her and Heke, that had to mean something.

"I am very glad to have these," Mattie said softly. "However they were come by."

She put the letters in her pocket and came down the porch steps and headed towards Bruce. He was standing in the field with his back to the house, looking out.

Mattie crossed the road and headed towards him, breathing the hot, dry smell the grass gave off, hearing the noise of insects as incessant and churning as it had been the hundreds of times she had heard it before.

"Bruce," Mattie called when she was closer.

Bruce turned around. “Mission accomplished,” he said. “That particular raccoon won’t be back bothering your garden, that’s for sure. He’s gone.”

“I am so relieved to hear that, you have no idea. Thank you, Bruce, so very much.” Mattie put her hand on his shoulder. “Ready to go?” she said.

Bruce nodded. He looked back towards the house, the hills climbing higher behind it. “This is kind of like the place we lived when we had dad,” he said. “Only here’s quieter.”

They headed back towards Mattie’s car, the dry grass whipping their ankles.

“Bruce,” Mattie said. “You know, I have to come up here from time to time, to see to the house. Maybe you’d come with me, give me a hand.”

“Doing what?” Bruce said.

“Chores,” Mattie said. “Rake up the yard, sweep the porch. I’ll do the inside, you could do the outside.”

“Okay,” Bruce said. “I like it up here. And I could keep away any animals you didn’t want around the place.”

“Yes,” Mattie said. “That’s right. You could do that.”

38

TURNER PARKED in the lot behind the market, where his big, flush, finned Caddy made the other cars look puny and in need of a wash. The lot was full but quiet, a momentary lull in the day. Turner hadn't been here for a long time, not since he'd moved out to the Ward place. Now he had people who did this kind of thing for him—shopped, cooked, cleaned. But it was the day of the barbecue, the come-one-come-all he was throwing to announce his candidacy for the senate seat his aged second cousin was vacating. Everything was set, ready to go, a line of grills fired up, smoke hanging over the yard and the old orchard beyond it like a mile-long marquee, but Turner was here because he didn't think there'd be enough hot dogs for the kids.

He was about to step on the mat and open the supermarket's magic-eye door, but a girl came through then, pushing a loaded cart, so he stepped aside, waiting for her to pass. The cart bumped and jangled. He looked up at the posters fixed to the plate glass—Broccoli, 2 for $2—thinking, briefly, about broccoli.

"Hey," the girl said. "Hi."

Turner's eyes snapped to her, then back to the broccoli sign. "Hey there!" he said. "How are you? Good to see you." He was about to step around her, when she said, "You pretending not to know me?"

"Of course I'm not," Turner said, hearty-voiced, though he still didn't know her. He met people all the time, hundreds of them, but then the way she stood there behind him, planted, hands on her hips, made him take a closer look. Sylvie.

"Oh my," he said. "I didn't realize it was you." That feeling she'd called up in him not so long ago came back, a recollection, not a fact, but still. He remembered. Fast heart, light head. Now, though, there was a drag on it, a weight, as if what he remembered was shameful.

"I didn't recognize you," he said.

"Well, I'm bigger," Sylvie said, and put her hands on her belly and smiled, as if the baby was a secret between them. Turner fidgeted. He looked at the next sign over: rhubarb.

"How are you?" Turner said. "It's been a long while."

"It has," Sylvie said. "I'm good. Livin in town now."

"You are?" he said. "And I moved out of town."

"I know," Sylvie said. "Well, I heard about it. That other time, we thought it would be the opposite, that I was the one would be going."

Turner didn't answer. "That other time," as if there'd been lots of conversations between them.

"You didn't go too far, though," Sylvie said, and Turner said, "Feels far. State of mind," and tapped the side of his head. Sylvie looked down at her feet, over her belly and down, as if she didn't get what he was talking about. There had been intimate moments between them and also, there had been nothing.

"Well," Turner said, and gestured toward the doorway. "I best be—"

"We was about to move our own selves, me and Cass, then we didn't. Opportunity came our way, so—" She shrugged.

"I guess you could say the same about me," Turner said. "Opportunities more or less presented themselves." It sounded to him as though he'd just corrected Sylvie's sentence; it must have sounded that way to Sylvie, too. She pressed her back against the brick wall of the market and looked away from him, out towards the parking lot.

Turner waited a moment, then he said. "I best go. Nice to see you." He didn't know if he should touch her as good-bye, touch her shoulder, take her hand in both of his. He hesitated, then he did neither. He smiled. He stepped around Sylvie and headed into the store.

"Hey," Sylvie said. "Mind if I ask you something?"

Turner stepped outside again, one foot still on the rubber mat where the magic-eye apparatus was embedded. The door stayed open, but he could feel it shivering, wanting to close.

"Would you ever live up the hill, to where Heke's house is? I mean, if it was available to you?"

"Not Heke's house anymore," Turner said. "That's Miss Mattie's house now."

"I know that," Sylvie said. "I know whose house it is. That's not what I asked you."

"Would I ever live up there? I wouldn't," Turner said. "Too quiet. Too far away."

"Yeah," Sylvie said. "I liked that about it. Not too many people did. Well, bye." She was the first to walk away. Turner watched her. The day was overcast, heavily gray, but the light that touched Sylvie shone through her hair and the hem of her skirt where he could see her legs moving. Not too long ago, the sight would have paralyzed him. He knew it to be true, he remembered it, though it wasn't something he could conjure.

"Hey," Turner called after Sylvie. "You come on out to my barbecue later. You hear about that?"

"Everybody heard about it," Sylvie said. There were signs up all over town, taped to the lampposts and telephone poles and inside shop windows. Plus, it was the kind of thing people talked about. Big party. Free beer and free food.

"You coming?" Turner said. "There's buses, you don't feel like driving."

"Maybe," Sylvie said.

"You should," Turner said. "You shouldn't miss it. Be a good time. Big doings."

"What's it for?" Sylvie said. They were a distance from each other now, Sylvie almost down to the curb, Turner still half in, half out the magic-eye door, far enough away so that their voices had to be raised.

"Political campaign," Turner said. "Keep it under your hat. Nobody knows about it yet."

"Everybody knows," Sylvie said.

"Really?" Turner said. He didn't know whether to be pleased or disappointed. "Oh well. Be fun anyhow."

"Why you having it up to your house?" Sylvie said. "You're not afraid all those people will wreck it?"

"No," Turner said. "Gets wrecked, fix it up again. That's what houses are for. And anyway, I like company."

Photo by Emily Schmidt

EDRA ZIESK is the author of two previous novels, *Acceptable Losses* (SMU, 1996) and *A Cold Spring*, as well as many short stories. She is the recipient of fellowships in fiction from the National Endowment for the Arts and the New York Foundation for the Arts. She lives in New York City with her husband and daughter.